VIRGIN FLYER

LUCY LENNOX

Cover Art: Steamy Designs

Cover Photo: RafaGCatala

Editing: One Love Editing

Beta Reading: Leslie Copeland

KEEP IN TOUCH WITH LUCY!

Join Lucy's Lair
Get Lucy's New Release Alerts
Like Lucy on Facebook
Follow Lucy on BookBub
Follow Lucy on Amazon
Follow Lucy on Instagram
Follow Lucy on Pinterest

Other books by Lucy:
Made Marian Series
Forever Wilde Series
Aster Valley Series
Twist of Fate Series with Sloane Kennedy
After Oscar Series with Molly Maddox
Licking Thicket Series with May Archer
Virgin Flyer
Say You'll Be Nine

Visit Lucy's website at www.LucyLennox.com for a comprehensive list of titles, audio samples, freebies, suggested reading order, and more!

AUTHOR'S NOTES:

The idea of a "silent hook-up" has been percolating in my head for quite a while. I loved finally being able to make a complete novel out of it.

Special thanks, as always, to the people who help me present the most polished version of my work possible:

Leslie, May, Sloane, Shay, Chad, Victoria, and Ed were especially helpful this time around.

And thanks to Crystal Lacy for bringing those damned pineapple candies to GRL from Hawaii.

1

TEO

"Who the hell is still a virgin at age twenty-six?"

Chris asked the question, gesturing with his overfull beer glass and sloshing some of the foam onto the sticky table below. "I told her that was bullshit. Any guy who claims to still be a virgin at our age is just lying to get into her pants quicker. Or he's got an embarrassing little problem in his pants. One of the two."

As our friends laughed around the crowded table, I hoped the dim lights of the bar hid my splotchy face. My cheeks were so hot they'd probably steam outside in the frigid January air, but in the crowded space of the neighborhood pub, I began to sweat.

Jay's laugh turned into a giggle as he reached out to high-five Chris. Jay was noticeably drunker than the rest of the group since he'd gone out for birthday drinks with his coworkers before meeting up with us at the pub. His tie was half-untied, and his black hair stood out in messy spikes. "And if he was gay... dude would have even less chance of still claiming a purity ring." He turned to me with his trademark grin. "That 'virgin' crap is heteronormative bullshit. Teo, am I right or am I right?" He moved his palm over to me for another high five.

I glanced at Chris, wondering how it was even possible my best friend of twenty years didn't know I was still a virgin. But of course I knew the truth. It was because I'd lied to him years ago in a fit of anger and jealousy.

"You're right," I said with as much fake enthusiasm as I could.

But deep down, I'd always wished Chris knew me well enough to see the truth, that I'd been holding out for someone special instead of giving up my virginity to some random hookup. That I'd been holding out for *him*.

"Anyway," Chris continued, "I told her to dump his sorry ass and find someone with more experience in the bedroom. Someone who knows how to find a woman's special spot. Someone like me."

Groans and cheers came from around the table as another one of our friends shoved him good-naturedly in the shoulder. Chris raised his hand to get the server's attention for another pitcher of beer even though his glass was still full enough to leave thick puddles all over the table.

As the boisterous conversation turned predictably toward lewd references and tall bedroom tales that I couldn't really participate in without lying to my friends' faces, I wondered just how many more nights like this I could take. How many more *years* like this I could take. There came a point where I needed to admit defeat. At this rate, Christopher Edward Banks III was never going to be mine. He was never going to give me a chance as long as I was a boring virgin with no experience and he was still trying his hardest to be the good little straight boy his parents thought he was.

I thought back to the night of our high school graduation when we'd been in Veronica Monteserra's enormous backyard, stretched out side by side on the thick, cool grass looking up at the stars. He'd held my hand and told me he loved me. Even though it had been ten years, I could still feel the soft caress of his thumb as it moved back and forth across my skin.

Chris met my eyes across the sticky barroom table. "You okay?" he asked, leaning forward so we could hear each other better. His forehead crinkled in concern, and my heart did its usual silly flutter.

I swallowed and nodded before trying to reassure him with a small smile. "Long day at work, that's all."

His frown deepened. "Have you thought about my offer to come work for us? I hate thinking about you in that place. It's depressing."

"Your great-aunt lives there," I reminded him for the hundredth time as the server leaned against me to place the pitcher of beer in the center of the table. "It's one of the nicest senior care facilities in the city. Your grandfather told me he'd rather me stay at Wilton to look after her instead of following him around the office all the time."

Chris's blue eyes flicked up at the server and narrowed for a split second before he looked back at me.

"It's the waiting room they put you in before your appointment with the Grim Reaper," he muttered. "You deserve better. You're talented, Teo. And no one recognizes it there."

"I love what I do. I love taking care of people."

Chris's face softened. "I know. You take care of me, remember?"

I tried not to give him a goofy, lovesick grin. It was true. I cooked for him when he worked late, and sometimes I ran little errands for him when he was too busy, like picking up his dry cleaning or groceries. It was exactly the kind of thing I enjoyed doing for the people I cared about. Grandpa Banks always teased me for being born in the wrong era. And the wrong gender. "You'd have made someone a nice housewife back in the days when that was an acceptable thing to be," he'd said on more than one occasion.

And he was right. The idea of having a husband and family to take care of was appealing to me. It was one of the reasons I didn't feel completely comfortable when Jay and our other gay and bi friends started raging against heteronormativity. I felt like maybe I wasn't the "right" kind of gay man if what I wanted was the same life my parents had.

The server's hand landed on my shoulder after he finished setting down more platters of appetizers someone must have ordered. "Need something else, cutie?" he asked, meeting my eyes with a crooked smile.

I looked around the table at my friends. "Anyone need anything?"

Everyone seemed happy enough, so I turned back to him. "We're good. Thanks."

He pursed his lips and walked away. When I turned back to Chris, he was laughing.

"What?" I asked.

"Dude, he was flirting with you. The man's had his hands on you all night."

I glanced back in the direction of the server, but his back was to us as he waited at the bar for more drinks.

"I don't think so."

Jay snorted. "Oblivious."

"Right?" Chris asked with a laugh. "He never notices when men are trying to pick him up. If it weren't for Grindr, he'd probably never get any action." He winked at me.

"I don't use Grindr," I said. Since when did he think I hooked up with a bunch of random men? "Are you kidding?"

"Yes." He met my eyes and held them. "But maybe you should."

The words hit me square in the chest like well-aimed darts. My throat felt thick, and my fingers tingled. I glanced around at our group of friends, but no one seemed to notice the heated moment that had just happened between us.

"I think I will," I said through my teeth as I met his eyes again. "Good night."

I stood up and reached for my jacket, ignoring his sudden protests that he was "just kidding" and I should "stop being so sensitive."

Just when I thought he might actually come after me, someone at the table said something funny that caught his attention and he was back to laughing with our table of friends.

As I walked out into the frigid Chicago night, I reminded myself that they were actually *his* friends. I'd stayed home in Carpentersville and gone to community college first before being able to afford my bachelor's degree in nursing. During those years, I'd come to the city many times to visit Chris in college and meet his friends. So when I'd finally gotten a good placement at a nursing home in the city a few years ago, I'd felt like I already had a good group of friends here.

They'd always welcomed me and made me feel included, even though they had fancy degrees from expensive universities and came from the kind of wealth I'd only ever seen in Chris's family.

As I made my way down the stairs to the train station, people jostled me from all sides. All I wanted was my bed and the companionship of my cat. Well, my *two* cats. Only, one of them wasn't really mine. My next-door neighbor had gotten her for her daughter before discovering the daughter was allergic. So she'd asked me to keep Waffles at my place so her daughter could visit it whenever she wanted.

It was fine. Waffles and Socrates gave each other as much healthy respect as could be expected in a 540-square-foot studio apartment. But at least it was all ours. No sharing. That had been my one requirement when I'd moved to the city, even if it meant a couple of additional stops on the train at the end of the day.

When I finally settled into a seat on the train and felt the familiar jostling as it pulled away from the platform, I let out a breath.

It wasn't like I'd intentionally set out to still be a virgin in my late twenties. There'd been... oh, about a hundred and fifty *thousand* instances in which I would have liked to have had sex in the past ten or twelve years, but the person I'd wanted to do it with hadn't been willing. And for some stupid-ass reason, doing it with anyone else felt like cheating.

I knew it was ridiculous. Pathetic, even. But I hadn't wanted to fuck some random stranger. I'd wanted to have sex with Chris. And I'd wanted it to be special. It was the reason I'd refused to sleep with him until he was ready to come out to his family and commit to a real relationship.

I rubbed my hands over my face. Fuck special. At this rate, I was going to die a virgin. Even when Chris finally came to his senses, if he found out I was still a virgin, he'd surely lose respect for me or think I was weird. At the very least, he'd be annoyed by my inability to give him the experience he deserved.

Every time I'd imagined having sex with someone else, I'd thought about the futility of the get-to-know-you dance that would inevitably come with it. There was no reason to get-to-know the guy or date the guy when I knew my future lay with Chris and only Chris.

The time had come for me to make it happen with or without him, but I'd be damned if it was going to be some awkward transaction with excruciating small talk. No, if I was going to do this, I wanted to at least pretend it was special. I wanted to be treated like I mattered, like I was worthy. It couldn't be some quickie Grindr hookup where the man was out the door before the cum dried. I wanted the whole night, as if he was truly my boyfriend and actually gave a shit the way I knew Chris would be with me once we were together.

I pulled out my phone and started planning.

2

———

JACK

I plastered a smile on my face and stood in the cockpit door as the passengers deplaned.

"Thank you for flying with us," I murmured over and over. "Have a great weekend."

No less than two women and one man hard-core flirted with me, but I tried my hardest not to reciprocate. I'd learned early on from a fellow pilot never to shit where you flew. There were plenty of fish in the sea to fuck without putting your job in jeopardy.

When I caught the eye of a little boy screaming and trying to pull out of his mother's hand, I squatted down and crooked my finger at him. His eyes grew wide, and the screaming came to a sudden halt.

"I'm looking for someone to help me make sure the cockpit is ready for the next flight. Do you know anyone who could do that?" I asked. "They'd have to be on their best behavior and have eagle eyes to look for anything out of place like a forgotten jacket or a leftover coffee cup."

He nodded and looked up at his mother. I shot her a wink, and she returned it with a grateful smile and sigh.

"Um... I can help you," he said hesitantly. "I'm good at finding things. Even things I'm not supposed to find."

I reached for his hand and lifted him up on my hip before turning and stepping back into the cockpit. I pointed out the usual elements that fascinated kids and asked if he saw anything out of place. After helping the boy's mother take some photos with her phone, one of the flight attendants handed the boy a set of plastic wings before waving them off.

By the time the plane was empty of passengers and the ground crew were going through the seats to clean up, I spared a few thanks and nods at the rest of the flight crew and bolted down the jetway. I was ready for a break, the kind with hard muscles, wiry chest hair, and a nice hard dick.

So maybe I was a cliché. I didn't exactly have a lover in every port in the traditional sense of the phrase, but I certainly used the hell out of my hookup app as soon as I stepped out of whatever airport I'd flown into for the night. There were benefits to being a commercial airline pilot, and arranging anonymous fucks in random cities was definitely one of them.

But when I walked out of O'Hare into the frigid sleet to wait for the shuttle to the hotel, I wondered if I had enough mental energy to handle one more stranger interaction today. It had been a long day, but it had been even longer since I'd gotten off. Due to a hectic string of long trips and even longer days, it had been over a week since I'd had any action, including my own hand. It was only midafternoon, and I wasn't due back at the airport until ten the following morning. I envisioned a nice steak dinner with a bottle of wine. Even better if I could find someone interesting to share the meal with.

I thought back to the super-flirty senior flight attendant I'd spent the last three flights with. His constant chatter was easier to handle in small doses, but after several flights in a row of him telling me in graphic detail all about his recent vacation to a clothing-optional resort in Jamaica as well as his extended family reunion over Christmas in Houston... well, maybe a quiet dinner alone would be better after all.

Holiday travelers were already their own special kind of crazy with ten times more kids and non-seasoned fliers. Complaints were always up, and airports were more crowded. It was like everyone who'd never flown before had splurged just this once for tickets to see Grandma, and they expected to be treated like a king for the hundred and fifty bucks they'd shelled out to get from Kansas City to Chicago. My nerves were shot, and my ears still rang.

A nice dinner, a quick fuck, then blessed silence in my own clean hotel room.

My finger froze on a listing.

Wanted: one night of lovemaking with absolutely no talking. I just want to be held and loved on without chitchat or expectations. I prefer to bottom and would desperately like to be taken care of and treated like I'm the most important thing in your world, at least for a little while. Please stay all night and hold me, but don't be surprised if I'm gone in the morning. No names exchanged.

I read the entry over and over. Emotions weren't something I did. While I frequently fantasized about having someone waiting for me at home, my schedule didn't allow for settling down that way. I'd learned that the hard way. Twice.

Plus, I loved my job. I felt energized by traveling to different cities and meeting all kinds of different people. Sometimes I felt like I'd hit the jackpot with my career as a commercial airline pilot. The job had given me a steady paycheck and benefits, the ability to see more of the country I'd grown up in, and several good friends. When I wanted a man in my bed, all I had to do was call one up on my handy app. Relationships and actual dating were unnecessary.

But this guy? This wasn't someone looking for a relationship. It was someone looking to pretend for one night only. Did I want something like that?

Hell yes.

For one night only, I could pretend to have it all. Lavishing someone with attention all night and imagining they were my special someone sounded like an interesting departure from the anonymous fucks I was used to.

I read it again as the shuttle bus pulled up.

The needy emotion pouring out of the ad did something to me. My throat tightened and my heart thunked around in my chest. Maybe this was exactly the kind of one-night stand I needed. Even if the emotions were pretend, they'd be there.

And not talking? Man, that would be a treat after the shitty flights I'd just completed. Quiet, slow fucking without strings attached or awkward small talk. I could get on board with that quite nicely, in fact.

I clicked the link to respond.

His username was NurseTee which made me assume he was a nurse. I told him I was free to meet at 8:00 p.m. if he was still interested. He quickly wrote back:

NurseTee: *You're okay with no talking?*

FlyGuy: *Absolutely. Have had enough talking for the day anyway.*

There was a hesitation before he responded again with hotel room information and a time. A couple of hours later when I arrived at my favorite steak house downtown, I received another message.

NurseTee: *You're okay with condoms?*

I smiled, wondering if this was his first anonymous hookup or something.

FlyGuy: *Yes. Do you need me to bring them?*

NurseTee: *No. I have them. Unless... you need a special kind, or...?*

I laughed again. Was he a size queen fishing for information? In hopes maybe my dick was so large I needed special-order condoms?

FlyGuy: *Whatever you have is fine. See you soon.*

After sitting back and enjoying a nice glass of red wine while I waited for my food to arrive, I read the news and checked some ice hockey scores on my phone. A text message from my sister, Millie, popped up.

Millie: *Where are you?*

Jack: *Chicago. Will be back through South Bend in a few weeks. Dinner?*

Millie: *Yeah, sure. Kirk wanted me to ask if you heard back about that job.*

My brother-in-law owned a skydiving operation and was always trying to lure me over to work for him. I wasn't interested in that kind of work, but I had considered moving from the large airline to private charters.

I thought of the job interview I'd had the week before at Teterboro.

Jack: *Not yet, but it didn't sound like they were willing to pay enough to make it worth the switch to private.*

Millie: *Well, that's too bad. Maybe you can find something closer to here.*

While there were several airports in the nearby South Bend area that accommodated private jets, the opportunity for those jobs was minuscule compared to being based out of the Newark/New York area. Hell, even Chicago would be a better option. Besides, I wasn't quite sure I wanted to move quite that close to home. I was still single and gay after all.

Jack: *We'll see.*

Millie: *You're not going to get as much as a United pilot does, but think of the quality of life, Jack.*

It was an argument she'd made to me many times before. Supposedly private corporate pilots had predictable schedules which made for a better work/life balance. I wasn't sure what she meant by that considering I already had a stellar work/life balance.

I thought of my hookup app and how convenient it made my life. It was like having a universal gym membership and being able to visit any of their hundreds of locations all around the world without losing training momentum. As long as I had good books in my bag, the internet on my phone, sex on demand, and decent restaurants to feed me, well, I was pretty damned happy regardless of what city I laid my head down in.

Jack: *I'm about to cut into a perfectly cooked filet before meeting a beautiful man in an expensive hotel overlooking Lake Michigan. I think my quality of life is pretty damned good, Mills.*

Millie: *Grindr won't grow old with you.*

Jack: *Who says?*

The server approached my table to ask if I wanted another glass of wine. I shook my head with a smile of thanks. While I was generally both large and strong enough to hold my own with any man I met up with, I did make a point of not hooking up with strangers while under the influence, just in case. Falling asleep and waking up without any cash left in my wallet wasn't a risk I wanted to take.

Millie: *Kirk met a cute guy at work.*

I took a bite of my steak and bit back a groan of satisfaction before typing my response.

Jack: *Good for him. Tell him to hit me up if he needs any tips.*

Millie: *Shut up. He says you'd like him. The guy plays in an amateur hockey league and has a killer body.*

Jack: *Your husband needs a hobby.*

Millie: *His name is Jefferson Plenty. He reminds me of Ty.*

I took a sip of my water. It wasn't the first time my sister had threatened to set me up with someone, but I got the sense she was serious this time if she was invoking the name of my most serious relationship.

Jack: *No thank you.*

Millie: *He volunteers with kids in one of those Big Brother deals.*

I rolled my eyes. Of course he did.

Jack: *Do-gooder. Ew.*

Millie: *WTF. You cook for your elderly neighbor.*

I thought of Elaine Stickley next door who ate cold soup straight from the can. It gave me the willies.

Jack: *It's easier to cook for two than one. She just gets my leftovers.*

Millie: *Liar. You're a do-gooder too. You weed Mom's yard every time you visit.*

Jack: *Only because it's embarrassing to see the state of her lawn.*

Millie: *And you weed the neighbor's lawn too.*

I sighed.

Jack: *They're all slackers. Gotta go. You're getting on my nerves.*

I put my phone down and focused on enjoying the rest of my meal. I overheard a couple arguing at a nearby table about what color to paint their dining room, and I thanked my lucky stars I didn't have either a spouse or a dining room. My loft apartment in Newark was bright and clean with huge windows and an open-floor plan. The twenty-minute bus ride to the airport was even better. Hell, I'd lived in the unit four years already and still hadn't put any art on the walls, much less thought about changing the wall color.

I finished my meal, paid the bill, and pulled on my heavy wool coat.

Dessert was waiting for me only a few blocks away.

3

TEO

I was terrified.

My hands wouldn't stop shaking, and I worried I was sweating enough to stink. Also, how long was a douche supposed to last before nerves negated the effects?

I shook my hands out and paced back and forth in the hotel room. I'd splurged on a nice room on a high floor with a gorgeous view of the river. Not that I could see much of it now that it was dark, but it had been pretty before the sun had gone down. Now it was mostly city lights.

I stopped pacing and pulled the curtains closed. No one needed to watch what was surely going to be an utter disaster. Another good reason I'd laid out the no-talking rule. It would hopefully prevent the man from asking what the hell my problem was. Also, I didn't want him to ask about my experience or lack thereof. My hope was to... somehow cover up my virgin status by acting like I knew what I was doing.

I did not know what I was doing.

Thank goodness for Google. Thank goodness for porn. Hell, thank goodness for Grindr if I was being honest. No matter how much of a fool I made of myself tonight, I wouldn't have to ever see the guy again and he'd never know my real name. I'd even locked my wallet and other personally identifying items in the hotel safe just in case.

Embarrassingly, I'd also texted Jay and told him where I was in case I was murdered and/or kidnapped. He'd asked me why I'd never used him as a wingman before, and I'd piled on more lies, saying I'd never needed backup until a bad experience the month before. Then, of course, he'd wanted to ask me all about my close call. I'd mumbled something about bad poppers and hung up.

I didn't even know if guys used poppers anymore, and I sure as hell knew I was too much of a dork to be a popper user. Jay had probably immediately called Chris to ask him about my bad popper experience. Even now Chris could have been trying to get ahold of me to make sure I was all right.

I raced toward the closet to get my phone out of the safe, but tripped over my own foot on the way there and sideswiped the TV table with my hip, hard.

"Fuck," I hissed, looking down at the offending piece of furniture. And that's when there was a knock on the door.

I slapped a hand over my mouth to keep from yelping. Was it too late to cancel? What if I was so nervous I couldn't get a hard-on? What if...

He knocked again.

Oh god. It's happening.

I took a deep breath and strode toward the door as confidently as I could fake being. After shooting one last warning look over my shoulder at the TV table, I reached for the handle and pulled the door open.

My eyes had never before been gifted with such a sight.

I blinked and was surprised to see him still standing there. Tall, broad, handsome as hell. He had dirty-blond windblown hair and was dressed in a dark wool coat over a white button-down shirt open at the collar. I could see darker blond chest hair in the vee of his shirt and a prominent Adam's apple under dark evening stubble. I wanted to lick it. I wanted to sniff it. I wanted to climb up his large body and beg for him to touch me. My stomach dropped. This was unexpected.

My jaw had also dropped, and maybe drool had escaped too. Just when I was about to tell the man he had the wrong room, he reached out to shake my hand but then pulled it to his lips for a kiss instead. He took his time dropping soft kisses up the inside of my arm until he was close enough to reach an arm around my back and pull me in for a real kiss.

A full-on, lips-on-sexy-lips kiss.

I may have let out a little whimper, just a tiny one before realizing that if he was kissing me—a stranger—without saying a word, maybe he was in the right room after all. And, hell, even if he wasn't... I was probably okay with that.

I kissed him back with all I was worth, clutching the thick, soft wool of his coat lapels and holding him close. He smelled like winter air mixed with late-in-the-day cologne and something that reminded me of airplanes. Maybe he was a businessman in town for work and had just come off a flight. Or maybe he lived here and had just returned from visiting family somewhere for the holidays. His username was FlyGuy, so it made sense.

Why did it matter? It didn't. I ran my arms around his neck and threaded my fingers into his thick hair. He was taller and broader than Chris, but had similar hair. I tried to remind myself that's who I wanted to imagine myself with tonight, but it wasn't easy. This man didn't smell like Chris, and he had a different kind of physical presence and confidence altogether. I wasn't sure how I felt about it, but I was willing to find out.

He moved me into the room and let the door close behind us. I didn't pay much attention to our surroundings, as distracted as I was by the taste of his tongue on mine. It was minty but with a hint of alcohol like maybe he'd had a drink with dinner. His stubble lightly scratched my face in the best way, and his large hands moved up to cup my cheeks. I noticed one oddly pointy canine tooth that made his imperfect smile perfectly endearing.

He pulled back to stare at me for a beat before smiling wider and leaning in to press the softest kiss on my cheek. And then one on my other cheek. And then one on my forehead.

I stood there and drank in the attention, falling immediately into the simulated boyfriend experience as if it was real. I wanted it to be real, and I wasn't going to waste a moment of the pretense reminding myself it wasn't.

He clasped my chin with his finger and thumb before pressing another soft kiss to my lips and then stepped back to pull off his coat, never breaking eye contact with me.

I wanted to babble. My mouth was itching to ask him if this was all right, if he was sure, if I was a disappointment. I had to press my teeth tightly together to keep from breaking my rule within the first five minutes.

As he removed items from his pockets and set them on the table, he continued watching me with a soft smile and warm eyes. It was sweeter than I'd expected. I'd been worried the guy would disregard my plea for romance and just barge in here expecting a straight-up fuck. So the eye contact both put me at ease and made me flutteringly nervous.

Was I supposed to undress? Or... or offer him something to drink? I wasn't even sure what to do with my hands, so I simply clasped them together in front of me and held on for dear life.

Once his pockets were empty of his phone and wallet, I expected him to begin unbuttoning his shirt or pulling open his belt, but he reached for me again instead, pulling me close and nuzzling his nose and lips into the side of my neck. His hands moved around to my back and rubbed slowly up and down as he nibbled and sucked a path along my throat and down into my collar. I buried my fingers in his hair again and closed my eyes. The sensations swarming me were too good to keep to myself. A few gasps and sighs of pleasure escaped me which seemed to encourage him.

His hands moved down to the top of my ass. By now my dick was hard and leaking. I'd never been so turned on in my whole life. How in the world had I waited this long to have a man's hands on me? All this time I could have been enjoying anonymous fucks like this while I waited for Chris to come around?

I groaned again. Making out with another man was my new favorite thing.

He turned me around so that my back was against his front and his lips were on the nape of my neck and his hands moved across my chest and abdomen. I placed my hand on top of his and hesitantly moved it down to my aching cock. Was that okay? I wasn't sure what the protocol was, and I didn't want to come across as a bossy asshole. But he seemed to take it in stride, grasping my erection and squeezing it firmly. I dropped my head back onto his shoulder and pressed my hips forward into his grip.

I could hear his short breaths in my ear and feel the warm air against my skin. The scent of his body and the solid shape of him behind me were everything I'd ever dreamed of. His whiskers caught the hair on my head as he moved to kiss my temple.

My heart was going to beat right out of my chest with an embarrassing splat. Somewhere in the back of my head I realized that if I felt like this with some random stranger, I would probably lose my mind when I finally had sex with Chris.

The stranger grunted in a deep voice as he pressed his palm down against my dick again. He yanked my shirttail out of my pants and pulled it over my head before setting it on the nearby desk. Then he wrapped his arms around my front again and returned his lips to the side of my face and neck. His fingers brushed along my stomach and chest, raising goose bumps in their wake.

The man was an expert at seduction. He must have taken some kind of training course. There wasn't a single nerve on my skin that wasn't standing up and saluting him. I felt like every hair on my body was connected to jumper cables.

I reached back to grasp his hips. The fabric of his navy slacks was fine and soft like he shopped at Brooks Brothers. Again, I wondered what kind of businessman he was, but it didn't matter. In my imagination he was an international man of mystery, flying around the world solving high-level problems in exotic locations.

And he'd stopped in Chicago for one night in order to give me pleasure.

His body was warm beneath the fabric of the slacks, and I was tired of not feeling his bare skin.

I turned around to face him, fully planning to undo his own shirt buttons, but as I turned, I felt the long, hard ridge of his erection.

My eyes must have widened comically, because a deep rumble of laughter came out of him, and he reached for my face with his hands again to give me small, reassuring kisses. The little chuckles that came on the tail end of his laughter helped put me at ease. I got the feeling he wasn't laughing at me, but more like...

He was simply happy to be there in the moment, just like I was.

4

———

JACK

NurseTee was adorable but had clearly been nervous as hell. As I continued to remove his clothes, his wide eyes reminded me of a panicked woodland animal at the sound of a cracking branch.

He was smaller than I expected, but model-gorgeous and sexy as fuck. I wondered if my taller, broader frame intimidated him at all. I'd wanted to reassure him while also respecting his no-talking rule, so I'd softened my smile and held out my hand when he'd first opened the door.

He'd taken it carefully, sliding his smooth palm into my larger grasp and blinking up at me through dark lashes. His pale green eyes had rings of darker green around the edges. I couldn't stop staring at them. When I'd brought the back of his hand up to my mouth and held it against my lips, his pupils had widened and his neck had flushed pink.

From the first moment I'd seen him, I'd wanted to kiss and touch him everywhere. After starting off slowly in order to ease him into it, I finally hadn't been willing to wait any longer. I'd stripped off his shirt to reveal a slender, fit body, and now my hand was returning to feel his hard dick through the front of his pants. I couldn't keep my mouth off him.

As I moved more openmouthed kisses slowly up his winter-pale skin, I heard a quick intake of breath. *So fucking sexy.*

I turned him back around to face me and leaned down to take his rosy lips with my own.

Even though I'd kissed him already, I nearly groaned in response to the sweet taste of him again. He was timid, but he clearly knew how to kiss. His lips were dark pink and full, warm and soft. We kissed for a long time before I couldn't keep from running my hands all over him again. I squeezed his pert ass and pulled him tightly against me. It was on the tip of my tongue to tell him how sexy he was, how responsive and adorable, but I didn't. He'd requested no talking, and I wanted to respect that.

As I moved him around to kiss the back of his neck and feel the shape of him, he was like putty in my hands. It was clear he wanted me to take charge, and I was completely comfortable doing so. I wasn't sure if it was a natural effect of our age difference or not. He seemed to be in his midtwenties at the most whereas I was past my midthirties. It didn't make much difference to me in a random hookup. As long as he was legal and willing, how old he was didn't matter much for a one-night connection.

Having only one night with this gorgeous young man was going to be a challenge, I could tell. There was so much I wanted to do to him. Where I'd been tired and overwhelmed earlier from the long work shifts, being with this sweet and sexy man was energizing. I imagined being able to spend hours this evening drinking my fill of him.

When I pulled back from nibbling on his neck, I noticed how dazed and kiss-drunk he looked. I couldn't help but grin. I nudged him back toward the big bed and continued undressing him slowly. Our eyes stayed locked together, and a million thoughts went through my head.

What's your name, sweetheart?

Why isn't there someone at home waiting to lavish you with attention?

How can I tell you how beautiful and sexy you are if I can't talk to you?

The last one was easy. I would show him with my mouth and hands how much he turned me on.

Once he was completely bare, I raked my eyes over him which caused him to blush deep crimson. His dick was uncut, and the deep blush head peeked out from the sheath. I wanted to suck him off and fuck his sweet, tight ass at the same time.

I quickly removed my own clothes and tried to ignore the way his eyes widened when he stared down at my dick. Instead, I started at his ankles and slowly began caressing his skin and dropping open-mouthed kisses up the insides of his legs until reaching the smooth, creamy skin of his inner thighs. By the time I looked up at him, he was gasping for breath and his dick was jumping and leaking.

God, he was delicious. I nuzzled his sac and ran my tongue along the warm skin at the base of his cock, inhaling the masculine scent of him. His quickly indrawn breaths were like benedictions, and feeling his dick jerk against my mouth was perfect.

I feasted on him until I worried he'd come too soon. He'd specifically mentioned bottoming, so I had to assume he was expecting anal. Since I'd noticed lube and condoms on the bedside table, I leaned up and spent a few minutes kissing his mouth again before reaching for the supplies and pulling them onto the bed beside him.

His eyes glanced over at the items and then back to me. He seemed nervous. I could tell he wasn't used to random hookups, and it meshed with how new his profile was in the app. Normally, I tried not wondering too much about the strangers I connected with, but this time I couldn't help but wonder what his story was. Why now? Why hook up with a stranger if it made him this skittish?

It wasn't that he seemed reluctant to have sex with me. On the contrary. He seemed eager and anxious. If I'd gotten any sense that he was doing something against his better judgment, I'd have stopped.

He reached up and grasped my face, pulling me back down for more kisses. As soon as his plump lips were back on mine, my brain fizzled out. He smelled like soap and a simple lemony aftershave, clean and pure in a way that seemed to fit him.

We made out for a while longer, pressing our dicks together and humping each other while exploring our mouths as if our very lives depended on it.

By the time I finally cobbled together enough brainpower to spread lube at his entrance and begin fingering him, I was panting almost as much as he was. My heart hammered in expectation, and the soft sounds of his whimpers filled the hotel room. His body was tight and hot, welcoming. I couldn't remember if I'd ever been so eager to be inside another person's body. Was it the silence? Did that add to the excitement?

Or was it the bone-deep impression this man needed me?

His body was hungry for touch. Skin pebbled with goose bumps wherever my hands grazed him, and when I held him tightly against me, he sank into my embrace with a deep sigh. I wanted to give him everything, but I was only there for one night.

So I made that one night count. I played with my fingers in his ass until he broke his no-talking vow and whispered, *"Please."* The soft sound tightened my chest. After rolling on a condom, I moved up again to kiss him while I moved between his legs and bent his knees over my arms to get the right angle.

Pushing inside of him almost short-circuited my brain. He felt so fucking good—impossibly tight and hot—and his body was small enough for me to fuck him with my forearms resting on the mattress on either side of his head. I looked down at his flushed face while I thrust into him. His eyes were glassy and wide, his lips were puffy and red from my beard, and his previously tidy, dark brown hair was sticking up everywhere from my hungry fingers.

I clenched my jaw against orgasm, begging my balls to hold off until I could give the man beneath me the pleasure he deserved.

His smaller hands came up to clasp the sides of my face, and he held me there. I stared at his magnetic green eyes until I felt his body tense and warm jets of fluid hit my front. He'd come untouched, and it was enough to skyrocket me into orgasm immediately.

"Oh fuck," I cried, forgetting the no-talking rule and losing my ever-loving mind with the feel of coming deep in his tight body.

As my brain clicked back online, I noticed the feel of his strong legs wrapped around me, the warm wetness trapped between our bellies, and the affectionate fingers that moved through my hair. His mouth pressed small kisses into my neck as our breathing slowed back down.

I pulled back and looked down at the stranger who'd given me such a powerful orgasm. His eyes were already half-lidded with drowsy afterglow, and my cock was telling me to pull out and clean up.

But I wasn't ready to separate from him so soon.

Eventually, I got up and disposed of the condom before returning to the bed to clean him up. Once I'd finished, I moved him under the covers and climbed in behind him, pulling him into the little spoon position in front of me and holding on tightly.

How the hell was I supposed to let this sweet man go after only one night? And why was I having this reaction when I was so damned experienced in one-night stands?

I never succumbed to what-ifs and thoughts of more. Ever. I'd learned a long time ago that turning a fantastic night in bed into more was a recipe for heartache and trouble.

Regardless of my past and those unspoken rules, I fell asleep still high on the man in my arms, imagining what it would be like to take him out on a date. In my daydreams, we'd have a ton of things in common and spend hours talking and laughing over coffee. In my daydreams I didn't live in another state and have a job that kept me away from home most nights. Clearly, there was no future with him, but I couldn't help but want to learn the guy's name. Maybe I'd find a way to convince him to simply share a cup of coffee with me in the morning.

Sometime later I awoke to warm wet suction on my cock. I looked down at sleepy green eyes peering up at me a little apprehensively from halfway under the big white hotel comforter. I shoved the bedding aside so I could watch him suck me off. His hair was a mess, and I threaded my fingers into it without thinking. I groaned and squeezed my eyes closed, arching up into his mouth as gently as I could in search of more of his hot mouth.

He gagged and winced but continued licking and sucking me. I thumbed away the tears that escaped and almost told him what a good job he was doing and how sexy he looked with his lips wrapped around my dick.

I remembered the no-talking rule.

He seemed so damned eager to please, but I didn't want to forget his plea to be treated like the most important thing in my world. I lifted his chin until he let my cock fall from his mouth, and then I sat up and pulled him into my lap for some kisses. He fit against me perfectly and felt amazing straddling my hips with his slender legs. I ran my hands along his thighs and noticed, not for the first time, that he was in good shape. It was clear from his fit body and clear skin that he took good care of himself which would make sense if he was a nurse.

After kissing all over his mouth, his cheeks, his chin and neck, I flipped him over until he lay on his back beneath me. Where to even begin?

I dropped a kiss in the center of his chest and then moved over to suck on the pink disk of his nipple until it pebbled against my tongue. After repeating the same attention on his other nipple, I moved down to suck his cock. I nipped and tugged at the foreskin with my lips, running my tongue around it and getting my fill until I felt his fingers tighten in my hair in warning. I swallowed him as deeply as I could, and he arched off the bed with a cry. His release hit the back of my throat, and I swallowed.

As soon as he came down off his orgasm, he scrambled to reciprocate, but I held him down and kissed him stupid instead. After a while, I grabbed another condom and slid into him from behind as we lay together on our sides. I held him tightly against my front and sucked on the skin of his nape and shoulder as I thrust in and out of him slowly. He reached for my hand and threaded his fingers through mine, clasping it to the center of his chest. When he turned his face back for a kiss, I pressed my lips to his and thought for a brief moment that all was finally right in my world.

It was pretend. I knew it wasn't real. But just for a moment, I wished to hell it was.

When his body tightened in release and I heard his sweet voice cry out, I felt my own orgasm race to the surface. Heavy breathing filled the room, and my sexy stranger kept a tight hold on the hand he held over his heart. Suddenly he turned around and threw his arms around my neck, kissing me like he was running out of air and I was the only one who had some to spare. It took me by surprise, but I held him close and kissed him back, trying desperately to give him what he so clearly needed.

Finally he calmed down and our kisses slowed and gentled until we were asleep in each other's arms again.

But, just like he'd warned in the ad, in the morning I woke up alone.

5

TEO

Leaving that beautiful dream man asleep in the hotel bed was one of the hardest things I'd ever had to do. Not only had he been warm and solid against me, but he'd held me tightly as if I'd truly been special to him. As if we'd been lovers or partners.

The way I'd always dreamed Chris would hold me.

And of course when I left the hotel, all I wanted to do was call Chris and tell him about my incredible night, about losing my virginity and having sex with a stranger. But I would never, ever do that. First of all, I'd never admit it had been my first time, and secondly, somehow talking about my night with FlyGuy would make it feel cheaper than it was.

I rolled my eyes as I pushed out of the hotel's front doors and into the frigid Chicago morning. I might as well have been a teen diary writer with the way I was swooning over my "first time." God, I needed to get a grip and move on.

It was done. Good. Virginity lost, *check*.

I ducked into the first Starbucks I came to and ordered a giant latte. At the last minute, I added a slice of pumpkin bread because apparently I'd somehow also gotten rich overnight.

I rolled my eyes again and stepped back out onto the street after grabbing my order and tipping the barista, determined to return to my apartment and get on with my life. Did I take a little pride in the fact I was acutely aware of my ass in a way I hadn't been before? Maybe. Did I finally feel like a real gay man for once in my fucking life? Definitely.

I'd spent all night with a naked dick, not my own, pressed up against me. My face stung with beard burn, and my balls felt a bit sensitive. I wondered if I looked different. When I passed the next reflective storefront window, I snuck a glance at myself.

My hair looked like I'd been electrocuted.

I regretted the tip I'd given the barista. Any twink worth his salt(-rimmed margarita glass) would have given me some kind of warning about the hair situation before letting me out of the coffee shop. Asshole.

Nevertheless, I noticed a little swing in my step as I made my way to the nearest train station and back to my apartment. Waffles and Socrates voiced their disapproval on my overnight disappearance the minute I walked through the door, so my first order of business was feeding the beasts. After that, I stepped into the bathroom intending to take a shower but stopped myself when I noticed a small red mark on my collarbone.

I ran a fingertip over it and grinned. In high school, the drum major in our marching band had started dating the most popular baseball player at our school. One night Cade had shown up at marching band practice wearing Jackson's baseball team hoodie like some big badge of honor. It was his way of flaunting his new status as Jackson's boyfriend. Or maybe it was Jackson's way of claiming Cade as his own. Either way, I remembered feeling envious. The hoodie was "proof" there was a relationship there.

That's how I felt looking at my very first hickey. And if a photo of it ended up on my phone to record it for all eternity, it was nobody's business but my own.

I pretty much floated through the rest of my day, dressing in my favorite jeans and sweater, walking to the market for the week's groceries, and even splurging on a little bundle of daisies that were on sale in the produce section. Waffles would probably shred them the minute I put them in a jelly jar vase, but at least the flowers would be a nice change from the gray winter sky outside my window.

Late in the day, I got a text from Chris asking me to meet him at one of our favorite sports bars to share some wings and watch the hockey game together. My heart kicked up in excitement as I responded I'd meet him in thirty minutes.

When I walked into the pub, I saw him right away. He sat at a booth halfway down the side wall of the restaurant and was scrolling through his phone. The gray-and-red checked scarf I'd given him for Christmas was still wrapped around his neck, and seeing him in it made me feel warm inside.

"Hey," I said, peeling off my coat and sliding into the booth. "Hope you weren't waiting long."

He looked up and smiled, setting his phone down and stretching his neck from side to side. "Nah. I was visiting Hattie, so it took me a while to get here."

The news surprised me. He rarely had time in his busy work schedule to go by Wilton Manor to see his great-aunt.

"How was she?" I asked, pulling the menu open on the off chance there'd been any changes in the past week. There hadn't. "Did she have good color in her cheeks?"

Chris's forehead crinkled in confusion. "I don't know what that means."

"Did she look healthy or pasty?" I couldn't tell him she'd had a little anemia last week, but I was curious to know if she was coming out of it since they'd started her on iron supplements.

"She looked normal. Like she always does. I don't know. What are you getting? Want to split the big platter?"

I nodded. "Did your dad go too? And Grandpa Banks?"

Grandpa Banks was good at checking in on his sister, but his son Mike rarely made it over there to see her. Mike was CEO of the family business and even busier than Chris. They owned a very large medical consulting company which was why both Mike and Chris were always offering for me to come work for them. They claimed they wanted my help with the medical consulting, but I worried my full-time job would actually be personal nurse to Grandpa Banks.

I adored Grandpa Banks, but his biggest medical challenges at the moment were diabetes and mild dementia. If I came to work as his nurse, I'd be more of a babysitter than a medical professional.

Chris nodded. "Yeah. It's Hattie's birthday. We brought her a cake."

I opened my mouth to correct him. Hattie's birthday wasn't until tomorrow. The entire staff had already signed a card, and my supervisor had ordered special Chicago Cubs pennants to pin up in her room. But before I could say any of that, our server came by to deliver our beers and take our food order. By the time she'd left, Chris was telling me about a big hospital contract his dad had closed.

"Dad asked me again to get you on board," he continued. "Said to offer you whatever it takes."

I finished a sip of my beer before asking what he was talking about.

Chris smiled affectionately at me and reached his hand across the table to clasp mine. "Babe. Focus. We want you to come work for Banks Consulting. It's time."

I met his eyes and got lost in them. One time I'd teased him about using those eyes against me like the snake from *The Jungle Book*. When I looked into Chris's eyes, I almost never said no.

"I really love my job," I argued for the millionth time. "The reason I wanted to go into nursing was because of the patients. At Banks, I'd be working at a desk in an office."

His warm hand held mine tighter, reminding me of the night my mom had been rushed to the emergency room our senior year of high school and Chris had held my hand all night, waiting to find out what was wrong with her. He'd called in his dad to make sure we had the best doctors available. When it turned out to be a gallbladder attack, Mike had helped get Mom in with the best surgeon in Chicago.

Not only had they always been there for me, but I owed them. Still, I hated the idea of saying goodbye to my patients at Wilton.

Chris moved his leg under the table until our calves were resting against each other. "Teo. Just think of all the good you'll be able to do, helping optimize policies and procedures at hospitals all over the world to ensure more patients will get better care."

He had a point. If I went to work at the consulting company, I could help a greater number of patients get quality nursing.

"What if I hate it?" I asked.

"What if you love it," he responded with a grin and a wink. "Plus, just think. We can go to lunch together practically every day. I'm dying to take you to that sushi place I keep telling you about. And you can play nurse with Grandpa when he needs his insulin shots."

I blew out a breath and looked around the bar, not really focusing on anything, more like thinking things through and trying not to fall under the known effects of my best friend.

"I'll think about it," I finally said. "Put together a formal offer." I locked eyes with him. "And make it worth my while."

Chris's eyes widened. "Oooh, look at Mr. Big Shot standing up for what he deserves. I like it. You should do that more often."

I laughed, feeling lighter than usual. Instead of taking his words as a jab, I took them as encouragement to continue standing up for myself.

Chris let go of my hand and sat back in the booth, taking a slow sip of his beer and studying me. "You seem to be in a good mood. Did you do something fun last night?"

I thought back to my night. The word fun was woefully inadequate.

"Yes." I couldn't help but smile like a lunatic.

"Spill," he said with a laugh. "This isn't like you. Did a new Star Wars movie come out or something?"

"I..." I hadn't intended to tell him. In fact, I'd been relishing keeping FlyGuy all to myself. But when Chris mentioned a new movie as the probable excitement in my life... well, I couldn't stand not correcting him. "Last night I had sex with the hottest guy ever," I blurted.

We stared at each other across the table for several long beats before the server arrived with the giant wings platter.

"Enjoy, fellas," she said before racing off again.

I reached for a little plate from the stack and began selecting wings from the platter to put on it.

"You... what?" Chris asked with an awkward chuckle. "Dude, you never talk about your sex life. I was beginning to wonder if you were even getting any."

I shrugged and bit into a piece of chicken. "You know me. I don't kiss and tell." I met his eyes to see if my words meant something to him. To see if they reminded him of the time we'd made out at Wesley Kincaid's house the night of his older brother's pool party. Chris had convinced me that telling anyone we'd kissed would ruin his future at the family business.

It hadn't stopped him from kissing me in secret every chance he'd had. No, that had come when I'd shown up at his college dorm room to surprise him for his birthday and found he was already being well celebrated by a woman *and* a man in bed. I'd learned the hard way that it wasn't necessarily my gender that was the problem, it was my desire for commitment and loyalty.

Chris simply wasn't ready yet. And if I ever came across actual wild oats, I planned on burning them with poison fire.

"But you're kissing and telling now," he said. "Why the change?"

I took another bite of my food to keep from admitting the real reason, that it had been the first thing *to* tell. "You asked," I said simply, realizing another truth. He'd never wanted to hear about my hookups, and now that I thought back on the past several years, I saw the truth of it plain as day.

"Are you dating this guy?" He selected another wing from the platter as if this was all just a normal conversation between bros. "Gonna see him again?"

There was no doubt in my mind I wanted to, but I'd shot myself in the foot with my insistence on anonymity. After offering the guy a chance at a complete no-strings connection, I could hardly go crawling back begging for his name and phone number now. In fact,

I'd had to delete my entire account from the app just to keep from doing exactly that.

"I don't think so," I said. "It was just a hookup." The noise in the pub had gotten louder since we'd sat down, and there were more people crowding around the bar nearby. I began to feel oddly jittery.

"Good," Chris mumbled between bites. I wasn't sure I'd heard him correctly.

"What? Why?"

He shrugged. "You know how you are. You probably already have feelings for the guy. And if it was just a hookup, the last thing he's looking for is a relationship." He continued to eat his food while I watched him. When he realized I wasn't eating, he stopped and wiped his hands off on a napkin before sighing.

"Teo, you have a bleeding heart. It's one of the reasons I love you. But it gets you into trouble, and I hate seeing you hurt."

His comment hit me like a slap in the face with a pillow. On the one hand, he told me he loved me. On the other, he was implying... what? That the man wouldn't want more than a hookup with me?

"What does that mean, exactly? That I'm not relationship material?" I glanced around the bar out of habit to make sure there wasn't anyone we knew there. "Because I'm pretty clear on that after ten fucking years of you sending me the same message."

Chris's brows shot up. "Woah, what the fuck? How is this suddenly about us?"

"I'm tired of waiting." There, I'd said it. "I'm ready to settle down. With or without you."

My entire body felt like it had been jolted by a stun gun. I practically vibrated from nerves now that the unintended ultimatum had been thrown out there.

Chris took his time cleaning his hands with a little wet wipe from a packet on the table before looking up at me. "Come to work with me, and let's see how we do spending that kind of time together."

I searched his expression for more meaning than his words were giving me. "Then what? What if we do well?"

His face relaxed into a warm smile, the same affection he'd given me consistently over the years and the expression that had always made me feel seen. "If we do well, I'll ask you out on a date. A real one."

He knew me well enough to know what my next question would be, so he held up a hand to stop me. "And I'll tell my father about it. About us."

It was too good to be true. "Really?"

Chris reached out and grasped my hand again, squeezing it with reassurance. "Really. But in the meantime, we're just friends and coworkers, okay? I don't want to rush things."

"Meaning...?"

"If you and I are going to be together soon, that means this is your last chance to sleep with anyone else," he said with a chuckle, sitting back in the booth and running a hand through his hair. When his eyes finally met mine again, he looked determined. "Because when we finally get together, I'm not going to want to share you with some random anonymous fuck from a hookup app."

I walked out of there later that night feeling lighter than air, like I was finally on the cusp of having everything I'd ever wanted. Maybe the job wasn't exactly what I'd envisioned when I'd become a nurse, but if I was soon to be part of the Banks family, I could probably change the position to be what I wanted it to be. And it would be worth it if I finally got to be with Chris.

I fell into daydreaming about my new life with Chris and how long it would take working together before he'd ask me out. Somehow, though, before falling asleep, my mind drifted back to FlyGuy and how his large, warm hands had felt moving over every inch of my body.

I tried to replace him in my memories with Chris, but it didn't work. When I finally fell asleep, it was the handsome stranger from the hotel room that made love to me all night long.

6

JACK

By the time I finally landed in South Bend for an overnight stopover long enough to visit my sister and Kirk in nearby La Porte, I thought I'd be over my silent hookup.

I was not.

For some reason, the dark-haired stranger with the gorgeous green eyes wouldn't get out of my damned head. He was the first thought I had in the morning and the last thought at night. When I closed my eyes, I could almost taste the salty-sweetness of his skin and smell the lemony scent that was strongest under his jaw.

I couldn't remember the last time an anonymous fuck had left such an impression on me, and I had to laugh at how ironic it was that the man I knew the absolute least about was the one I was most obsessed over. That had to be it. That had to be the reason I was so intrigued. Maybe if I'd had the usual small-talk bullshit with him, he'd have come off as a normal guy rather than this exotic kind of mystery man.

Even when I flew into Chicago again, I refused to look NurseTee —or anyone else—up on the app. I didn't do repeats for several reasons, the biggest of which was the fear of expectations or accidentally starting any kind of relationship. Besides, the large cities I flew through were big enough to provide me with hookup opportunities without revisiting the same man twice. And if not, it was a reminder that I could stand to spend more time alone. It wasn't like I looked for a man to sleep with every night. I didn't.

"Yoo-hoo," Millie said, waving a hand in front of my face. "You with us, big guy?"

I blinked and looked around at the crowded waiting area of the Italian restaurant closest to their house. "Yeah. I'm here. Why'd you tell them there were four of us? Please tell me you didn't invite Ty."

"Not Ty," she said.

Millie's husband got a maniacal look on his face.

"Shit," I muttered. "Please, no."

"You're going to love him," Kirk promised. "He's the coolest guy ever, and he knows someone who manages corporate jets out of Midway. It's not South Bend or La Porte, but at least it's closer than Newark. And I'll stop pressuring you to come work for me at the skydiving center."

"Humans weren't made to jump out of perfectly good planes, Kirk," I said for the millionth time. There weren't many things I was scared of, but skydiving was at the top of the list. But then I realized that he might have been asking me for a different reason. Kirk and Millie's business partner had turned out to be worthless. He'd done jack-all to help the company and then had bailed the minute Kirk had confronted him about it.

I put a hand on his shoulder. "Are you struggling? Do you need me to come—"

"No. Hell no. Don't say another word," Kirk said, still smiling despite the lines of stress I could see on his face. "Things are a little tight right now, but that's why we're letting you pick up dinner."

I nodded but shot him a suspicious look. "Dinner for *four*..."

Kirk's face lit up, erasing the lines and returning his grin to normal. "I invited a great guy. You're going to love him."

Millie winced and shot me an apologetic look. "I couldn't say no. Look how excited he is," she whispered. "Do me a solid here."

I glared at her. "You owe me big-time."

She closed her eyes and nodded. "Agreed."

Just then, a tall good-looking man made his way through the crowd by the door to shake hands with Kirk. "Sorry I'm late. My mom called with an urgent Google problem." His wide grin was easy, and his blue eyes flashed with humor. "She kept entering search terms, but none of them worked. We finally figured out her internet was down. God knows how long she tried searching before calling me."

He turned to me with a friendly smile. "Jeff Plenty. You must be Millie's brother, Jack."

I shook his hand and returned the smile. "I am. It's nice to meet you."

As soon as the hostess called for our table, Millie and Kirk strode ahead while Jeff held me back and leaned in to speak softly. "Sorry if this wasn't your idea. I adore your sister and was anxious to meet you, but I don't want you to think I have any expectations."

In addition to being handsome and fit, he was kind and thoughtful. It was no wonder Millie and Kirk wanted me to meet him.

I put my hand on his lower back to urge him forward so we didn't lose track of Millie in the crowded restaurant. "I'm always happy to meet a friend of my sister's."

We had a great meal with engaging conversation and lots of laughter, but for some reason that was the extent of it. Here was a man who ticked all my damned boxes, but I still wasn't in the mood to take him back to my hotel room.

After saying goodbye to Millie and Kirk in the parking lot, I turned to Jeff and held out my hand. His face dropped a little, but he shook my hand with a smile.

"Can I get your number?" I asked. "I had a really nice time tonight, but I've been working my ass off lately and could use some sleep."

It was all true. I'd enjoyed his company at dinner and could imagine future nights out with the four of us. Surely next time, I'd want to take him back to my room and find out how good that fit body looked naked.

He smiled and pulled out his wallet, sliding out a business card.

"My email and cell number are on there. Shoot me an email and I'll connect you to my friend at Midway. And... let me know the next time you're in town?"

I leaned in and pressed a kiss to his cheek, noticing the dark spicy tang of his cologne. "Absolutely."

When I returned to the hotel room by the airport, I took a long hot shower. And when my dick got hard from stroking it, I wondered if I'd made a mistake not inviting Jefferson Plenty back to my room. My mind flashed to NurseTee, the beautiful muscles of his shoulders and arms and the desire pooled in his eyes as I stroked into him. God, I couldn't stop thinking of him. The little noises he made, the needy way his hands clutched at me, the absolute conviction I had that the man needed someone to give him the exact love he was looking for.

I groaned and pounded my fist on the shower wall. This was nonsense. I was making up stories in my head like a soap opera writer. For all I knew, the man came up with various hookup scenarios every week or even every night and played a role.

But I knew that wasn't true. He was clearly inexperienced and unsure. No one was that good of an actor. And his body had been tight as fuck. When he'd gagged while giving me head, he'd been both embarrassed and surprised. God, I wanted him again. I wanted to teach him how good sex could feel. I craved the chance to do more with him, get my hands and mouth on him one more time.

I jerked off to the image of Tee on his knees for me, sucking and gagging while looking up at me with those gorgeous eyes and spiky wet lashes. My orgasm was swift and strong, causing me to accidentally inhale some of the shower spray and wind up choking and gasping for breath as I came down too quickly from my high.

I couldn't help but see it as some kind of metaphor for my life.

AFTER THE FIFTH straight week of not feeling like arranging for a hookup, I started to wonder if it was possible to experience a midlife crisis before the age of forty. I dragged my ass home to my apartment and decided to spend my entire three days off by buying a bunch of groceries and learning how to make my mother's prune and olive chicken dish. When I got up Saturday morning, I knocked on Elaine's apartment next door. The older woman answered with a big smile.

"There's my jet-set neighbor. Where've you been off to lately? Anywhere exciting?"

I noticed she was freshly made up and dressed for the day. "I'll tell you all about it over dinner if you're free. I'm on my way to the market and wondered if you needed anything or wanted to come with me."

Her whole face lit up. "Just the kind of offer I was looking for, sweet man. Having a bit of the cabin fever if you want to know the truth."

"Then maybe we need to stop somewhere for a coffee and pastry on the way and make a morning of it. What do you say?"

We spent a nice morning wandering the neighborhood, sharing a box of pastries, and collecting groceries. When we returned, Elaine joined me in the kitchen to keep me company while I prepared the marinade for the chicken.

"You know," she began, "at some point you might consider a different job."

I glanced up at her from chopping the prunes in half. "Why? I love my job."

One of the reasons we'd bonded so quickly after I'd moved in was because I'd discovered she'd been a flight attendant for United for forty years before she'd retired. We'd spent hours swapping stories of crazy flights and customers.

"Your job won't keep your bed warm at night," she said with a twinkle in her eye. "Ask me how I know."

"You sound like my sister. She's been encouraging me to change over to private charters. Find something more predictable. I interviewed for one several weeks ago, but the pay wasn't good enough." I went back to chopping. "And I think if I'm going to make a big change like that, I might want to move closer to her and Kirk. They're trying to get pregnant, and it would be nice to be closer to them."

Elaine made a thoughtful sound before taking a sip from the glass of ice water I'd given her.

"What about you? Do you want children?" she asked. She already knew I was gay despite the fact I never brought men home to my apartment.

I shrugged. "I go back and forth. I think it would depend on the guy I fell in love with." I thought about it for a minute. "If I met someone who didn't want kids, I'd enjoy taking advantage of our freedom to travel and go out for nice long dinners. But if I met someone who wanted a family, I could see myself enjoying that life too, you know? It's weird. If you'd asked me even a year ago, I would have said no kids."

She smiled and hummed her agreement. "You know I never want to get in your business, Jack. But I don't want you to turn around one day and have regrets."

I looked up at her and saw the truth of her words in her eyes. "What's your biggest regret? Not settling down? Not having a family?"

Elaine shook her head. "Falling in love with someone who was in love with someone else. I wasted twenty years thinking he'd change his mind. By the time I met Raymond, I was past my prime. They wouldn't even let us adopt."

Heavy silence fell between us until she finally flapped her hand at me. "That's not to say we didn't take advantage of our independence. Did I ever tell you about the time we went on one of those spiritual retreats in South America where they give you psychedelic drugs?"

And just like that, she was off on another adventure story. The subject of conversation was officially changed, but her words stayed with me longer than she probably realized.

Pretending with NurseTee had broken something open in me, and Elaine had looked right at the pile of leftover debris that spilled out and pinpointed the problem.

I was lonely. And maybe all of the women in my life were right.

Maybe I was ready for more.

Later that night, I pulled out Jefferson Plenty's card and gave him a call.

7

TEO

It had been almost four months since the night with FlyGuy that I still couldn't get out of my damned head. I'd entered into this odd sort of reality where I worked hard and flirted happily with Chris during the day but fantasized about my mysterious stranger at night.

At first, I wrote it off as a byproduct of my first sexual experience. Of course I carried a little torch for the first man I'd ever slept with. From everything I'd ever heard, that was normal, especially if the first time had been amazing. But then I began to wonder if there was more to it than that. Was it possible I'd had some kind of special chemistry with FlyGuy? The question began to nag at me until one night, after a late night of drinking and watching a late basketball game at Chris's place, I got the bright idea to sign up for the app again to see if I could find FlyGuy and arrange another night together.

When I couldn't find his username anywhere on the app, I chalked it up to having had too much to drink. But in the light of the following day, there was still no one with the username FlyGuy. I'd started a new account, so it couldn't be an issue of him blocking me. After scrolling and searching until my eyes bled, I finally deleted my account again and uninstalled the damned thing.

"Why are you growling at your phone?" Chris mumbled,

wandering out from his bedroom in nothing but low-hanging pajama pants. I glanced over at Jay, who was still dead asleep on the couch opposite the one I'd slept on.

"Nothing. You have any eggs? I'm going to make some if you do."

Chris scratched his stomach, drawing my eyes to the dark blond hair of his happy trail. He was sexy as hell, always had been. As he walked past me to the fridge, I was blessed with a view of his round ass and muscular back. The faded silver scar on his right shoulder blade was from the time he'd shimmied under a fence to retrieve our football from a neighbor's yard. He was so familiar and beloved, it hurt.

"I'm taking Grandpa Banks to see Hattie during our lunch break today," I said before standing up from the barstool to join him by the stove. "Do you want to come with us?"

When I brushed past him, I leaned in to catch a whiff of his scent. He smelled different than normal, like he was using a new soap or aftershave.

"Nah. I have to work through lunch. We're trying to close that hospital in Frankfurt, and I have some more work to do with the legal team on the contract."

I reached out to run a finger along his lower back above the waistband of his pajama pants, but he swatted my hand away with a hiss. "Jay is right there."

My face flooded with heat. "So? He's asleep. Also, he's gay. It's not like he's going to judge you for—"

"Knock it off, Teo," he snapped in a harsh whisper. "We agreed to just friends for now, remember?"

I glanced at the sleeping form of our friend before looking back at Chris. I noticed the front of his pajama pants were tented which was sending me a totally different message than the one from his mouth.

"I've been working at Banks for three months," I said softly. "I thought you said—"

He let out a deep sigh and put his hands on my shoulders. "I know. I know what I said. But I'm just... Dad is working me to death on this German deal, and Grandpa wants to have his finger in every piece of it even though he should be long retired by now. As soon as the deal is all closed and contracts are signed, we'll talk. Okay? Right now I just..." He glanced in Jay's direction before lowering his voice even further. "I just need you to be the one area of my life where I don't feel so much pressure. Can you do that for me?"

I stepped forward and gave him a hug. "I can do that," I said. "Of course. I'm sorry. I didn't mean to pressure you."

His hands rubbed up and down my back. "I know, Tee. You're my one safe place, and I love that about you."

I swallowed around the lump in my throat, grateful that he recognized that I didn't mean to pressure him. I simply wanted to be with him the way I'd anticipated for so long.

He pulled away and tapped me on the nose. "Now. I'm starving. You make the eggs, and I'll start the coffee."

After a nice breakfast, I headed home to shower and change before heading to work. As had been happening more and more lately, my workday turned quickly from consulting input on current projects to keeping an eye on Grandpa Banks. It took three instances of being asked to come get him out of Chris and Mike's meeting with the lawyers before I finally decided to duck out early for our visit to see Hattie.

At Wilton Manors, everyone at the senior care facility greeted me with big smiles and a warm welcome. I'd made a point to stop by and visit with my favorite patients and coworkers as often as I could, but it hadn't been enough. A lot had happened since I'd left my job there. Mrs. Singh had passed away, leaving Mr. Kelly devastated. The Johnson twins had been forced into separate rooms when Judy's dementia had turned a corner into violent behavior toward Jackie. And my favorite nurse tech was pregnant with twins.

We knocked on Hattie's door and walked in when she called out.

"What's that?" she asked, nodding toward the little pot of daffodils I'd brought her.

"First sign of spring. Thought you could use it," I said, setting the pot down on the table next to her recliner. Her face lit up with a smile, and she reached hands out to both Grandpa Banks and me.

"Sit and tell me everything that's happened since I saw you two last," she said.

I let her brother take charge of the conversation, but when he began to tell her about the German deal the company was signing, my ears perked up.

"Marie's parents are buried in Wiesbaden," he explained. "She always wanted to go back someday for a final visit, but she declined too quickly to make it."

His wife had passed away after having several strokes while Chris was in college. I remembered her as being very quiet but extremely kind. "I forgot she was German," I said.

His smile was full of memories. "Yes. She grew up outside of Frankfurt. Her nephew is one of the administrators at the hospital we're talking to there. That's how this consulting opportunity started. I keep explaining to Mike and Chris that if I could just go meet with him in person, it would make a difference. I met him several times when he was growing up. He's always had a good head on his shoulders."

Hattie asked more questions about his trips with Marie to visit family, but it didn't take long before Grandpa Banks and I both noticed her fading.

"We'll head out and let you rest before lunch," I told her, standing up to help Grandpa Banks out of his chair. "I'm going to make this guy earn his lunch with a walk first."

She snickered at her brother. "I finally got the Teo monkey off my back and onto yours, hm?"

He leaned over and kissed her cheek. "He's good company. Takes excellent care of me too. Your loss."

She winked at me. "And that's the truth. Come back soon, all right?"

"Of course," I said, leaning in for a gentle hug. She smelled so familiar, like the body lotion I'd spent hours rubbing into her skin when I'd worked there. The scent pulled back memories of how good it had felt taking care of her. I remembered overnight shifts where the woman in the suite next door to Hattie's would wake from nightmares and ask me to sing the Happy Birthday song over and over again to help her fall back to sleep. After several nights of hearing me singing, Hattie had finally asked me why Mrs. Cohen wanted that particular song. "Because it reminds her of being around her family," I'd told her. "And they haven't been to see her in over six months."

Sometimes I'd gotten a stern reprimand for spending so much time in with the patients rather than letting the CNA's handle some of those tasks, but I couldn't help myself, not when they needed someone and I was there.

As I walked back through the halls of Wilton Manor with Grandpa Banks and waved to my old patients and some new faces, I realized just how much I missed giving them the care they deserved. I glanced over at my current patient and realized I hadn't spent enough attention making sure all his needs were met.

"Grandpa Banks, are you okay with walking back? It's a little chilly, but the sun is out."

"You going to let me get a Philly while we're out?" he asked with a grin.

"Ah, what the hell. I could go for a Philly too. But let's walk there. I really could use the exercise."

As we made our way out to the sidewalk, I felt his eyes on me. "Been working hard, huh? How they treating you over there?"

"Not gonna lie, it's hard work, Grandpa Banks. I'm not sure it's for me long term."

"How many times in the past six months have I asked you to call me Gordon?"

It hadn't been six months, but he was right. "It's not easy," I admitted. "I think I'd have an easier time just calling you Grandpa."

I'd meant it as a joke, but his warm hand squeezed through the arm of my jacket where he held on to me for support. "Then call me Grandpa, son."

I put my hand on top of his and squeezed back. We walked in silence for a moment until crossing the street to the park on the lakefront.

"Teo, why did you leave Wilton? Honestly, it surprised me. Don't get me wrong, I enjoy your company immensely, but... you seemed happier when you worked at the home."

"Yeah." I took in a breath while I thought about my answer. It wasn't like I could tell him about my desire to spend more time with Chris. "I actually like the consulting work itself just fine, and obviously I enjoy taking care of you too. It's being stuck behind a desk that I don't love. Hopefully, if I put in my time and get more comfortable with everything, I can travel more and go on-site to the hospitals."

Grandpa Banks—*Gordon*— was quiet again while we navigated our way to one of our favorite benches. It was a gorgeous spring day, and I could feel him relaxing in the warm sun.

"I met a guy," I blurted.

He turned his head toward me slowly.

"I'm gay," I added. "But you knew that. I think. I mean... at least we talked about it once. When you asked me why Billy Porter was wearing a dress and we had this whole conversation about sexuality and gender identity. Remember? Oh god," I groaned. I covered my face with my hands. "Never mind."

His hand came up to squeeze my shoulder. "Relax, Teo. Of course I remember. But I've always known you were gay."

I blinked at him. "You have? Then why did you look so surprised when I said I'd met a guy?"

He studied me for a moment. "Well, I thought all this time you were in love with my grandson. Honestly, I never thought I'd see the day where you finally gave up on him."

To say I was shocked was a massive understatement. "I've loved Chris for twenty years," I admitted, feeling actual nausea at saying the words out loud to the Banks family patriarch.

He pursed his lips. "I thought maybe you finally came to work for us because of that. Because of him."

I felt like I was standing on a wet log in the middle of a swift-moving river. Suddenly I wasn't sure if I was talking to the man who'd been my own surrogate grandfather for years, the man who was the head of the supposedly homophobic Banks family, or my boss.

"That's about right. But I see how important the work is," I hedged.

He threw back his head and laughed so hard, he began coughing. When he caught his breath, he turned to face me. The look of fatherly affection was a pleasant surprise. I'd always felt appreciated by him, but I'd wondered if that was more recently because of my position as his nurse than anything else.

"Life is too short to wait and see," Grandpa Banks began. "If a life with Chris is what you want, fight for it. Make it happen."

"Wouldn't you and Mike... I don't know... have a problem with him being in a relationship with another man?"

His forehead wrinkled in confusion. "Why would we have a problem with Chris being gay? My brother Rod is gay. Mike's college roommate, Oliver Poole, is gay. You know Oliver. He and his husband, Jordan, come to the Christmas party every year. Jordan manages one of the theaters downtown, but I can never remember which one."

I felt like someone had kicked the wet log out from under me. "Uncle Rod is gay? Since when? How did I not know this? Are you sure?"

He laughed again, and it was good to see. I cared about his happiness and worried sometimes about him becoming lonely without his wife there to keep him company.

"Yes, I'm sure," he said. "But you're welcome to ask him. Better yet, ask Emmanuel." He bounced his eyebrows at me in a knowing gesture.

"Emmanuel his *nurse*?" I cried. "Inappropriate! Jesus, Grandpa. Gross. That's a problem in so many—"

Grandpa Banks cut in. "Calm down. Emmanuel has been his partner for ten years, long before he started caring for Rod's health full-time. I guess you came along after we lost Rod's first partner. They were together a long time, so it took a while for Rod to grieve. But Emmanuel is good for him. Keeps him young."

I filtered everything I knew about the Banks family back through my brain with this new information. My own internalized bias was clear. I'd assumed Rod's grief had been due to losing a wife.

"But..." I didn't even know where to begin. If the Bankses didn't have a problem with Chris being gay, what the hell was the holdup on our relationship? "Then why..." I swallowed around a newly forming lump in my throat. I couldn't even say the words. They might break my fucking heart right there on the banks of Lake Michigan.

"Teo, tell me something. Did you ever read Napoleon Hill? The *Think and Grow Rich* books?"

I shook my head. "No, but I've heard of them."

"Well, that man had lots of optimistic sayings. He was kind of the king of self-help. But one of the things he said has always stayed with me. 'The starting point of all achievement is desire.' In other words," he said, moving to stand up from the bench, "if you want it, make it happen."

He stayed quiet during the rest of our stroll through the park toward the Philly restaurant. It gave me time to process his words and realize that, while I wanted to know Chris's reasons for stalling, the end result was the same. I wanted him in my life as my partner, my future. And it was time I took action to make it happen.

WHEN WE GOT BACK to the office, it was humming with activity. "What's going on?" I asked Chris when I led Gordon around the corner to the executive hallway.

Chris glanced past me to his grandfather. "They're ready to sign, but Andreas wants you to bring the paperwork in person."

Gordon's face lit up. "Excellent. Let's get to work to make that happen."

He turned to pat my hand and thank me for lunch and the visit to see Hattie before he turned to join Chris and Mike in the large conference room at the end of the hallway. I turned around and made my way back down the hall to my cubicle in the area I shared with a handful of other junior consultants.

A couple of hours later when I went to find Gordon to check his blood glucose, I discovered all three of the Banks men had left for the night.

"Oh, there you are," Mike's assistant said, standing to wave me down. "Mike and Chris had to meet some clients for dinner, but they wanted to make sure you were all set for tomorrow."

I blinked at Mike's assistant. "Tomorrow?"

He nodded and rustled through some papers in a folder before handing me a single sheet of paper. "I emailed this to you as well. It's the itinerary for your trip. Chris and Mr. Banks will meet you at the plane at four. It leaves out of the private terminal at Midway." He reached over to the side table next to his desk and grabbed a simple leather document case. "Here are the legal papers you need. Chris had to leave before I had them ready. Be sure to give those to him at the airport. Let's see... what else?"

He looked at me like I had any idea what he was talking about.

"I don't understand," I said when no more information seemed forthcoming. "What trip?"

"To Frankfurt. They told me you'd be accompanying Mr. Banks as his personal nurse."

We stared at each other for a minute. On the one hand, I was furious this had been decided without discussing it with me. On the other... I was going on a trip to Germany with my best friend.

Except he, and everyone else who'd ever met me, knew I'd never flown before because I was absolutely terrified of flying.

I took the leather portfolio from him in a shaky hand and tried returning his smile. "Thanks. Have a great weekend."

That evening was spent frantically searching for my barely used passport that I'd only gotten once for a weekend road trip to Canada, packing for the unexpected trip, and making last-minute arrangements with my neighbor to look in on the cats. I texted Chris to ask him to call me when his dinner was over, but I didn't hear from him.

The following day, I still didn't hear from him, and now he wasn't answering actual calls either. It wasn't until I was walking out to the private jet that afternoon—with complete and total conviction I was going to puke my guts out if I didn't calm down—that I finally heard from him.

"Are you already here?" I asked, looking forward to the solid block of time I would get to spend with him overnight. I hoped to god he'd let me hold his hand. At least during takeoff and landing.

"Teo, fuck," he said as out of breath as I felt. "Sorry about all this. I'm not going to make it. I need you to—"

I interrupted him with a squawk. "What? What do you mean you're not going to make it?"

"Listen, this is great news, actually. Last night when we were at dinner, Dad ran into an old friend who introduced us to the CEO of MedPoint. They're the third largest hospital chain in the US. We've been trying to get an appointment with them forever. Anyway, they've agreed to meet with us, so I can't go to Frankfurt with you."

I'd stopped walking and stood still at the bottom of the airplane stairs. He had to be pulling my leg. "You're not coming?"

"It's fine. Grandpa can handle it. The signing is just a formality anyway. We've already hashed out the details with their legal team."

That wasn't the point.

A uniformed woman about my mother's age smiled at me from the door of the jet. I recognized the jacket in her hands as Grandpa Banks's, so I assumed he was already on board. I closed my eyes for a minute and took a deep breath. This was going off the rails. My stomach was going to revolt. There was no way I was getting on that plane without my best friend.

"Chris... it's not that, it's... I'm terrified of flying, and... and I just wanted to talk to you about... about us."

"Us?"

I winced, realizing this was a terrible time to bring it up if I wasn't going to be able to see him in person again for an entire week. But I couldn't wait any longer for some answers. And I needed something to distract me from one of my biggest fears. "Why didn't you ever tell me Uncle Rod was gay? Or Oliver Poole? You made it sound like your family would freak out if they found out you were bi."

The noise from other airplanes was loud enough for me to put a finger in my other ear so I didn't miss his response. I was desperate for any little scrap of evidence he hadn't spent the past ten years stringing me along for some other reason.

There was a pause before he answered. "You said you wouldn't pressure me, Teo."

"It's been over ten fucking years! At what point do I read the writing on the fucking wall and give up? Every reason for your hesitation went up in smoke when I realized it wasn't your family who were the problem. Tell me what's holding you back, for god's sake." I pressed my palm to my forehead and gritted my teeth against the pain in my chest. I'd been such an idiot. "If it's that you don't want to be with me... please just tell me and let me go. Let me stop hoping for something that's never going to happen."

His voice was softer this time, the familiar comforting voice of the friend who'd been by my side since I was six years old.

"I love you. You know that. But I'm just not ready to settle down yet. I don't understand why we can't just have fun together first."

I lowered my voice. "Fun, meaning sex?"

"Yes. Just think of all the shit we could be doing right now if you just... Jesus, Tee, if you just relaxed for once. How can you go out and sleep with some random fucking stranger and not me?"

His question surprised me, not only because I hadn't realized he'd been thinking of me that way, but also because he kind of had a point. It only took me about a second to remember the reason.

"Because I wouldn't be able to stand sharing you," I confessed. "And I can't believe you'd be okay sharing me either."

The flight attendant caught my eye again, and I realized they were waiting on me to board so we could get underway. I wasn't going to let the Banks family down, and I especially wasn't going to let Gordon travel overseas without someone to help look after him. I climbed the stairs and dropped into the first seat, not even bothering to find Gordon until I finished the call with Chris. I didn't want to give Chris any excuse to cut our conversation short.

I heard shuffling and muttering through the phone and wondered where he was and what he was doing.

"Chris?" I asked, since he hadn't responded.

"Yeah, sorry, I'm just—"

The loud clunking sound and vibrations alerted me to the closing airplane door. I glanced up at the flight attendant preparing to begin some kind of safety presentation. I could see the narrow cockpit door still partially ajar and the pilots moving around getting settled.

"I'm going to have to go," I said. "They just closed the airplane door."

"I'm not ready to settle down yet, Teo. That's the reason. We're only twenty-six for god's sake."

I sighed. "Yeah, well, I am ready."

The bitterness was clear in his voice. "Then maybe you should find someone else to do it with."

A deep rumble of laughter caught my attention from the open cockpit door.

"Maybe I will," I said, absently, recognizing the familiar stubbled jaw and pointed canine tooth in the smile of the laughing pilot.

I didn't hear Chris's words over the sound of the roaring in my ears. The pilot turned to close the cockpit door and met my eyes. Time stopped and my stomach plummeted. There he was. The stranger I'd given myself to, the man who'd kept me company in my daydreams for months and held up as the standard by which all future bedmates would be judged.

FlyGuy.

While we stared at each other in disbelief and my entire world seemed to jangle unexpectedly, the efficient flight attendant reached back and pulled the cockpit door closed, cutting off our eye contact and beginning the stopwatch on an eight-and-a-half-hour flight to Frankfurt.

For the next eight hours I would have to sit there knowing that my sexy stranger was less than ten feet away from me.

And the man I thought was my future seemed bound and determined to become only my past.

8

JACK

It was him. I'd know those sweet light green eyes anywhere. My lips remembered the warm curves of his skin and the taste of his kisses. He'd looked just as surprised as I was when we saw each other through the cockpit door.

I forced myself to concentrate on the task at hand. We needed to get this plane in the air. The sooner we got to Frankfurt, the sooner I'd be able to beg him to give me a few minutes of his time to get his contact information. In the meantime, the captain's voice snapped in my headset, helping keep me on task through taxi and takeoff. Once we were settled at cruising altitude, my mind wandered back to NurseTee. Had it really been him?

The surprised doe eyes had been unmistakable. The man was sexy as hell and irresistible. I wondered why he was flying to Frankfurt. Did he have family in Europe? Or business? And if he was a nurse the way I'd assumed, how could he afford to fly in a private jet? The only other passenger I'd seen was the elder Mr. Banks, whose company owned the plane. I'd already met some of the other family members who worked for the company, so I didn't think Tee was part of the Banks family. But maybe he worked for the company with Mr. Banks?

Maybe Tee was the older man's nurse. But what if he was more? Mr. Banks could be Tee's sugar daddy for all I knew. How would that make me feel? It certainly could explain his need for the sexual hookup with me.

Even if he was alone, he'd been so adamant about no contact during our hookup, would it be unfair of me to approach him? Maybe I would have to approach cautiously and assess his body language.

My skin itched with the need to climb out of the flight deck and talk to him, but I couldn't. I'd only been in this job for a few weeks, and I was still anxious to prove myself as focused and dedicated even though I was sure my fellow pilot wouldn't mind. I'd already figured out this captain was diligent and professional but didn't take his job too seriously. It was one of the things that had attracted me to the position. I hoped to learn about work/life balance from pilots like him, and I'd already enjoyed the few trips Nate and I had flown together.

He'd been an Air Force pilot who'd gone on to fly for Delta. We'd already shared several stories of our time in the service as well as crazy flights and crazier passengers in the few trips we'd taken together, but thankfully, he'd told me not much unexpected happened in this executive jet side of things. His wife, Brenda, who happened to be our flight attendant on this trip, agreed with him. It was quieter and more predictable.

And so far, it had been. Until about two and a half hours into this flight. It started with a sudden thump in the left engine. Alarms began sounding.

"What the hell was that?" Nate asked.

"Bird strike?" I asked. "That's what it felt like, but aren't we too high?"

We reacted quickly, assessing the situation and going through memory actions to extinguish the fire in the engine. Brenda called up to report a smoke smell in the cabin.

"Hang tight," I told her. "Fire in port engine, but it's out now. We'll divert somewhere to take a look." There was no way we'd risk crossing the ocean under these conditions.

Another several thumps and we were without our port side engine completely. Alarms for the starboard side engine flared as well, but they were only warnings so far. It all happened so fast. We went from effortlessly cruising north of Quebec City to deciding to divert to Goose Bay to suddenly wondering if we were even going to make it to an actual runway before having to bring the plane down in the middle of nowhere.

"Fuck," Nate muttered, scrambling over the controls. We were both well trained for this, but a real-life crisis was very different than simulations.

Aviate, Navigate, Communicate. I kept reminding myself to prioritize according to everything I'd been taught.

As the plane tilted and bumped in our efforts to make it to the snowy Goose Bay airport, I couldn't help but think about the sweet man I knew in the cabin of the jet and how he, Mr. Banks, and our flight attendant were counting on Nate and me to get us on the ground safely.

"Not going to be smooth," Nate clipped over the headset. "Tell Brenda to prepare."

I gave her the update, letting her know to prepare the passengers for a very bumpy landing. In addition to the difficulties in landing a plane on the one engine when the other was alarming too, we were also coming in much heavier than normal with so much fuel left in our tanks.

As the air traffic controller guided us in with a steady voice, we dropped through several air pockets which only served to ratchet up the tension and make controlling the plane that much more difficult. By the time we came screaming down the runway, we were both drenched in sweat and relying on everything we knew to keep the plane steady while we came to a stop.

While Nate worked to shut everything down as quickly as possible, I told Brenda to evacuate the passengers, taking care to grab any jackets and blankets on the way out. Then I radioed our request for medical and fire response just in case they were needed. The air traffic controller promised they were already working on it, and within moments, I saw a red pickup truck with a giant tank of what I could only assume was fire foam on the back racing across the tarmac toward us.

Nate and I grabbed the bare essentials and hustled out of the cockpit and into the frigid night air to meet up with the fire response unit. When I got to the bottom of the stairs, I noticed Mr. Banks clutching his chest and struggling to breathe. Tee and Brenda were both helping him, but I could tell by the look on Tee's face it could be more than a panic attack.

I raced over to the fire truck just as the driver was stepping out. "We need an ambulance quickly," I shouted. "One of our passengers is having trouble breathing."

He jumped back in the truck and reached for his radio, but I could already see the reflections of red lights blinking around the side of the building. Sure enough, an ambulance pulled directly onto the tarmac and headed toward us. After double-checking there wasn't a fire danger from the plane, I waved the ambulance close.

The first responders helped assess the situation and quickly loaded Mr. Banks onto their gurney for transportation to the hospital. "It's only a few minutes away," one of the EMTs told me. "Simon can give you a ride when you're ready."

I didn't know who Simon was, but it wasn't important. For now, my job was to stay with the plane and try to protect Mr. Banks's asset while he was hopefully in good hands at the hospital. I locked eyes with Tee.

"Are you going with him?" I asked hesitantly. It was strange to speak to him after so many hours of being together under a no-speaking rule.

He nodded. "Yeah. I'm his nurse." His eyes were wide and worried, and his face was pale. I strangely wanted to pull him into my arms and tell him everything would be okay.

"I'm so sorry," I said instead.

"For what?"

I gestured to the plane. "I don't know what happened, but..."

His hand reached out to gently grip my upper arm. "No, I think his symptoms started earlier, and I didn't catch them in time. You got us on the ground in one piece. You got an ambulance here before I even realized we'd need one."

I put my hand over the one he had on my arm and squeezed lightly. "Will you be okay by yourself until I can get to the hospital?"

His face relaxed a little bit. "Of course. Yeah."

The EMTs finished snapping the gurney in place, and I knew Tee needed to hop in so they could get going.

"I'm Jack Snyder," I said, holding out my hand.

"Teo Parisi," he replied, slipping his slender fingers into my grasp.

There wasn't time to exchange phone numbers or linger over the feel of his skin against mine, so I pulled away. "I'll meet you at the hospital as soon as I can. If you need me before then, call the airport and tell them to find me, okay?"

He moved toward the open bay door of the ambulance. "Okay."

Nate and I spent the next several hours dealing with inspections and assessments before determining that it had been a bird strike. We were going to need mechanical help before any chance of taking the plane back up.

"Apparently they have a good crew here who can come check it out in the morning if the snowstorm they're expecting holds off," Nate said, blowing out a breath of frustration. "So I guess we just need to find a place to get some sleep until then. The Canadian TSB is going to send someone out too. Probably be here around ten, I'd imagine."

The overnight airport manager was a man named Simon. He walked out to us from the airport building with two Styrofoam cups of coffee. "Brenda sent me out with these. She's arranged hotel rooms for you, and I have a car you can borrow when you're ready."

The fact this man was willing to let us borrow a car was a testament to just how small this town was. With less than ten thousand residents, Goose Bay was just big enough for two Tim Hortons and a hospital. Instead of stopping at the hotel, I asked to be dropped off at the hospital.

The nice woman at the reception desk directed me to a room where Mr. Banks seemed to be sleeping peacefully despite the number of tubes and wires snaking out from under his gown. Teo, on the other hand was pacing around the room with one hand on his phone and the other raking through his hair.

"Hey," I said softly. His head popped up and he stopped pacing. "How's he doing?"

"Oh, uh... not... not great. He, ah..." His face pinched in dismay. "He had a heart attack. And... and I can't get ahold of his family, and they don't have a cardiothoracic specialist here, and he would want one. I mean, he *needs* one, and they say they can—"

I stepped forward without thinking and pulled him into my arms, holding him tightly to me and whispering to him to take a breath. "Shh, it's going to be okay. He looks stable right now, so just breathe, all right?"

His body relaxed against mine, and his arms came around my back to return the hug. I inhaled the same lemony scent from my memories of him, only now it was mixed with the smell of antiseptic hand soap that seemed to permeate all medical facilities.

After he had a chance to catch his breath, I pulled back just enough to clasp his face in my hands. "I'm here. I'll help any way I can. If we need to get medical transport back to Chicago, I can start working on that right now."

He looked so tired and worried. I wished more than anything I could simply take him back to the hotel and hold him while he slept. But it was clear he wasn't about to leave Mr. Banks alone, and I respected that completely.

Teo ducked his forehead into my collar and kept his arms around me. "I was happy to see you on that airplane." His words were muffled, but they still managed to hit me square in the chest with a burst of relief.

"That makes two of us," I admitted, rubbing his back. "What did the doctor say about Mr. Banks?"

Teo stepped back out of my arms and moved closer to the hospital bed where he gently picked up Mr. Banks's hand. "They're not sure of the extent of the damage yet because they don't have a cath lab here. The closest one is in St. John's which means an hour-and-a-half flight. But if we're going to do that, I think he might be better off back in Chicago. So—" He stopped and glanced up at me before slowing down again. "So, I was hoping to reach Mike or Chris to see what they want me to do. But... they're not answering."

I checked my watch and saw it was four in the morning which meant two in Chicago. "If they have their phones on nighttime mode, maybe they'll only accept calls from family. Did they give you Mr. Banks's phone?"

Teo paused for a beat before saying, "I'm Chris's best friend."

I thought back to the guy I'd met twice before on previous trips since going to work for the company that managed Banks Consulting's Gulfstream. That man had been very different than sweet Teo. He'd been a stereotypical corporate type who'd acted like pilots and flight crew were invisible. It was a glaring reminder that I didn't know Teo very well, despite having been inside of his body. For all I knew, my impressions of him were inaccurate and he was as much of a corporate type as his friend. "Could he be out at a loud club or some-place he wouldn't be able to hear his phone?"

He frowned. "He's supposed to be prepping for an important presentation on Monday, but... I mean, I guess?"

We stood side by side and watched the man in bed continue to sleep through our quiet conversation. I could tell by the look on Teo's face and the way he was holding Mr. Banks's hand that he cared about the man very much.

"What decision would you make if he was your grandfather?" I asked.

Teo's eyes filled with tears, and his voice broke when he spoke. "I'd take him home and get him the best healthcare money could buy."

I clasped the back of his head and leaned down to drop a kiss on top of it. "Then that's what we'll do. Let me make a few calls so we can get him out before this storm hits."

He looked up at me with an expression of gratitude as I gently pulled away from him to escape to the hallway. As soon as I was out of the room, I pulled out my phone and called the concierge support line for the company I now worked for. A full day of my orientation training had been dedicated to meeting the higher standards of corporate jet fliers. Flying private planes meant interacting with the uber wealthy, and that necessitated a level of support I'd never known before.

It only took one ten-minute phone call before the plan was underway. When I returned to the room, Teo was speaking animatedly into the phone.

"But he's your family," he hissed. "Cancel the damned meeting, for god's sake. How could you not choose—"

He stopped talking to listen. The anger and disappointment was clear on his face, but when he glanced up at me, he tried to hide it.

"I understand," he said in a voice devoid of emotion. "I'll take care of it. Of him. Don't worry."

I gestured to my phone and gave him a thumbs-up so at least he would know the arrangements for Mr. Banks's transport had been arranged.

Teo lifted an eyebrow. "Hang on, Chris. Hang... hang on. Stop. Just give me a minute." He put his hand over the microphone and asked me what I'd found out.

"Dispatch told me there is an air ambulance traveling from Reykjavík to Chicago tonight that's willing to stop and pick Mr. Banks up on the way." Before Teo could get too excited, I held up a hand. "There's a catch. They can only take the patient. The other patient they're transporting is already on board with his whole family and medical personnel. The other option is to wait until around two in the afternoon for a replacement plane to come get both of you and take you back to Chicago. You would arrive in the early evening. In the first scenario, Mr. Banks would be seen in the cath lab tomorrow afternoon. In the second, he'd be seen the following day. With the second option you also run the risk of the snowstorm causing delays."

Teo nodded and put the phone back to his ear, relaying the information to his friend. When the conversation became heated again, I stepped out to give him some privacy. I wasn't completely sure, but it had sounded like the grandson had some kind of conflict which was making the arrangements more difficult. When Teo finally joined me in the hallway, he looked exhausted.

"We want to get him on the flight that's already in the air," he said. "Have him seen by the specialists as soon as possible."

I quickly called the dispatcher back and put in the request. It took twenty more minutes of coordinating, so I told Teo to go back into the room and get comfortable in the chair there until I had everything confirmed.

I called Simon back at the airport to let him know when to expect the plane, and then I texted Nate at the hotel to give him the update. After that, Teo and I spoke to the nurse on duty to find out how to transport Mr. Banks back to the airport via ambulance.

At some point Mr. Banks must have woken up because I heard Teo murmuring to him in the room. I glanced in to see Teo stroking the patient's forehead while he smiled down at him. His affection for the man was obvious, as was his gentle demeanor. My heart squeezed watching him care for the older man. I could see why he'd become a nurse.

I heard Teo promising Mr. Banks that Chris would be there to meet him at the hospital in Chicago. I wondered what he'd said to convince his friend to change his mind. It was really none of my business, but I couldn't help but feel a tinge of jealousy knowing the dismissive younger Banks I'd met a couple of times already was closer to Teo than I'd ever be. It didn't seem fair, somehow. But that was the price I paid to keep the lifestyle I had.

Just as I was about to go in search of a snack and some water for Teo, Simon called.

"That weather I told you about is coming in fast. Our window is narrowing to get this plane in and out before it hits."

9

TEO

I felt like a child: tired, hungry, unsure. I hated feeling this way. My entire life, I'd struggled with feelings of inferiority, but now I also felt vastly unprepared and relegated to being nothing more in this scenario than the hired help.

As I watched the red taillights of the sleek air ambulance jet rise into the pitch-black early-morning sky, I couldn't help but worry excessively. Gordon had looked so small and frail on the gurney, and sending him off with a plane full of strangers had been nearly impossible.

Jack had arranged everything, and he'd stood by my side while they'd loaded Gordon onto the plane. I'd found the head nurse and gone over everything about Gordon's care with her. She was a lovely British woman with insignia that identified her as part of an international air ambulance crew. I knew she had to be plenty capable, but it didn't stop me from covering all my bases.

After she returned to the cabin to check on Gordon, Jack introduced me to four other crew members on the flight, making sure to explain in a friendly way how important Mr. Banks was to me and how grateful we were for their help. It wasn't until I stood there, watching the plane fly away, that his actions had accomplished two things: he'd gently reminded them Gordon was important and loved, and he'd gently reminded *me* that there were several nice people on board the flight who would make sure Gordon was well cared for.

"Let's go to the hotel," he said quietly. "You must be dead on your feet. I know I am."

Snow flurries had begun on our drive to the airport, but the flakes were beginning to come down faster now. Since it was April, I hadn't brought a parka with me. Chicago hadn't been that cold, and I hadn't expected Frankfurt to be much different. But the weather on the northeastern coast of Canada was a different animal. A frigid animal.

I followed Jack back to the vehicle he was using and hopped in, grateful when the heat from the vents proved to still be warm since we hadn't been gone from the truck long. We pulled into the hotel lot and parked. The front desk had a room key waiting for Jack, but nothing for me.

"I'm so sorry," he murmured to me. "I thought they were arranging something for you too."

"It's fine. Nate probably knew I wouldn't leave Gordon alone at the hospital." I turned back to the woman at the front desk. "Can I get a room please?"

She bit at her lip and shot a worried glance at Jack. "Well, you see... it's the Winter Carnival and..."

I felt Jack's body shift next to mine, and part of me just wanted to lean myself against him and fall asleep standing right there.

"It's fine," I said, trying to rally. "I saw another hotel across the street, I think."

The woman winced. "We're all full, I'm afraid. We keep two rooms open for emergencies. Since the other pilot was able to share with the flight attendant, your friend here got the last remaining room. I can—"

"You can share with me," Jack said in a gruff voice. "It's no problem. Or... actually. You can have the room and I'll..."

I put my hand on his arm. "Don't be silly. Sharing sounds fine if you don't mind." I wanted to add that we'd done it before with no problem, but the situation was obviously different now.

Jack cleared his throat and nodded at the lady. "Thank you for your help."

I thanked her too and then followed Jack to the stairwell. My stomach flipped around, making me feel like I was at a teen party and the spinning bottle had just stopped at the most gorgeous member of the football team. Following Jack to a shared hotel room was like following the quarterback into the closet for five minutes in heaven.

My palms began to sweat.

Don't say anything or you'll open the chatty floodgates, I warned myself.

I didn't listen.

"Did you know climbing just eight flights of stairs a day lowers average early mortality risk by 33 percent?" I asked. "It burns more calories per minute than jogging. So you have all these people who think they can't afford to be healthy when all they need to do is find a simple flight of stairs."

Stop talking.

"In fact, stair climbing engages multiple muscles and improves balance. When I worked at a senior living center, we did stair climbing challenges all the time with the patients who could manage them."

Please shut up.

I took a breath and spoke even faster when I realized the door to our shared room was right there at the top of the stairs. "And even the people who couldn't manage the stairs saw benefits from something as simple as sitting calf raises. Did you know your calf muscles are considered a 'second heart' of sorts? So when those muscles fire, they help pump blood back toward the heart from your lower extremities. Keeping those muscles healthy is important, and people in sedentary—"

The moment I stepped through the door, Jack closed it and pressed me against it, stopping my idiotic babbling with his mouth. I whimpered against his lips and clutched at the front of his jacket to keep from tipping over in surprise.

His whiskers were a delicious combination of soft and sharp

against my lips. He smelled like coffee and airplane and faint traces of some kind of magical male fragrance that made me want to climb him like a clingy koala and never let go.

Jack pulled off my jacket without stopping the kiss, and before I knew it, I was kicking off my own shoes in a desperate attempt to get as naked as humanly possible just on the off chance he'd reciprocate and let me rub my body all over his.

I knew from experience he was covered in the exact right amount of body hair and his muscles were firm, but his abs were hidden under the sweetest little layer of belly fat that probably drove him crazy in a bad way but drove me crazy in a good way. I remembered exploring his body with my hands and tongue after I'd finally gotten up the nerve to do more than take, take, take.

"Can we...?" I mumbled the words against his lips but couldn't keep my tongue out of his mouth long enough to finish the question.

His hands yanked my shirt out of my pants, and his warm palms smoothed along my bare back, pulling me even closer to him.

"Naked," I continued with a gasp.

Jack moved his mouth down to my neck and sucked on the skin under my ear. My skin erupted in goose bumps, and the oxygen level in the room dropped suddenly.

"Jack." It was a plea for mercy maybe. "*Jack.*"

One of his hands plunged down the back of my pants and squeezed an ass cheek, pulling until I was on my tiptoes. My dick was hard and dripping, so I reached down to shove my pants and underwear off. Was that presumptuous? I wasn't really well versed in hookup etiquette.

An image of Chris popped into my mind, but I wished it away. I was still angry at him for any number of things and didn't want to think about him right now. I wanted to be touched and appreciated. If I could get Jack to act like he did that first night where he pretended to care about me... well, that would be even better.

Either way, I would take what I could get with him. Even a quick shared orgasm before sleep would be better than nothing. Way, way better than nothing.

Jack's finger slid between my cheeks and made me squeak in surprise. I wasn't used to being touched this way, intimately. He was the only person who'd ever had his hands on my body before, but he was still a stranger.

"You okay?" he asked, pulling back to check in with me. "Am I going too fast?"

His eyes were half-lidded and sexy as hell. His lips were plump and a deeper pink from the kissing, and I thought, once again, the sight of his late-night stubble might be enough to trigger my orgasm on its own.

"Uh-huh." I nodded.

"Oh," he said stepping back. "Sorry."

I squinted at him. "What? Oh, no! I thought... never mind. I'm okay. I'm more than okay."

His face softened into a smile, and he reached out to brush his fingers through my hair. "You're so fucking beautiful. It killed me not to be able to tell you that night. Your dark hair and your bright eyes... your perfect body and all this gorgeous skin... god, I just wanted to tell you over and over how much you turned me on."

My stomach flipped over. "Really?"

"Yeah," he said, pulling me back in close. "I'm sure you've heard it before, but... it's a relief to finally be able to say it out loud."

I swallowed. "I've never heard it before."

Jack tilted his head in confusion. "Your other boyfriends haven't told you how sexy and beautiful you are?"

Oh, shit. The last thing I wanted to do was admit he was the only person I'd ever had sex with. That was a one-way ticket straight to loserville.

"No, I mean. Yeah. Well, you know some guys aren't talkers, so..."

"They're idiots," he murmured before leaning in to kiss me on the lips again. He had the kind of magical kisses that made clothing disappear. I didn't know that was a thing, but it happened, and the next thing I knew, I was on my back on one of the beds, the cool comforter a shock to my overly warm skin.

An equally naked Jack was on top of me, raining kisses down my jaw to my shoulder and across my chest. I felt like I was grasping at him wildly with both hands and feet like one of those inflatable blowing things in front of car dealerships. No purpose, just frantic flailing.

He finally grabbed both of my wrists and crossed them on the pillow above my head, transferring them into one of his strong hands while the other hand felt up my chest.

I wish I bench-pressed. Did men apologize to other men for not being buffer?

I opened my mouth to say something, but an unintelligible sound of longing came out.

"I have you," he whispered between kisses. His hands continued to map my chest, sides, and stomach. "So good, so fucking good."

I wasn't even sure he knew he was talking out loud, but I liked it. This big, strong pilot muttering reassurances to me during sex was unexpectedly sweet, especially because nothing he was feeling was particularly good at all. It was all very Teo Parisi mediocre. I was that guy you didn't remember: medium height, medium build, brown hair. So, for him to say anything about being naked with me was good meant he was kind and generous.

Our dicks rubbed together deliciously as he moved his hips rhythmically against me. I arched up into him seeking more and more and more. I wondered if he was going to fuck me or if maybe I should try to suck him off. As soon as the image of his fat dick on my tongue came into my mind, my mouth filled with saliva.

"Suck you," I managed to blurt.

He froze in the middle of licking one of my nipples and looked up at me with a frown. "I'm sorry?"

"Your dick. Your cock." What part didn't he understand? "Your penis."

His face relaxed into laughter, and he laid his forehead down on my chest. "Teo, I thought you said 'fuck you.'"

"Ohhh. No. Well, I mean... I guess I could try, but—"

He lurched up and kissed me hard. "You're adorable. Stay right there."

Jack climbed off the bed and rustled through his bag before coming back with a small bottle of lube. I didn't want to think of why he traveled with it. Hopefully for masturbation only.

I rolled my eyes at myself. *Sure, Teo. Probably for masturbation only. Look at the man, for god's sake. He probably has a sailor in every port.*

That was corny enough, I had to roll my eyes again. Jack must have seen me because he furrowed his brow.

"No!" I said. "Not you. That's for me. I'm… never mind. Yes, that. Whatever you're going to do with that. Please do it. I consent. *Fervently.* I fervently consent."

He laughed and shook his head. "I'm beginning to understand your need for a silence rule before."

Before I could take offense, he winked at me and pressed a kiss to my cheek. "I'm joking. I'm so happy not to have a silence rule right now, I can't even express it in words. Which is ironic."

I ran my fingers through his hair, noticing the thick waves were just as soft as they'd been before. We locked eyes and stared at each other for a few beats while our lower bodies automatically resumed the dry humping we'd been doing before. Suddenly I felt Jack's hand gripping our dicks together with cool, slick lube.

"Oh god," I said, closing my eyes and arching my head back in bliss. "Feels so good."

I pushed my cock through his tight grip and held on to his wide shoulders to keep him from pulling away. It felt so good, so unbelievably sensual and exciting that I had a moment of absolute regret. Regret at wasting all the years I could have been doing this with other men, could have been feeling sexy and desired. Having someone as hot as Jack Snyder kissing me, touching me, stroking me to orgasm against his own hard cock… god, it was like something out of a dream.

"Want you to come," he grunted, his breath hot against my chest. "Let go, Tee. Come all over me."

The combination of the nickname and dirty talk blasted me over the edge. I cried out as my balls emptied, the feeling of release a combination of utter euphoria and relief. After a beat, I felt the warm splats of his own release on my stomach. It was so hot, so foreign and exciting, another bead of cum escaped me while my body contracted again.

"Ughgod," I gasped. I folded my legs around the back of him and pulled his face down to kiss me. We were breathing so heavy, it was more like holding our mouths together as we fought for oxygen, but it still gave me the intimate connection I craved.

"So fucking sexy," he murmured before kissing me more fully. "So hot."

I felt half-conscious, like I'd melted into the bed and would never be able to get up again. I'd been awake now for over twenty-four hours, and the adrenaline spike from the crash had made the exhaustion even worse. Would it be rude if I just closed my eyes and slipped away?

Jack began murmuring to me again, but I couldn't catch the words. At one point a warm wet cloth cleaned me up like something out of a Disney movie where objects were animated and sentient. Or maybe that was a dream.

When I woke up sometime later, I was plastered against a solid, masculine body that smelled like hotel soap and sleepy man. Would it be considered strange if I sniffed his armpit? His arm was bent up over his head, exposing the sexiest dark pit hair ever. Just as I was inching up to sneak a whiff, the phone rang, splitting the silence of the dark hotel room.

10

JACK

Watching Teo orgasm himself into a stupor had been intoxicating. The noises he'd made, the flush on his chest, and the way he'd clung to me had made me feel like some kind of sex god. He was so beautiful when he let go. I wanted to see it a million more times.

But when the phone woke us up, I knew we had a long day ahead of us that didn't include more shared orgasms.

"Hello," I croaked into the room's headset.

"Morning, Jack," Nate said. "I need to get the keys from you and head back to the airport. The mechanic and investigator are arriving soon, and I need to be there."

Teo began to shift away from me, but I pulled him back to my side and pressed a quick kiss against his messy hair.

I glanced at the clock and noticed it was almost ten. We'd only managed about four hours of sleep. "Yeah. Give me five minutes to shave, and I'll meet you in the lobby."

After I hung up, I put both arms around Teo and squeezed gently, wanting to imprint the feel of his body against mine on my memory.

"I have to go to the airport. Stay here and get some more sleep." I kissed the top of his head again before letting go. He reached out to grab my hand.

"Wait. Um... will you... what should I..." He winced and looked everywhere but at me before continuing. "Do you need help? I mean, not that I would know how to help with an airplane or anything, but... never mind." He chuckled and shook his head. "Never mind. That's stupid."

God, he was so vulnerable and sweet. Naive, almost. Or... something. Something that brought out an unexpected tenderness in me.

"Actually, yeah. You know what would be a huge help?" Teo's face lit up when I spoke. "Find out where we can meet for lunch in a couple of hours and text me? I think there's a restaurant here at the hotel, but I'm not positive. If Nate and Brenda come with us, we'll need a table for four."

He nodded and smiled in relief. "Got it. I can do that. Do you want me to pick something up and bring it to the airport?"

"Probably not, but I'll text you if things change. I don't want you to have to try and find a ride in this place. It's not the kind of town you can hail a cab in."

After making myself somewhat presentable in the bathroom, I raced to get dressed in the warmest clothes I had before meeting Nate in the lobby.

"How's Mr. Banks?" he asked, handing me a paper cup of coffee and a granola bar.

I updated him on everything that had happened overnight, including the family's decision to send him on home.

"Does the other gentleman still need to go to Frankfurt?"

I glanced at him as we hopped in the borrowed truck. "I... I don't know. I mean, I assume not because he was traveling as Mr. Banks's nurse, wasn't he?"

It was only a couple of miles to the airport, but since the roads had patches of snow and ice on them and I was driving a borrowed vehicle, I was extra careful. I'd driven plenty growing up in Indiana, but once I'd moved to Newark, there'd been years where the most driving I'd done was on vacations and visits home.

"No. It was my understanding he's a consultant for the company and they were headed to Germany to close a deal. If that's the case, we may need to make arrangements to charter another plane. Either way, we can't expect the guy to stick around here while we assess the engines."

He was right, and I was an idiot. It had never occurred to me to make arrangements for him to fly home. I should have done that while I had the concierge on the phone the night before making the air ambulance plans.

"I'll text him when we get to the airport," I promised. "Meanwhile, what do you think the mechanic is going to say?"

It only took thirty minutes for the mechanic to explain what had malfunctioned in the portside engine and tell us it could be fixed relatively easily. "I can probably get the parts up here by noon tomorrow, and then... I'd say the work will be done maybe noon the following day? Unless, of course, something unexpected happens."

The three of us met with the safety inspector, who went through the mechanic's conclusions and seemed to agree with everything. We made the requisite calls to the home office to make arrangements for the repairs, and then Nate called Brenda to arrange to keep our hotel rooms a couple more nights.

I hadn't heard back from Teo about whether he needed to continue on to Frankfurt or not, so I tried to keep from getting a little excited about the possibility of spending more time with him. I couldn't think of a better way to spend the next forty-eight hours than naked in bed with the sexy man.

When we were finally able to leave the airport and meet Teo and Brenda for lunch, I was starving. That had to explain the odd feeling in my stomach when I walked into the hotel restaurant and saw Teo. He'd obviously showered and dressed in clean clothes. He looked handsome in a navy sweater and jeans. His smile was genuine and friendly as he spoke to Brenda, who already sat next to him at a four-top table. The hostess who led us to the table seemed unable to keep her eyes off Teo, and I couldn't blame her. He was drop-dead fucking gorgeous, and I was honestly shocked he wasn't already in a twelve-way relationship with a dozen of the most beautiful and generous gay men in the world whose sole purpose in life was to lavish him with attention and love.

"Um, Jack?" Teo said, jerking me out of that mental image. His bright eyes looked at me, unsure, which made me smile automatically in hopes of putting him at ease. His cheeks flushed.

There was an awkward moment when Nate leaned over to kiss Brenda hello. Suddenly, I was faced with the obvious reality of not being able to let on that Teo and I were anything other than acquaintances from the ill-fated flight. I was very new at the executive charter service that managed the Bankses' Gulfstream, and the last thing I needed was for Nate to think I planned on sleeping with our passengers.

"Hi," I said, clearing my throat. "We just heard that Mr. Banks's plane landed and the transfer to Northwestern went smoothly."

Teo nodded. "Chris called me. I'm so relieved to know he's in good hands."

I took the chair next to him so Nate could sit next to his wife. "Did you get my text about Frankfurt?"

"Oh, uh, yeah. Sorry. That's actually why I called Chris in the first place. They don't need me to go. The client went ahead and signed the papers remotely. It's kind of a long story, but it was Grandpa Banks they wanted because of a family connection. We didn't really need to have the papers signed in person."

"Oh, good. Then..." I fiddled with my water glass. "You can head back to Chicago. We can help you find flights."

Teo glanced between Nate and me. "Is the plane grounded for a while?"

Nate cut in. "Not at all. They think it'll take about forty-eight hours for it to be ready. But we can probably get you back to Chicago on commercial flights sooner. I'll warn you though, it's a pretty long travel day. I think they stop in Halifax and Newark before O'Hare. Ten hours, maybe?"

Teo's eyes widened. "But we were only in the air for a few hours before we got here."

Nate continued. "Yeah. It's only about three and a half for us. The problem is all the stops and layovers doing it on the airlines. You have to go around your elbow to get to your ass. It's one of the reasons companies like Banks Consulting uses a corporate jet. That time is money when their high-level executives are the ones stuck in airports."

Teo glanced back at me before speaking to Nate. I noticed his cheeks flush again a little bit which only made my stomach feel funnier. "I don't really want to go by myself. Can I stay and ride back with you?"

"Of course," Brenda said, reaching over to pat his hand. "It's your plane, after all. You're the client. We just want to make sure you're happy and comfortable."

"Well, I have my computer, and I think the hotel has Wi-Fi..." He glanced at me again under his lashes, and I imagined lunging over the table and tackling him to the floor just so I could taste the lip he was currently biting on. "So if it's not a bother..."

"Not at all," I said in a gruff voice. "Happy to have you."

He blew out a breath and smiled at me. I really needed that server to come take our order before my stomach turned completely inside out from hunger. "Okay, good. Thanks. That's... thanks."

After we placed our orders for a shocking amount of fried food and the hostess came over to refill Teo's water for the tenth time since seating us, Brenda began making polite conversation with Teo by asking him where he was from and why he'd become a nurse. I could have kissed her for drawing out so much personal information from him.

He wasn't as shy as I'd originally thought. He chatted happily with Nate and Brenda, telling them about growing up outside of Chicago where his dad worked as a plumber and his mom stayed home and cooked for half the neighborhood. He had one sister, same as me, but his was older.

"She nags me," he said with a laugh. "But if it weren't for her, I don't think I would have made it through nursing school."

"How so?" Brenda asked.

He shrugged and took a sip of his water before answering. "She's an LPN. She wanted to become an RN, but then she got pregnant with my niece before she could finish more than the diploma program. So, since she didn't get a bachelor's degree, she decided to hound me to make up for it. I'm glad she did though. I love what I do." His brows furrowed a little bit. "Well, I mean... I..." He looked up and seemed to remember he was sitting with three practical strangers. "I love taking care of people."

Brenda patted his hand again and gave him a maternal smile. "I could tell. Mr. Banks was lucky to have you there last night. You were very calm under pressure."

He blushed and looked down, fiddling with the fork in his place setting. "I hope he's okay. If only I'd assessed him earlier. Maybe I could have—"

"Nonsense," Brenda said. "I saw you take his vitals and check his glucose once we got into the air. If you'd done more than that, he probably would have griped at you."

Teo's lip curled up a little. "You're right. He doesn't like being babied."

Brenda and Nate went on to share some stories of flying Mr. Banks over the past several years since they began working for the company. They had nothing but complimentary things to say about the older man, and Teo laughed and shared his own stories. By the time our food came, I felt like I'd gotten to know enough of him to confirm my first impression that he was a kind and sweet man.

The more I learned about him, the more I wanted to find out why he'd placed that ad several months before asking for the silent hookup. Why silent? And why did he need to resort to an anonymous hookup to get someone to treat him like he mattered?

It had also become clear that the reason he knew Mr. Banks so well was because Teo had been Chris Banks's best friend since they were in elementary school. That bothered me more than it should have. It *should* have been none of my damned business. And even if Teo was somehow my business, what did it matter if he was close friends with rich businessmen?

I forced Chris Banks out of my mind and focused on Brenda's

story about their son, who'd just gotten an impressive promotion in the Air Force. Before long, the meal was over, and Brenda and Nate were discussing meeting back up for lunch the following day.

Teo's sweet, unsure glance at me before answering made me smile. Hopefully that meant he wanted to spend that time with me. "Yeah, uh, sure. That sounds fine. The lady at the front desk said there were a couple of pub-type places close enough to walk to."

We said goodbye in the lobby before making our way to the room. Thankfully, Brenda and Nate's room was down a different hallway, so they didn't see Teo and I enter the same hotel room.

Once we were in the room, things turned awkward. Teo sat down at the foot of one of the freshly made beds and folded his hands in his lap.

"Um. Do you want to watch a movie, or..." He didn't look at me while he spoke. He kept his eyes riveted on his hands.

"I'm actually still really tired," I admitted. "Would you mind if I —" I gestured to the bed, and he hopped up like it was on fire.

"Oh! Oh, of course not. No. I'm sure you're tired. You didn't get much sleep last night." He pinched his lips closed and shook his head. "I mean, obviously. But still, it makes sense you'd like to lie down. Here, lie down." He held his hand out to display the bed behind him like a prize on a game show.

He was so fucking cute, I really couldn't keep my hands off him. I stepped up toward him slowly so he'd have time to dart away if he didn't want me in his personal space.

He stood still.

I grasped his face in both hands. His skin was warm and smooth. "Will you lie down with me?" I asked in a low voice.

He swallowed. "Um, yeah. If you want."

I grinned at him. "Oh, I want."

His face flushed pink. "That's not what I meant."

"Teo, tell me to stop," I murmured before leaning in to brush my nose against his.

"Don't want you to stop," he whispered back before reaching up to pull me fully into a kiss. We kissed for a long time, slowly and teasing. When I finally began working the clothes off him, both of us were plenty hard. I wondered idly what kind of god of aviation I'd somehow tricked into bestowing me this job that had led me right back into the arms of the sexy NurseTee.

Once we were both naked, I moved us onto the bed, covering him with my body when I realized he was cold in the wintery hotel room. He continued to shiver so much under my touch, that I finally got up to adjust the thermostat in the room.

"What are you...? That's not," he began before starting to laugh. "Get over here, silly man. I'm shivering because you're driving me crazy. Not because I'm cold."

I shrugged and grinned and climbed back on top of him, continuing my exploration of every single inch of him with my nose and tongue. Just as I was about to take his cock into my mouth, the fucking phone interrupted us again. Only this time it wasn't the room phone but Teo's cell.

And my cockblocker was, of course, Chris Banks.

11

TEO

I wouldn't have answered it if I wasn't worried about Grandpa Banks. But as soon as I heard Chris's ringtone, I scrambled out from underneath Jack and grabbed my phone.

"How is he?" I said after hitting the button to answer the call.

"How's who?" Chris asked. I could hear the sounds of the city in the background like maybe he was walking somewhere.

I paused a beat, confused that he didn't know who I was asking about. "Grandpa Banks."

"Oh, I don't know. Good, I guess. They're doing tests. We'll know more later. Dad's going to head over there now. I was calling to tell you we—"

"Wait, wait. You're not at Northwestern?" I didn't understand. He'd called me earlier to tell me Gordon's arrival had gone smoothly.

"No. Dad and I just finished our presentation. That's what I was calling about. It went great. I think we have a good chance at doing business with these guys, and they have—"

"You're not at the hospital?" I asked again. Maybe I hoped the answer would be different this time. I couldn't fathom my father or grandfather having a heart attack and not rushing to the hospital to be with them.

"No. I just told you. We were at the Firehouse restaurant where they have that private room with the big flat-screen. It was perfect for the PowerPoint, and they had a prime rib french dip you would have loved."

I tuned him out while he continued to talk about the meeting. Should I try to get back there so Gordon would have someone at his bedside? Would Mike and Chris be more attentive to the situation now that their all-important meeting was finished? I pictured Gordon going through the testing at the cath lab where he'd most likely only be sedated rather than put all the way under. If he needed any stents put in, I assumed they'd most likely do it during the cath lab procedure.

"Teo?" Chris interrupted my thoughts.

"Yeah?"

"You're really worried about Grandpa, aren't you?"

"Yes, Chris. It's serious. You didn't see the way he looked when he was clutching his chest and struggling to breathe. He's not young and strong. And the diabetes is a serious complication. Almost 70 percent of people his age with diabetes die from heart disease. He should have already been under the care of a cardiologist. I should have made sure he'd seen a specialist, and then maybe this could have been prevented."

"Hon, you've only been his nurse a couple of months," Chris said gently. The words didn't sit right with me.

"I'm not actually his nurse, Chris. At least... I didn't think I was?"

He paused. "No, that's not what I meant. Sorry. I only meant that you take such good care of him and you've only been around him enough to keep your eye on him for the past few months. Not that it's your responsibility. At all. I'm sorry I made you feel that way."

I blew out a breath. "Thank you."

"I'll head over there right now," he said. "I got so caught up in trying to get this new business, I guess I wasn't paying enough attention to how serious this was."

I smiled in relief. There was the man I knew. "Thank you. That would mean a lot to me."

"When are you coming home? Do you need me to send another plane to come and get you?"

"Probably day after tomorrow. We're waiting on some parts to have the plane fixed. If I fly home on my own, it'll take an entire day, so I'm just going to wait and come home with the plane once it's ready."

"You sure? I wish you were here. I miss you."

I glanced up at Jack, who had grabbed his own phone and was currently scrolling through it, probably to give me some modicum of privacy. But there was no doubt he could hear every word I said since I was only four feet away from him.

"Yeah. Me too." Except that wasn't exactly true. I missed him in the general sense of preferring to be around him and wanting to be with him, but I didn't want to leave this strange pretend world with Jack either. If there was a plane waiting on the tarmac right now to take me straight home, would I choose to board it?

"See you soon, Teo. Take care," Chris said softly.

"Yeah, uh, you too."

When we got off the phone, I felt conflicted. For twenty years I'd wanted nothing more than to be by that man's side. But now here I was finally getting to experience sex. Finally getting to feel what it was like to have a man look at me like I was someone desirable.

Did I want to pursue a relationship with Jack now, instead of Chris? No, of course not. For one, I hardly knew him. And secondly, he was probably never around. If there was one thing I selfishly knew about myself, it was that I wanted the white picket fence. I wanted a husband who came home to me every night and asked me how my day was. I didn't want a man who answered ads on an app for anonymous hotel room fucks.

As much as our encounter months ago had rocked my world, I hadn't fooled myself into thinking it was more than it was. And I wasn't doing so now either. Jack didn't seem like the kind of man who settled down, and even if he did, I couldn't in a million years imagine him choosing a dork like me to do it with. He was model-beautiful and the kind of person who walked through the world with built-in confidence. Even at the restaurant for lunch, the waitress had damned near shit herself when Jack had called her by her name.

He was charismatic and magnetic. Nate had bragged at lunch about how Jack had been one of the youngest United Airlines pilots to fly the A380. It made me wonder why he'd left the airline, but then again, I imagined there was much less hassle flying private than commercial. But what did I know?

"Everything okay back home?" he asked, setting his phone on the bedside table.

"Yeah, I guess. Mike and Chris aren't at the hospital yet."

Jack's brows furrowed. "I thought Chris promised you he'd meet the plane?"

I shrugged and tossed my phone on the bedside table, suddenly self-conscious about being naked in front of him. He was all broad and muscular while I was more on the skinny and pathetic side. Well, pathetic was too strong of a word. I did run most days, and I did push-ups and sit-ups when I remembered. But I'd never have a body like Jack's. He had the kind of body that men flocked to on Instagram.

"I guess he couldn't be bothered," I said before pulling back the covers and sliding underneath. "Well, that's not really fair. The truth of the matter is they had a huge client meeting at lunch and chose to go ahead with it and head to the hospital after. I guess they thought since Grandpa Banks was going to be busy with the testing anyway... And, really, this deal is important to the future of the company. It's a really big opportunity."

Jack moved around so he could slide under the covers too. He lay on his side with his head propped in his hand. "You and Chris are good friends, huh?"

I relaxed into the pillow. "Yes. Only most of the time I wish he would get his head out of his ass and grow up."

"Isn't he the sales director of a multimillion-dollar consulting company?" Jack lifted an eyebrow as if to make some kind of point. I wasn't quite sure what the point was.

"Yes. But that doesn't make him a grown-up. There's more to being an adult than being good at your job."

"Like what?"

I looked at him out of the corner of my eye. "Like a lot of things."

"Okay," he said, shifting around until he was sitting up against the headboard. "Tell me what you wish he'd do differently."

God, where would I even begin?

"Why are we talking about this?" I asked instead.

"Because you seem super frustrated by him, like he's letting you down. I'm curious why you have such high expectations of him."

I sat up too so I could flap my hands around in frustration. Apparently. "I don't think it's high expectation to want Gordon Banks not to be alone at the hospital right after a heart attack. I don't think it's high expectations for Chris to show up for an international fucking flight he promised to show up for. I don't think it's high expectation to follow through on promises to *be there* when a man says he's going to be there for you. He's a fucking promise-breaker is what he is."

Jack's eyes widened as I ranted.

"Woah. Okay. I can see why you're upset."

"Yeah," I said, petering out.

"What's the biggest promise he's ever broken to you?" he asked gently.

"He..." I wondered why I felt compelled to tell Jack the truth. "He..." But would it be rude of me to talk about another love interest with the man I was currently naked in bed with?

Jack reached out and took my hand. "I'm a dead end, Teo. Hell, after we get back home, you may never even see me again. Chicago is a big place."

I didn't like the idea of never seeing him again, but at least his words confirmed what I already knew to be true. He didn't have plans to ask me out when we returned to Chicago. Of course he didn't. And that was fine. It wasn't like I was looking for a boyfriend when all I'd ever wanted was Chris Banks.

"He promised me we'd be together," I admitted in a small voice. I sounded pathetic. There was finally an appropriate way to use that word accurately in describing me.

Jack looked taken aback. "He's gay?"

I shrugged. "I don't know. Bi maybe. He's only ever really dated women, thank god."

"What do you mean? He's only ever dated women, but he promised to be with you?"

It sounded weird when he put it that way. "We've been each other's everything for twenty years," I explained. "In high school we finally kissed and it was…" I thought back to how perfect and magical it had felt. "It was like everything falling perfectly into place, you know?"

"So what happened?"

I pulled my knees up and rested my arms on them, not looking over at Jack. I didn't want to see his reaction to my stupid story.

"He wanted to have sex, of course. What teenage boy doesn't? I did too. Badly. But he was dating a girl named Demi Woodley, and I'd already felt like an ass for kissing the girl's boyfriend. Even though I'd had him longer, so to speak." I groaned. "And believe me when I tell you I'm well aware of how ridiculous this all sounds. But in my defense, it was actually high school."

"So you asked him to break up with Demi first."

"No! Well, I mean, kind of. I didn't set out to make it an ultimatum, but I also wasn't going to be the guy who breaks the poor girl's heart. She loved him. They'd been together for like a year already." I sighed. "So I didn't ask him to dump her, but I said I wasn't going to sleep with him while he was dating her."

"And did they break up?"

I shook my head. "His parents adored Demi. They were good friends with Demi's parents and had already built Demi and Chris up as some kind of power couple who was going to go off to college together, then get married and give them all perfect little babies."

"Ouch. That's a lot of expectations on a high schooler."

"Tell me about it. He felt a ton of pressure. And I was around his parents plenty to see it firsthand, so I couldn't exactly blame him. Plus, I think he really liked her. He's… he's kind of the type of person who wants to have his cake and eat it too."

"Ah. I see."

"But the real reason, at least the one he told me at the time, was his inability to come out to his family. He's an only child, and he feels the expectations of the entire family on his shoulders, not to mention the family business."

"Mm."

I glanced over at Jack, who seemed to be making an attempt to be a good listener. It was clear from the tension around his lips he wasn't all that thrilled with the story.

"But then..." I thought about what I'd learned from Gordon about Uncle Rod and Oliver Poole. "And so..." I swallowed. How could I admit this out loud to anyone without having to face the truth? "Never mind," I finally said.

I chanced a peek at Jack out of the corner of my eye. He looked confused and upset. I didn't blame him since I felt the exact same way.

After several moments of awkward silence, I was considering faking a sudden coma when suddenly Jack hopped out of bed and reached for his clothes.

Oh great. He's leaving me.

I slid down between the sheets and pulled the blanket over my head.

12

JACK

This called for alcohol.

It was clear Teo had some things he needed to talk through, but he was having a hell of a time getting past his inner critic.

"I'll be back in a few," I said, before sliding on my shoes and grabbing my wallet.

After asking for help at the front desk, I headed out of the hotel and to a nearby liquor store. I grabbed some snacks and mixers, as well as a couple of touristy Goose Bay shot glasses before returning to the hotel.

When I entered the room, the soft sounds of snoring hit my ears. Teo was curled up in a small ball with his hands under his chin and his knees to his chest. His face was flushed with sleep, and his dark eyelashes rested against the smooth skin of his cheeks.

He was breathtaking.

I stripped off my clothes and slid into bed behind him, pulling him close and kissing the back of his neck. I was half-asleep within moments, relaxed in the knowledge that, for now, I was exactly where I wanted to be.

When I awoke to the feeling of his warm lips on my hardening dick, I sucked in a breath. "Oh fuck yeah," I murmured, reaching down to put my hand in his hair. He was good at this. I didn't want to think of what other dicks he'd sucked before mine, especially any that came between our first time together and now.

It reminded me I hadn't been with anyone in the months between our times together. Maybe it was because of my job change and the frustration and burnout leading up to it. Regardless, I was pumped as hell the dry spell was over, and my dick was even happier.

I lay back and enjoyed a few more vigorous pulls from his hot mouth before realizing this would be sixty-nine times better if I sucked him at the same time. I swiveled around and took him into my mouth, thrilled to see he was already hard as a rock.

The moaning whimper sound he made around my cock was scorching hot. Teo was incredibly responsive. I loved that he didn't stay quiet during sex. The sounds and movements he made jacked me up even more than simply feeling his body against mine.

Within minutes of sucking each other off, we were both coming, one after the other in a satisfying twist of bodies damp with sweat and warm from sleep. We both lay there panting after the fact, waiting to catch our breaths.

"I want to do that again soon," Teo said in a rough voice. "I could do that every morning and every night and be happy."

I ran my hand up his outer thigh to his round ass cheek and squeezed. That John Mayer song "Your Body is a Wonderland" popped into my head. "No complaints here."

His chuckle was pleasantly relaxed, unlike how stressed he'd been before I'd left on the alcohol run.

"I brought you something," I said, moving to get up from the bed so I could collect my goodies. "I thought we could play a little drinking game."

Teo stood up and reached for his boxer briefs. "I'm going to need some clothes on for this."

I started unpacking the paper bags. "I got a selection because I didn't know what you wanted. One of the perks of private air flight is being able to take liquid on board," I said with a wink. "So if we have leftovers, it's fine."

"Oh, pass me those crunchy things. What are those?"

I looked through the snacks and found something called Hickory Sticks. I tossed them over. "I was going to get ketchup chips as a joke, but then I thought maybe that was a bridge too far."

He'd put on underwear and a T-shirt, but he still looked cold. I tossed him my Colts hoodie. "Put that on," I muttered before slipping into some track pants and a long-sleeve shirt from my bag. "I'm going to get some ice from the machine."

"Gimme that chocolate before you go," Teo said, making the universal sign for gimme with his hands. I tossed him the caramel chocolate bar. "Wait, you didn't get Milk Duds, did you? Those are my favorite."

"No Milk Duds. But here's the bag if you want to see what else I picked out. I grabbed an assortment."

I left him pawing through the bag with half a candy bar hanging out of his mouth. When I got back to the room, Teo had put some music on with a small portable Bluetooth speaker and his phone. I didn't recognize it, but it was a kind of mellow electronic music that seemed a little bit familiar.

"Okay," I said, pouring two shots of dark rum. "We're each going to take a shot first to get us warmed up. Then we're going to take turns asking questions. For every question you refuse to answer, you take another shot."

"Why would I refuse to answer?" he asked, reaching for one of the tiny glasses and throwing it back.

"What do you think is the real reason Chris won't come out?"

Teo choked and sputtered on the rum, shoving the empty shot glass back at me. He fanned his face with his hands as he struggled to swallow. By the time he got himself under control, his moist eyes were shooting daggers at me.

"Give me another shot," he said.

I did as he asked. Once he swallowed that one and handed the glass back, he met my eyes. "My turn."

The warm spice of the rum still lingered on my tongue from the first shot. "Go ahead. I'm an open book, sweetheart."

We'd moved over to the sofa by the window. I dragged one of the blankets off the extra bed and tossed it to him. As soon as he'd wrapped himself in it, he studied me for a minute.

"Why aren't you in a relationship?"

"I travel too much," I said. "When you and I first met, I was a commercial pilot for United out of Newark."

"Why'd you change jobs?"

I leaned back and put my feet up on the low coffee table. "I grew up in La Porte, Indiana, and my family is still there, including my sister, Millie, and her husband. She's been nagging me for a while to get a job with better hours so I could have a life outside of work. When she told me they were pregnant... well, I decided it was time to move closer."

"So, you can have a relationship now?" he asked.

I held up a hand. "Slow down, Agent Parisi. My turn." I thought for a minute. "How does Chris handle you hooking up with other guys?"

Teo's cheeks turned pink, and he reached out a hand for a shot. I pulled the bottle back toward me. "No way, Tee. At this rate, you'll be shitfaced by the top of the hour."

He sighed and ran his fingers through his hair, leaving one bit sticking up in the most adorably imperfect way. "I... I mean... I don't. Hook up with other guys. He thinks I do, I guess. But I'd never really confirmed it until I was with you."

"What do you mean, you don't hook up with other guys? You hooked up with me."

His blush deepened. "Can we change the subject? I think it's my turn anyway."

I realized what he was trying not to admit, and my stomach plummeted. I reached for his hand. "Teo, how old are you?"

The blanket wrapped around him must have been fascinating, because his eyes were glued to it.

"Tee," I said softly. "It's okay. This is a judgment-free zone."

"How could it possibly be judgment-free? You can't help but have opinions about things."

"Well, no, but I care about you. And I don't want you to be upset." I squeezed his hand. "But you don't have to tell me if you don't want to."

"Twenty-six," he admitted softly.

I wasn't sure how to ask the next part. "And..."

He finally glanced back up and met my eyes. "And you were the first person I ever had sex with."

My heart suddenly felt too big for my chest. "C'mere," I murmured, pulling the entire Teo burrito over into my lap. "Do you have any idea how incredible that makes me feel? That I was the one who got to experience that with you?"

He narrowed his eyes at me. "Don't be an asshole."

I pulled his hand up to kiss it. "I'm being serious, even though I want to kick your ass for trusting a stranger not to hurt you. Was it okay? Did I hurt you? Did we do anything that you—"

His slender hand covered my mouth. "It was amazing. I couldn't have asked for better."

So many things began to click into place then. The way he wanted to be treated like he mattered. Wanting to pretend it was special. Wanting to spend the entire night together.

He'd wanted it to be with Chris. And he hadn't wanted some random stranger's small talk to burst the fantasy he'd tried so hard to create.

The knowledge I'd only been a stand-in for the ungrateful Chris Banks stung like a bitch.

"Did Chris know you were waiting for him?" I asked.

He shook his head. "He would have thought I was a total loser. When I finally figured that out, I realized I needed to go out and get some experience."

"And that's when you placed the ad."

Teo nodded and smiled. "And that's when I hit the fucking V-card lottery." Then he quietly added, "I'm so glad it was you."

I realized however Teo's plan started, Chris had been nowhere in the room with us that night. What had happened between the two of us would always remain between the two of us. It was something special that had nothing to do with Chris Banks.

I threaded my fingers through his hair over and over, enjoying the way the thick waves felt in my hands. "So what now? How do you plan on getting his head out of his ass?"

Teo leaned in and rested his head on my upper chest. "That's the million-dollar question, isn't it? He said if I came to work for Banks Consulting, he'd consider asking me out on a real date."

I bit my tongue to keep from snapping about that being blatant manipulation. I hated this guy more and more. He obviously didn't have any idea what a sweet, kind man he was passing over in order to continue a life of indulgence.

I held Teo to my chest while I leaned over and grabbed the rum and Coke I'd poured over ice. After taking a sip, I handed it to him.

"I wonder what he'd do if you had a boyfriend," I mused. Chris Banks seemed like the kind of guy who didn't share.

"Well, he did kind of freak out when I mentioned having sex with you."

I tried not to preen, but I had to admit the information made me feel good. "What did he say, exactly?"

Teo took two more swigs of the cold drink. I could tell the rum was finally taking effect since his speech seemed like it came through softer lips.

"When I said it was just a hookup, he said, 'Good.'"

"Why?"

He shrugged and handed the drink back before snuggling into my chest some more. "Guess he doesn't want me to get hurt. And hookups don't have expectations of more." He picked at the blanket threads again. "I'd like to think it's because he doesn't want to lose me to someone else, but I don't know if that's true or not."

"Do you want to know?"

Teo leaned his head back to look at me. "Why wouldn't I?"

I loved the feel of him in my lap. I loved hanging out with him in this hotel room at the edge of the world. It was a little bit like time out of time.

"What if you lay it down once and for all and he doesn't pick it up? Are you ready for that?"

He thought about it for a little while before straightening up and looking at me. "Yes," he said with a firm set to his jaw. "I'm tired of being alone, Jack. I want a partner. And if Chris isn't ready, then it's time for me to move on. I've waited long enough."

I leaned in and kissed him hard before pulling back. "That's the spirit. Reach out and take what's rightfully yours. You deserve happiness and love."

Maybe Teo wasn't the only one feeling the effect of the drinks.

"Let's make a plan to find out once and for all," I suggested. "But first, more shots."

By the time we cobbled together a plan, we were both three sheets to the wind and the plan involved mandatory sushi date nights.

"For me or for you? I mean him? For you and me or for you and him? I mean you and me? The sushi," Teo asked.

"I don't understand what you're asking me, cutie."

He waved his drink around so much it would have slung little rum-and-Coke puddles all over the place if the glass hadn't been half-empty. "The sushi nights."

"I think when we talked about pretending to be boyfriends to make Chris jealous, you said I'd need to take you to sushi because he knows how much you love it and that would be a thing boyfriend Jack would do."

He giggled. "Boyfriend Jack. I'm calling you that now. The whole thing, like a title."

Teo had moved so that he was leaning against the far side of the couch with his feet on my lap. I massaged his feet while we talked through the details of our evil plan.

"But if we're going to do this fake-boyfriend thing," I explained, "I need you to come fake it at my sister's house at least once. Maybe then she'll stop setting me up with Jefferson Plenty."

"You made that name up."

"Did not. In fact, Jeff was the one who helped me get this job."

"Mpfh." His nose crinkled adorably when he frowned. "Sounds like a douche."

I laughed. "Not a douche. In fact, he's a very nice man."

His eyes narrowed accusingly. "Then why not go out with him?"

"Who says I didn't?"

Teo's mouth dropped open. "What? When? Why? And... why?"

I pulled his slender foot up and began sucking on his toes. His eyes widened to match his open mouth. "Because part of my goal in changing jobs was to get a personal life, remember?"

His full bottom lip poked out in a pout. "And was he good in bed? Experienced with lots of advanced moves?"

I laughed against the smooth skin of his foot. "I didn't sleep with him. But I'm curious, can you give me an example of an advanced move, Tee?"

He waved his hands around again, nearly spilling more drink. "No! Jesus, if I knew advanced moves, I wouldn't... I wouldn't... I'd..." He seemed distracted by his own thoughts. "Can you teach me some advanced moves? Maybe we can do that while we're fake dating. That would be amazing. Like... like sex lessons. Sex sessions. Sexions."

"I want to eat your entire foot." When I scraped my bottom teeth against the tender arch of his foot, he yelped and pulled his foot back.

"Ticklish. Rude."

I thought about his sex lesson proposal. He clearly didn't need any kind of lessons, but if agreeing to it gave me the ability to return to his bed several more times before parting ways...

"Yes. I will teach you the advanced moves," I said solemnly. "But you must agree to be an enthusiastic and thorough student."

"I was top of my nursing class," he said absently. "I'll do you proud, Teach."

Teo's feet snuck back onto my lap, and I began massaging them again. "Maybe I need a grand gesture," he said after a while, looking up at the ceiling. "Like in those romance movies."

"What do you mean?"

"Haven't you... haven't you ever wanted someone to swoop in and just, like... flash mob you or something?"

"No. Definitely not." The very idea of a public declaration made me sweat. What if the person rejected you right there in front of the fucking Bean? No. No, thanks.

"I want a grand gesture one day," he said dreamily. "I want Chris to... just... forget about everything else for one shining moment of... of *Teodor Parisi is the center of my world*. Maybe write it in flowers on the Sky Deck or something, I don't know."

He was so cute. I could watch him all night long with his quirky grin and bright eyes. "And what grand gesture would you do for him?"

He snorted. "He'd be happy if I got him a chili dog and cold beer. It's the secret indulgence no one's allowed to know about." His eyes went wide, and he clapped his hand over his mouth. "Wasn't supposed to tell anyone."

I rolled my eyes. "A Chicago boy likes a hot dog and beer. That's espionage-level classified shit right there."

Teo dropped his hand. "I guess you're right. He's not really the grand-gesture type. Maybe most men aren't. But..." He shrugged. "It'd be nice to have some kind of proof once and for all that someone loves me enough to draw a line in the sand and say, you're worth a little embarrassment. You're worth a hundred bucks of daisies laced end to end in the shape of our initials. You're worth a moment on the Kiss Cam at the Cubs game."

I imagined leaning over and tasting his lips during a baseball game. "You're worth a moment on the Kiss Cam, Teo," I said. "And if he doesn't think so, you need to find someone who does."

He was quiet for long enough, I wondered if maybe he'd passed out on me. I continued to run my hands up and down his calf muscles. After a while, he spoke softly. "Boyfriend Jack?"

"Mm-hm?"

"You promise you'll give me lessons?"

Now I was the one half-asleep. I was so comfortable there with him, warm and buzzy from the drinks and good company. "What kind of lessons, babe?"

"Mm... not just sex lessons, but... but maybe boyfriend lessons too?"

I opened one eye to peer at him. "What kind of boyfriend lessons?"

He lifted one shoulder, shifting my worn-out hoodie until I could see a peek of his creamy skin through the neckline. "Like how to go on dates and stuff. I've never done any of that, and he's dated like... everyone."

"I don't know if I'm such an expert on relationships, Tee. Every time I've ever tried dating anyone, it's gone horribly wrong."

Teo sat up straighter and then sort of tipped forward and let his momentum carry him until he was sitting in my lap again, curled up against my chest. He smelled like cinnamon and chocolate from a weird candy called Chicken Bones I'd picked up as a joke.

"I should probably feed you an actual meal," I murmured into his hair.

"No, tell me about the dates. The guys you dated, I mean. And why they didn't work out."

13

I mostly wanted to get closer to him so I could inhale his cologne. When Jack had run out of there earlier that morning to meet Nate, he hadn't had time for much more than a splash of cold water and a quick brush of his teeth. At lunch, he'd smelled like airplanes and snow mixed with the faint remnants of the hotel shower soap from last night, but I'd noticed when I'd woken up from my nap, he'd smelled like some kind of sexy cologne.

And the thought he'd put it on for my benefit drove me nuts. I could never ask him about it, but I sure as hell could suck it in like my life depended on it.

"Did you put on cologne?" Shit, I wasn't supposed to ask him about it.

Jack's lips quirked up in a smile. "Yes. I wanted to get in bed with you, but I didn't want to smell like avgas when I did it."

I turned up my nose. "I don't want any guy to smell like gas in bed with me."

The rumble of his laughter vibrated through me. "Duly noted. However, I might point out how unrealistic that preference is in the big scheme of things. Maybe you should consider going straight. For all I know, women have better bed manners. But I was talking about aviation fuel."

"Oh. But why aren't you telling me about your previous relationships? Are you trying to change the subject?"

I had spent plenty of time talking about my own past, my sister and her teen pregnancy with my niece, Bella, and my parents' continued conservatism even though they tried to be supportive of my "lifestyle." But now it was time for Jack to spill some beans.

Jack sighed, the spicy air of his alcohol breath warm and rummy against my face.

His arms tightened around me before he shifted to get more comfortable. "Let's see. First there was Adam. He was probably the one my mom would have voted for. Came from a good family in my hometown of La Porte and got a job in New Jersey after college. Our moms knew each other from church, so when he got settled into his place in Maplewood, he looked me up. I want to say we dated on and off for like a year, year and a half?"

That surprised me. I couldn't picture Jack in a steady relationship long-term. Which was kind of depressing. "Really? Jesus. What happened?"

"I'd wanted to become a pilot since I was a little boy. My dad's best friend, Wayne, was a pilot for Cummins, so he managed to help me start working on my pilot's license when I was still in high school. I went to community college for two years while I worked on accumulating flight hours, then I transferred to Indiana to finish my degree in Aviation Flight Technology. After that, I got a job with a regional airline out of Newark. I busted my ass, desperate to get to the next step. I took every flight I could, and I tried fitting in advanced certification courses too, anything to get up to the big planes faster. The result was... I was never around. I was always in the air or in a classroom. As Adam finally said, it never ended. My career was always out there demanding more attention than I gave him. And he was right."

"But didn't he understand it was temporary? I assume once you got on with an airline you'd have more say over your flights?"

"He knew me well enough to know I'd probably always want

more. After the regional jets, I wanted the big airliners at United. After United, I wanted to become a captain, then senior captain. Then I'd get the big international flights and be gone or home and jet-lagged. It was a future he wanted no part of. And I didn't blame him, really."

I leaned in and tasted the rounded knob of his collarbone with the tip of my tongue. It tasted really nice. "I guess I can see that. Who was next?"

He sighed. "Next was Rico, who I actually really liked a lot. He made me laugh, and he made the best homemade pizza ever. He lived in the Upper West Side, had a ton of money, and worked his ass off for an investment banking firm. I thought since he was ambitious too, we'd do just fine."

I picked up his hand and started fiddling with his fingers. "So what happened with Rico?"

"He invited me to his company holiday party at a fancy place in Chelsea. When I came to his place to get dressed, he surprised me with a new suit which should have tipped me off since we'd only been dating about six months. The suit probably cost an arm and a leg, but it fit like a damned dream. Rico looked amazing too, and I felt great heading out with him for the night."

I could tell this wasn't going anywhere good. "Obviously something happened. Did you rip the suit? In the butt? Leaving your crack exposed to his boss? Hold on..." I held up a hand and closed my eyes. "I'm picturing a sexy jock so they got the full monty. God, I wish I'd been there."

Jack poked his fingertips in my ribs until I squealed and batted his hands away.

"*Anyway*," he said, "it all went great. I met his boss and all of the coworkers he'd told me so much about. They were very friendly and complimentary, telling me Rico raved about me in the office all the time. We had a gorgeous dinner, tons of very nice wine, which went straight through me. So I went to the men's room at one point, and that's when I overheard Rico's closest work friend talking smack about me. He said if Rico had to be gay, at least he'd taken everyone's advice and found someone attractive enough to introduce to the clients. He also said he couldn't believe I was a Columbia graduate and a United captain when I looked more like a flight attendant with a degree from an online school."

Even though I'd begun sobering up, I was still confused. "But you went to community college and state school like me."

"Yep," he grumbled.

"So the guy's coworkers were asshole snobs. So?"

Jack's fingers moved absently through my hair. "So, not only was I not a Columbia grad, I also wasn't a United captain at the time. This was years before I even came anywhere close. I was lucky to have the job flying regional jets. Honestly, I just assumed it was a misunderstanding until I mentioned it to Rico and he freaked out about it. He asked if I'd told them the truth, and when I said they hadn't known I was even in there at the time, he'd let out a breath of relief. That's when I realized that he'd spun this big story about me that was all bullshit. And he'd done it because he was embarrassed by my real situation."

I turned around in Jack's lap and hugged him tightly. "Fucking asshole," I muttered into his warm neck. "I want to punch him for you."

"After that, I had trouble trusting anyone. I gave up for a while until I met a guy named Ty. Are you bored yet?"

"No. I like learning about your past. I want to go back and hug past Jack." I squeezed him again and kissed the side of his neck, taking the opportunity again to lick him a little. God, he tasted amazing. Like Mother Nature had sprinkled in some gourmet shit when she finished putting him together.

"You'll like this one, actually. Ty was awesome. *Is* awesome. Cute, smart, funny, kind. We met on a ski trip that a pilot buddy of mine had invited me on. The trip had started as this annual trip to Sugarloaf in Maine with his college friends and had grown into a big free-for-all where they rented out this cheap-ass hotel and invited everyone they knew to make it a big party week. It was so much fun. I hadn't done something like that in ages, so I had a blast. Ty was part of the original group of college friends, and he'd brought his two brothers along on the trip too."

For some reason, I didn't like hearing about this perfect man and his fancy ski trips. But I liked feeling like a jealous asshole even less. "Go on."

"We totally hit it off. Flirted all week and finally made out on the last night." He chuckled. "You would have appreciated the moment. It was all snowy and romantic. We were sitting on a bench late at night at the bottom of the slopes."

I put my hands over my face. "I don't need the details."

He laughed again and kissed my temple. "He lived in Manhattan, thank god. So when we got back home, we started dating. We did everything together, and I appreciated his great group of friends. About six months into our relationship, we hosted a dinner party at his place and I brought my sister, who was visiting from Indiana. She totally hit it off with Ty's brother, and the two of them started dating long-distance. Ty's brother is a pilot too, so we hit it off. After that, the four of us got together regularly and had lots of fun. I used my flight benefits to bring Millie to New York as often as we could manage, and the four of us would see shows, go out to eat, or just hang out at Ty's apartment with takeout and a movie. It was the closest thing I've ever had to feeling permanent."

"Did you love him?" I asked.

"Definitely. And his job was in travel too. He was a corporate event planner, so he traveled all over, putting on events or checking out venues for future ones. He loved to travel, so once we'd been together a little longer, we started traveling together. We went to Italy and Hawaii, Banff and Vancouver. I finally got to enjoy some of those places with a boyfriend instead of just wandering around on my own between flights."

It all sounded so perfect, I started to feel a little uneasy, like I was the "other man" or something. How could they not still be together if it was that good? "Did you catch him cheating or something?" I asked.

He grinned. "No. Ty is definitely not the cheating type. It was the opposite actually."

"What's the opposite of cheating?" I wondered out loud.

Jack looked down at me. "Proposing."

"Oh," I squeaked, feeling even more intensely jealous than before. "Oh."

He pressed a kiss to my lips and lingered there for a moment before pulling back. "Yeah, *oh*. But I wasn't ready. I... I didn't have the same kind of dream of settling down that he did. He wanted us to move in together and play happy gays. Ty loved nothing more than us spending all day Saturday shopping, cooking, and decorating for a dinner party with friends or putting on an elaborate Sunday brunch."

"That doesn't sound so bad," I said, even though it kinda did to me. "But, I mean... I'm the kind of guy who'd rather stay in pajamas and eat onion dip out of a can while binge-watching Netflix. Um... not that I do that kind of thing or anything. Gross."

Jack snorted. "That sounds like my kind of day. Relaxing instead of stressing about cleaning the bathroom and arranging the decorative sticks just so in their vase."

"What are decorative sticks?"

"I'm not really sure, but Ty had several different sets."

"Did you ever try to get him to spend your days off the way *you* wanted to? You know, try some of the couples communication all the books talk about?"

"Definitely. But I always felt like I was disappointing him or at the very least, boring him. And when he asked me to marry him, all I could see was a life ahead of us, made up of little moments of disappointing him." He looked down at me. I could see the sadness left over in his eyes. "So I said no. Hardest thing I've ever had to do."

My heart hurt for him, for both of them, really. It was a reminder that you can love someone but not be able to be with them. And you could love someone who wasn't your best match.

"I'm sorry."

Jack snuggled me closer. "Me too. It still weighs on me. Every time I see him, I feel like I'm still letting him down."

I sat up and looked at him. "Wait. You still see him?"

"He's kind of my brother-in-law. Millie married Ty's brother, Kirk. And now Millie and Kirk are expecting their first baby, so I'll probably see Ty even more often. It's the first grandchild on both sides."

"Oh. Well, shit."

"Mm-hm. It was almost as hard to tell my sister about the breakup as it was to break up with Ty in the first place. She was furious. She'd spent two years happily planning our joint futures together. We'd live next door to each other and help with each other's kids. It didn't matter that Ty and I didn't live in Indiana. Millie always treated that like a small bump in the road instead of a major obstacle. It's been six years and Millie still gives me hell for breaking up with Ty."

"And now you live in Chicago," I said. "So you're much closer."

He nodded. "And Ty is supposedly interviewing for jobs in Chicago to move closer to them too. Their parents are gone, so Ty and Kirk are each other's only remaining family."

Great. Perfect Ty was going to move to Chicago and be closer to Boyfriend Jack. Fucker.

"Maybe things will work out now that you're in a more predictable job," I suggested. I pulled out one of the peach gummy rings I'd been snacking on and slid it over his ring finger. "Maybe you'll decide to settle down after all and find someone to put a ring on."

He sucked the gummy candy off his finger in a lewd gesture. "Enough about me. Let's talk about you. I think it's time to go find some dinner since you keep snacking. Clearly you're hungry." He winked before pressing his lips to mine and kissing me silly. The taste of sugary peach was delicious on his lips.

We didn't quite make it out of the room in time for dinner.

Or breakfast.

Or lunch.

14

After twenty-four hours in the hotel room together, we decided to venture out into the small town of Goose Bay. We'd learned from the woman at the front desk that there was a winter carnival on, so we followed her directions to the town's sports complex in time to take advantage of the chili cooking competition. There were craft and vendor booths set up and a DJ playing music.

"How do I decide if I don't like this because I don't like chili or I don't like it because this particular chili is bad?" Teo asked.

I glanced over at him. He was wearing my Colts hoodie again since all the clothes he'd packed were more suitable for business meetings in Frankfurt than a cold Canadian winter carnival. It was huge on him but still pretty damned cute. "I thought you were vegetarian?"

He shrugged and took another hesitant bite of the chili. "Depends on my mood. I should be. It's better for you as long as you eat healthy and like legumes."

I used my own chili spoon to point at his bowl. "That's a bowlful of legumes you don't like."

Teo tossed the half-eaten chili in a nearby trash can. "I think I need a sweet treat to cleanse my palate."

I laughed. "You're a sugar addict. I've never seen anyone eat as many sweets as you, especially someone who has such a tight body."

His cheeks pinked up. "I've been putting on weight since changing to an office job. I should probably stop with the candy now. At my old job, I was on my feet, moving around, lifting patients. I took several patients for walks every shift, even if it was just around the corridors. Now I spend so much time at a desk, I'm surprised my ass hasn't flattened to giant pancake size."

I made a big production of looking back at his ass. "No pancakes here. Just a gorgeous pair of—"

Teo poked me in the side even though he was laughing. "Stop. It's a family event."

"Trousers," I finished. "Jeez. What did you think I was going to say?"

He poked me again. "I'm wearing ratty jeans and a hoodie long enough to cover both my pancakes and my chicken legs, thank you very much."

"Well, let the record show I enjoy pancakes *and* chicken legs, so there."

We wandered around the craft booths, stopping here and there to pick up some local treats. Teo got particularly excited when he discovered an older couple selling hand-spun yarn. He chatted with them for a solid twenty minutes, asking about their farm and sheep, their yarn dying process, and the best kind of projects to make with the ball of light, creamy yellow yarn he'd picked out.

"Do you sell needles too?" he asked excitedly. Once they'd helped him put together what he needed for what I now saw was a simple baby hat, they wished us both well on our new baby.

"I think some wires got crossed there," I whispered to him as we walked away.

"Whatever. I've always wanted to try circular needles, and this is the perfect excuse. If I can cast it on before our flight tomorrow, maybe I can keep myself distracted during the trip home."

"You know how to knit?"

He looked at me with furrowed brows. I noticed, not for the first time, he had a small, dusty brown birthmark the shape of Florida by his hairline near the part in his hair. "Did you think I just bought yarn and needles on a lark?"

I'd been staring at his eyes again. Irises so oddly light green, they reminded me of flying over the crystal clear waters of the Caribbean Sea.

I cleared my throat and stepped into line for a couple of hot chocolates to keep us warm on the trip back to the hotel. While it was early spring back in Chicago, it was definitely still full-on winter here in Goose Bay.

"I assumed it was a gift for your mom or your sister," I admitted. "Ignore my blatant sexism."

"No, it's fine. I learned from one of my patients a while back. Her arthritis had gotten too painful to finish the last half of a scarf she'd started for her twelfth grandchild. She'd hand made scarves for all the other grandkids, and this was the last one. After one of my shifts, I offered to stay and try to finish it for her. It turned out to be a blast. We were laughing so hard. It took me probably... I don't know, two weeks of working on it here and there. And once it was finished, I was hooked. I don't know how to do anything fancy, but I like having something to keep my hands busy when I watch TV."

I pictured Teo sitting next to a patient in a nursing home knitting up a storm while they gossiped about a game show on television. It was easy to imagine him like that, enjoying listening to old stories and genuinely appreciating time spent with them.

"I play silly games on my phone," I admitted. "I spend a lot of nights in hotels, so I'll find something on TV but then play Candy Crush or Words With Friends or 2048. My old neighbor Mrs. Stickley used to tell me she thought our generation was raised with too much multitasking and that's why we always had to be doing too many things at once."

Teo narrowed his eyes at me and grinned. "*Our* generation?"

It was our turn to order, so I told the young man behind the counter what we wanted and pulled out some cash to pay for it. After he handed us the two cups, I offered to carry Teo's paper gift bag in exchange for giving him his drink.

He handed it to me without thinking and began blowing on his cocoa as we headed toward the door to return to the hotel.

"So, yeah. You're a little younger than I am," I began with a smirk. "No need to rub it in."

"I figured if you were flying the big planes for United, you had to be at least... what? Midthirties?"

Teo's grin was adorable.

"Fine. I may be just a hair older than you are," I said, shifting the paper bag handles over my arm so I could take a sip of the hot drink. "But I'll have you know, there's a 777 captain who's only twenty-six years old."

"Is it you?" Tee was captivating when he teased me. It made me want him to do it more often.

"No, smartass. It's not me. I'm..." I made a big deal out of looking around to make sure no one could hear me before leaning over to whisper, "Thirty-six."

The sound of Teo's giggle, muffled behind his hand, was the best thing I'd ever heard. I loved making him laugh. I reached a hand over and ruffled his hair. "Laugh all you want, young Padawan."

He batted my hand away and ducked out of my reach, still laughing. "If it makes you feel any better, you're aging *very* well."

The look he gave me made my dick hard. "You're going to have to carry me back if you don't stop looking at me like that because I won't be able to walk."

He batted his eyelashes at me. "Looking at you like what? Like you're a mouthwatering side of aged beef or a delicious glass of aged whiskey?"

I put my arm around his shoulders and drew him close, muttering under my breath about disrespecting one's elders. We teased each other all the way back to the hotel room where I immediately pushed him face-first onto the desk, yanked his pants and underwear down to his ankles, and proceeded to show him with my tongue, my fingers, and finally my hard dick that some things did indeed get better with age.

15

TEO

I was in heaven.

Sure, I'd emergency landed in the middle of nowhere Canada, but I'd stumbled into a sex-fueled dream I never wanted to wake up from.

Except my ass hurt, and I had beard burn on my inner thighs that stung like a bitch.

"No more," I muttered, tossing the half-empty bag of baby carrots onto the coffee table. "I liked the candy better. This healthy shit is for the birds."

Jack nudged my thigh with his foot from his spot at the other end of the small sofa. "Need I remind you, getting the healthy shit was your idea?"

"Because candy and chips—not to mention festival food—were going to lead us to an early death." I winced at the memory of Grandpa Banks and his heart attack. "I'm going to call Chris and see how Gordon is doing."

When I got him on the phone, Chris sounded happy and much more grounded than before. "How is he?" I asked.

"Much better. His color is better than I've seen him in a while. I still don't understand how his cardiologist missed this if he was in that bad of shape."

"His last visit with a cardiologist was a year ago. He was scheduled next month for a full workup. Even his regular checkup with the GP was probably ten months ago." I'd asked him for all of his medical records when I'd started keeping a closer eye on him at the office. "The only doctor he'd seen recently was the endocrinologist. Not exactly the best person to catch heart disease."

Chris's voice softened. "You were right, Tee. I should have been there when he landed. I feel awful. I should have let Dad handle the meeting on his own."

It was nice to hear him sound more like himself, but I wondered what had caused the change. "What makes you say that now?"

"I've been spending some time with him, and it just brings up a lot of good memories. Dad and I were asking him questions about how he started the business originally, and it was fascinating."

I remembered one of my lunchtime walks with Gordon when the winter weather had finally started tapering off. "His dad wanted him to become a doctor like himself."

"Yeah. I never knew that. And he was too squeamish. That's hilarious. He said the closest he ever came to becoming a doctor was—"

"Marrying a nurse," I finished with a laugh. "Medicine was a big deal in your grandmother's family."

There was an odd silence, and I felt bad for interrupting him.

"How did you know those things?" he asked. "Sometimes, I feel like you know my family better than I do."

"Sorry," I said automatically. "I don't know... I guess I just ask too many questions. I'm nosy like that. You know this about me." I tried to make a joke of it, but the truth was, I listened to what Gordon and Hattie said. Over the years of working with elderly patients, I'd learned just how common it was for people to tune them out. It was similar to the way some people were with children. A lack of patience maybe. The words didn't come as quickly and clearly anymore, so you had to be patient and learn to slow down. That wasn't Chris's strong suit, nor had it ever been.

"You have a big heart, Tee," he said softly. "I don't deserve you."

His words touched me, but there was also something new there. A little sliver of awareness I'd never had before that this was a common occurrence between us. Just when I was at my most disappointed or angry in Chris, he'd turn into the perfect, thoughtful best friend. He'd say things that made me feel appreciated and adored. It was just enough to reel me back in again.

I pushed the thoughts away, because they made me feel nervous and scared. If my subconscious thought there was a chance Chris was being deliberately manipulative, I didn't want to hear about it or face it.

I closed my eyes and shook my head, hoping to clear it of any more unhelpful revelations. A warm hand clasped the back of my neck and squeezed. I opened my eyes to see Jack's concern in the divot between his eyebrows. Without thinking, I crawled over into his lap and curled against his chest.

"I gotta go, Chris," I said. "We're, um... I mean I... I'm meeting the pilot and his wife for dinner."

It was a total lie. My face flooded with heat, and I tried like hell to ignore Jack's body tensing beneath mine.

"Yeah, no problem. I'm heading out to meet Hannah and Jay for a beer. Will you still be home tomorrow? I miss you."

That was the second time he'd said such a thing to me recently. I felt like I was in an alternate universe where I was suddenly having sex and Chris was now showing affection and interest in me. The phrase *Absence makes the heart grow fonder* kept spinning through my head on a loop. Was that what this was?

"That's the plan." My voice sounded weird and squeaky, but then again, I always freaked out a little when thinking of getting on that plane again. Okay, a lot.

"Let me know when you get in."

When the call ended, I realized he'd never said a single word about my fear of flying or asked me if I was scared about the return flight after everything that had happened. That was disappointing, mostly because my fear of flying had been a strong presence between us growing up. In middle school, Chris had once invited me to join his family for a trip to the beach in Florida, and I'd said no because it required a plane flight. In college, he'd invited me to join his friends for a trip to Mexico. Again, I'd declined because of the flights required. I was a chickenshit, and it was embarrassing. But now I'd finally, finally done it. I'd gotten on a plane, for *him*, for the company, and it had lost a damned engine and had to emergency land in a tiny town on the coast of Canada. And he hadn't acknowledged any of it.

"Whatever," I muttered, putting my phone on the coffee table and nestling back against Jack's chest. "Hey, do we still have any of that rum?"

Jack's hands moved into my hair and began working their magic. He didn't answer my question about the rum, but he used his fingers to distract me.

"Do you want to talk about it?" His deep voice rumbled through his chest, making me want to beg him for more. I didn't care what he said as long as it rumbled against me in that sexy as hell way.

"No." I sounded like a child, but then again, I felt like a child. When would I be old enough and wise enough to stop having unrealistic expectations of people?

Jack continued playing with my hair until I was half in love with him. I'd always craved physical affection, and having it for the first time was one of the most eye-opening realizations about what I'd been missing by not allowing myself to connect with other people romantically this whole time.

"That feels so good. Please don't stop." *Don't ever stop* is what I wanted to say, but I at least still had enough self-control not to blurt out all of my thoughts.

"Are we meeting Nate and Brenda for dinner?" Jack asked hesitantly. I felt like an ass for my lie on the phone.

"Not that I know of," I said without looking up at him. I let out a sigh. "I couldn't bring myself to tell him I needed to go so I could beg a sexy pilot to fuck me over the desk again."

"Mm. The tips of your ears are pink. Methinks you're not used to using such sexual language, sweet newbie."

"Maybe so. And also, I can't actually get fucked again tonight without possibly needing medical attention." I'd meant it as a joke, but Jack shifted until he held my face in both hands. The concern in his eyes made my throat tighten.

"Are you hurting?"

I shook my head. "Not too bad, but I might if we pushed it. Is... is that okay? I'm sorry if—"

He pulled me in for a hard kiss, shutting me up quite effectively and erasing all memory of whatever it was we'd been talking about. By the time we came up for air, my lips were tender and my dick had been sucked. Somehow, he'd managed to come too, but I wasn't sure how.

I was laid out buck naked on the bed—with the exception of one sock still on my foot—and Jack was whistling a tune as his own naked ass headed toward the bathroom.

"What just happened?" I croaked.

"I distracted you," he called over his shoulder.

"My balls hurt," I called back. "They've never worked this hard in their lives," I muttered under my breath.

Jack came back in the room with a white washcloth in his hands and a shit-eating grin on his face. "That's one of your advanced lessons. Testing the limits of your body to know what you're capable of. Also, taking advantage of your youth while you still have it."

He leaned in to wash me off with gentle caresses even though there wasn't much to clean up since he'd swallowed it all. I wasn't complaining.

"You seem to be keeping up just fine and you're ten years older than I am," I reminded him.

"I've been training for this for years, rookie."

I hated thinking of him with other men, but I knew it was a fact of life. And, hell, he wouldn't have answered my ad if he wasn't the kind of guy out there looking for random hookups.

"So, how does that work, exactly?" I asked.

"How does what work? Training for marathon sex weeks?" He laughed and moved us both under the covers until I was pressed up against his side with my head on his shoulder. It was my new favorite thing. It made me feel like I had an actual boyfriend, and I refused to feel like that little dream of mine made me pathetic.

"No, I mean... like... hookups. Finding someone on an app and arranging to have sex. Do you..." I trailed off as I thought about how to word what I wanted to ask.

Jack rubbed my back. "You can ask me anything, Tee. It's okay."

"I don't know where to start. Like, how do you know who you can trust? And how do you greet them at the door? Do they want to kiss or just... get right down to business? If you're not trying to get to know each other like a date, is it more like a game of pickup basketball where you just sort of nod and fist-bump the stranger and then get down to it?"

I could tell he was biting his tongue against a laugh, but he still took my questions seriously. As he began to describe what it was like to hook up with a stranger, my stomach dropped into this mucky green jealousy place I didn't like.

"Never mind," I blurted. "Not... no. I mean, no. I changed my mind. I don't..." I shook my head. "Sorry. I don't think that's for me anyway, so it's not something we need to talk about."

He leaned his head back to look at me and then tipped my chin up with his fingers to make me meet his eye. "Does the idea scare you?"

"It's not that. I'm just, um, tired. You wore me out. And I'm nervous about tomorrow. And now I'm rambling, but I really don't want to talk about it anymore anyway. We could always see what's on TV or you can play your word games on your phone while I doze and drool all over your pecs."

Jack's warm fingers traced down the side of my face to my jawline. It was such a tender gesture, so at odds with the man who claimed to prefer anonymous sex to emotional entanglements. I wanted to punch those men in his past who'd hurt him. But then again, I wanted to hug the poor guy who'd proposed. I thought maybe I'd never be able to recover from such a horrible disappointment. Imagining you had a future with someone like Jack Snyder and then having it ripped away from you seemed like the worst kind of heartbreak.

Maybe it was a good thing my future was with Chris instead of someone like Jack. Chris was comfortable and predictable. I knew him like I knew myself. The only scary unknown with Chris was wondering when the hell he was going to finally come to his senses and commit.

WHEN IT WAS FINALLY time to fly back to Chicago the following day, my fear of flying overtook all common sense.

"You look like you're going to vomit," Jack said in the morning as we packed up our things.

I avoided making eye contact by refolding all of the clothes in my suitcase for the third time. "I'm not the best flyer."

"Meaning, you're scared of flying?"

"No. I *was* scared of flying. Then I actually went up in an airplane and had to emergency land after the engine crapped out. Now I'm utterly terrified of flying."

There was silence for a moment. "Wait. Teo, are you saying this trip was your first time in an airplane?"

I would have answered him, except my socks weren't bundled quite right. I went to work correcting the misbehaving pairs.

Jack pulled the socks out of my hand and gently tilted my chin up until I was looking at him. "Tee. Please tell me that wasn't your first flight."

"Okay."

His face fell. "Shit. Are you serious?"

I shrugged. "I figured if I was going to pop my flying cherry, I might as well choose an exciting flight for it. Heart attack and engine failure at the same time, in addition being pretty sure the pilot was the stranger who popped another cherry of mine too. At least I have a story to tell my grandchildren."

Jack snorted softly and pulled me in for a hug. "I'm so fucking sorry. God. You probably never want to get in a plane again."

That was an understatement. "Well, it helps that you're the one flying it," I admitted. "That's why I didn't want to fly home by myself. At least this time if I have a breakdown, the only person who'll see the ugly cry is Brenda."

"Do you have any Xanax or anything?"

I shook my head. "Actually, studies show that while taking those meds can lower your anxiety, they actually exacerbate your fear of flying in the long run. Seventy-one percent of people in one study who took Xanax on a flight had significantly increased anxiety, an increased heart rate, a desire to leave the plane, and panic on the next flight they took."

Why did I turn into Professor Facts and Figures every time I got nervous? "Sorry," I muttered. "Ignore me."

He kissed me on the forehead and then met my eyes. "Don't be sorry. I'm a pilot. That's great information for me to have. Is there anything I can do to help alleviate your fear?"

When Jack had told me about his previous relationships, he'd always made himself out to be the bad guy. Too ambitious to make things work with Adam, not educated or prestigious enough for Rico, not mature enough to commit to Ty. I wasn't quite sure why he took all that on himself, but he was wrong. His concern for me was proof of how thoughtful he was. Plus, he'd treated me like a precious treasure the entire time we'd spent together in Goose Bay, not to mention how tenderly he'd made love to me the first night we'd gotten together so many months ago.

"Just knowing you'll be there in case anything happens is good," I said. "I downloaded some podcasts to listen to in hopes it'll help distract me."

"Okay, well, all you have to do is speak up if there's anything you need. I can tell Brenda would love to mother you if given half a chance, so let her take care of you too."

We finished packing and made our way to the airport. Once on board the plane, I strapped in and tried to concentrate on some focused breathing techniques for relaxation. I'd already downed a couple of bottles of water to stay hydrated and put in my earbuds to play some of my favorite songs until we were in the air. I closed my eyes and tried to float away with the music in my ears. All of the thunking noises and vibrations associated with closing hatches and doors made me shake even worse until I was regretting not having Xanax after all. Future Teo might have hated me for it, but present Teo would have adored me.

Someone's hands grasped mine, and I opened my eyes to see Jack squatting in front of me. His handsome face was lit with a giant smile. God, he was stunning. I still couldn't believe a man like this would give a man like me the time of day, much less time with his naked body. "Hey, I brought you something." He pulled out a handful of individually wrapped candies. They were little yellow balls that looked lemony. "These are pineapple hard candies from Hawaii. They're one of my favorite things, and every time I visit there, I stock up. I want you to suck on one of these while we're taking off. Close your eyes and think of warm beaches and tropical breezes. Feel the sand between your toes and hear the whoosh of the ocean."

I took the candy from his outstretched palm. "Thank you. I'd ask you to divert the plane there, but that would make the flight ten times longer, and I can't handle that right now."

He squeezed my hands and stood, reaching down to run fingers through my hair before returning to the cockpit. I wasn't even sure he was aware of how often he ran his fingers through my hair. Whenever we lay together or snuggled up to watch television, his fingers always found their way into my hair. I loved it and preened like a cat every time he did it.

I took a deep breath and popped a candy into my mouth, hoping like hell it had Xanax-like side effects.

16

———————

JACK

I'd already informed Brenda about Teo's fear of flying so she could keep a special eye on him and make sure he was hanging in there. It didn't keep me from checking in with her several times during the flight though. By the time we crossed into US airspace, I was pretty sure Nate and Brenda both knew something was up between me and the client.

I just hoped it didn't get me fired. If there was one thing I'd decided on this unexpected trip, it was how much I enjoyed working for Douglas Aviation. They'd handled the emergency with professionalism and efficiency. There hadn't been any unnecessary drama or blame involved in the mechanical failure, and they'd already scheduled me for more flights as soon as we returned.

I spent most of the flight back to Chicago wondering how things would go between Teo and me. Did he really want me to be his fake boyfriend, or had he changed his mind? Would it be awkward? What if he needed me for something and I was out of town?

By the time we landed smoothly at Midway, I was keyed up and angry at myself. *This.* This was why I'd given up on relationships. I hated worrying about the other person and wondering if I was letting them down. I hated feeling like I wouldn't be good enough or they somehow deserved better. It was so much easier just to stick to casual sex and not get feelings involved. Even a fake relationship was bringing up some of these old feelings.

Maybe it was a good thing I was turning right around and heading out on another trip later this evening. I was scheduled to fly a client to Houston for a talk he was giving at a mobility expo. Rourke was in a wheelchair and had some really unique adaptations to his single-pilot Cessna. I'd flown him a couple of times before and got along with him well. It would hopefully be a straightforward trip, but I still felt odd parting from Teo after so much time glued to each other in Goose Bay.

Sure enough, the goodbye was awkward as hell. Nate and Brenda were there, so the most I could do was an odd kind of handshake. I met Teo's eyes and gave him the biggest smile I could, but then he was walking away from us.

And all I could do was watch him go.

It only took two days back in my regular routine before my skin began to feel too tight. I couldn't figure out what the problem was, so I assumed it had something to do with my job. After taking Rourke to Houston and back, I was rotated to fly a different corporate jet, taking six agriculture executives to a conference in Las Vegas.

Out of habit, I reached for my phone app to scroll through Grindr. None of the men got me half as excited as the memory of Teo did. Plus, I reminded myself I had a boyfriend now. Even if we weren't really dating, it would be rude to sleep around on him. What if someone saw me and it somehow got back to Chris or Teo himself? No. I'd content myself with a nice dinner and maybe call Teo when I got to my hotel room.

I went to a little Indian place not too far from the hotel where I was staying next to UNLV and the airport. I'd flown through Vegas a million times and had my list of favorites, but somehow it wasn't quite as good as usual. I'd never had a problem dining on my own before, but tonight's dinner seemed extra quiet for some reason. There were plenty of people at the restaurant—a mix of students and locals—but I still felt odd, like I was separated from everyone else by a transparent glass wall.

I pulled out my phone and texted my sister.

Jack: *Bored in Vegas. Thinking about going to see Thunder From Down Under.*

Millie: *Tell me you're joking.*

Jack: *I'm joking. But I would like a good Netflix recommendation if you have one.*

Millie: *That new Ryan Reynolds action flick was good. Why aren't you out hooking up with some pretty Vegas boy?*

I took a sip of my wine and thought about what to tell her.

Jack: *I kind of met someone.*

My phone rang two seconds after I hit Send on the text.

"Tell me everything," she said. "Oop, wait. Mom's birthday dinner is Saturday at my house. Bring that champagne she likes. Okay, go. Name?"

I smiled at her familiar bossy tone. "His name is Teo, short for Teodor. His parents are Italian. His father is some kind of specialty plumber who was moved to the States with an Italian faucet company when Teo was a baby and his sister was just getting ready to start kindergarten."

The server came by to top up my ice water, and I shot him a grateful smile.

"Anyway, so he's a nurse, and he—"

"Woah, woah." Millie's voice held a teasing smile in it. "So far I know more about this Teo guy than I ever knew about Mr. Corporate Snob."

"Rico. The man has a name."

"He doesn't deserve a name," she grumbled. "But so far, I like this Teo. Go on. What does he do for work?"

"Like I said, he's a nurse. Well… he *is*, but right now he's working for a medical consulting company rather than practicing."

My sister hummed with understanding. "Mm, he prefers the corporate side of things. Management, maybe."

I thought about it. "No. I don't think so. I think he prefers working with patients, especially the elderly. I'm not really sure why he changed jobs." Which, of course, was a lie. But I'd be damned if I was going to admit out loud that Teo had done it for Chris. "He's smart and kind. So freaking sweet too. He cares so much about his patients, and he has that same gentle nature that makes for a perfect nurse. You remember Vickie Young who lived around the corner and went to work for hospice? And how we thought that was just perfect because she was seriously the kindest human being on earth? He's like that."

There was silence on the phone while I took another sip of my wine. Just when I was getting ready to tell her more about him, she cut in.

"You really like this guy. It sounds serious."

"Pfft. No. Don't be ridiculous. You know me. Never again. Or at least not for a very long time." I took another quick slug of wine. Maybe telling Millie it wasn't serious was the wrong way to pretend he was my boyfriend. "I mean… never say never, right? But… probably not. Or at least… I'm not in any hurry. And neither is he. We're just… going to see how it goes." *Good job, Jack. Stellar.*

"Well, I for one can't wait to see him. Bring him on Saturday and we'll put him through Snyder initiation."

"Oh. Oh, no. No, no," I stammered. "He can't—"

"Jacqueline, I'm not taking no for an answer. Bring him Saturday night or I'm telling Mom you're in love."

"But I—"

"Gotta go, Kirk just got his hand caught in the pretzel barrel again."

The phone call ended before I could tell her that, in no uncertain terms, Teo Parisi was not meeting my family on Saturday night.

"I NEED you to meet my family Saturday night," I blurted an hour later when I got him on the phone.

Silence greeted me, and I wondered if the call had accidentally disconnected.

"Did you… is this… Jack, is that you?" Teo asked in mock confusion. "Are you being held against your will somewhere? Blink once for yes and—"

"We're not on FaceTime. If we were, you would have just seen me not blink. You would have also seen the stark terror in the whites around my eyes." I threw myself back into the mountain of crisp white bed pillows in my peaceful hotel room. The lights and sounds of Vegas were dimmed by the thick, tinted glass and sheer curtain in front of the windows. "It's a long story, but I thought it would be good practice at the whole pretend-boyfriend thing."

"Liar. Your sister roped you into something. Admit it."

"She's so bossy," I whined. "Say you'll come with me. There will be fancy champagne and my sister's famous spinach puffs that are basically worth meeting anyone's mom."

"Are your parents homophobes?"

"Um no? But they are trivia nerds, and they'll low-key test you on your trivia knowledge to determine whether or not they'll want you on their team the next time the family does game night."

"That doesn't sound so bad."

"Babe. You're… you're new. All right? So just… if my dad asks you any baseball statistic or like… the name of the man who invented Kevlar or something—"

"It was a woman, actually."

I barked out a laugh. "Oh my god."

"Stephanie Kwolek in 1966. She was trying to perfect a lighter fiber for car tires."

My heart did a little *ka-thunk*. "Tell me something else. Your big brain is turning me on."

I could hear Teo shifting in his seat as he chuckled warmly over the line. I missed his sweet face.

"A baby puffin is called a puffling. Isn't that the cutest thing ever?"

I squeezed my eyes closed. Since when did I get this goofy over a man I barely knew? Maybe since I hadn't had sex in too long. "*You're* the cutest thing ever. And I want to fuck you so badly right now I can hardly see straight."

"Oh." Teo swallowed. "Um. That would be nice, actually. When will you be back from Vegas?"

I reached down and palmed my cock. Just the sound of his voice made me hard. "Two days."

"Can we... I mean, can you... come with me to a thing?"

"What thing?" As if the answer would ever be no to any question he asked that might result in me clapping eyes on him again, much less touching him. "And how is Mr. Banks?"

"He's doing much better. They put stents in—wait, I think I told you that part already—and he's back home in his apartment. They're not sure how his recovery will go because he has chronic issues, but so far so good. I've been staying with him to keep an eye on him."

That was the Teo I knew. "Of course you have. He's lucky to have you."

"I'm lucky to have him. He's always treated me like family. And he gripes at me like family. I'm trying to cut salt out of his diet, and he's being a total bitch about it." He laughed softly. "I found this salt substitute a nurse friend of mine recommended and put it on his potato last night. He loved it. Then I used it in the soup I made today. So far it totally has him fooled. I can't decide whether or not to tell him about it just so I can have the satisfaction of seeing his face."

"Is Chris giving you time off work to make up for looking after him?" I suspected I knew the answer to that, but I wanted to make sure Chris wasn't expecting him to be nurse to Mr. Banks and a full-time consultant too.

"Oh yeah, of course. It's not a problem. I'm handing off my two projects to another nurse consultant so I can be here with Gordon full-time for now."

"Good. I'm glad he's recovering well so far."

The conversation change had understandably deflated my dick, so I turned on my side to get more comfortable. I wanted to see him, so I pressed the button to turn the call into a FaceTime one.

He accepted, and suddenly I was looking at the pale skin of his throat above a soft-looking red sweater.

"Ooop, sorry," he said, angling the camera up with a soft laugh. "Better?"

He was grinning adorably, and his eyes looked bright and happy.

"You're beautiful," I said without thinking. "So fucking gorgeous." I reached a finger out to trace the one wild curl above his ear.

His face flushed. "Charmer. Why aren't you out there using those smooth moves to seduce the men of Vegas back to your hotel?"

"Because I'd rather be alone in my room talking to you," I admitted. "Besides, I have a boyfriend, remember?"

He blushed even deeper pink. "Right. So, um, that reminds me I was getting ready to ask you if you could come to a thing with me Friday night. As... as my date. You know, my boyfriend, or whatever."

Teo's dark eyelashes fluttered around while he avoided looking at me.

I grinned at him. "Of course I will. What's the thing?"

"A Cubs game. The company has a box, and a bunch of Chris's and my friends are going."

"Box seats at Wrigley? Twist my arm."

He smiled back and finally looked at me. "Okay, yeah, it's pretty cool. Good. Thank you."

I wanted to hold him, reach out and pull him against my body so I could remind myself what he felt like, tasted like, smelled like. It made me feel strangely unmoored, like I was drifting away from an anchor that was meant to keep me steady, safe, protected.

"Are you getting enough sleep?" I asked, clearing my throat. "Are you eating?"

The look on Teo's face was affectionate and soft. "Yes, Daddy."

I couldn't hold back a laugh. "Don't ever say that to an actual Daddy Dom or he will squirrel you away, and I'll never get to see you again."

"Just you, then," he teased. "Oh, and maybe my real dad."

"Ewww. Now I'm never getting hard again. Take it back."

We continued to talk and joke, flirt and tease, until I realized several hours had passed and it was well past midnight in Chicago. I could tell Teo was getting drowsy, and our conversation had already slipped into that sleepy, slow kind of meander that was more about not wanting to say goodbye than anything else.

"You need to get some sleep, baby," I said, the endearment slipping out without me realizing it. When I heard myself say the word, I almost choked on my tongue. I'd called him "babe" before, but never like this. Never in the tender kind of way that made me feel exposed and vulnerable, as if my real feelings for him couldn't stay hidden even though they should have. Teo's eyes widened. We stared at each other.

"See you Friday?" he asked hesitantly, as if I'd somehow changed my mind while we talked.

"Absolutely. Just let me know where to meet you. I'm looking forward to it."

And I was. Not only could I not wait to see Teo again, but the idea of claiming him in front of Chris, even if it wasn't real, was selfishly exciting.

I counted down the hours.

17

TEO

My hands were sweating. Come to think of it, so was my back. And under my arms, and probably... there he was. I stood outside the Wrigley Field gate beside Chris and a couple of other guys from work when I spotted Jack making his way toward us through the crowd.

"I can't believe you invited the company pilot," Chris muttered, not for the first time.

"He doesn't work for Banks," I reminded him under my breath. "He works for Douglas Aviation."

"Same difference."

My heart skittered around the closer Jack got, but when he spotted me and grinned a huge, gorgeous smile... well, let's just say I was sweating in even more places after that.

"Hi," I said, stepping forward to greet him. My legs were on a different speed plan than my brain, so I kind of stumbled into his arms by accident. He held me tightly for a beat before pulling back and laying a kiss on me.

Oh god. *Ohhhh godddd.* His lips... his now-familiar taste... I wanted to melt into him and kiss him for the rest of the night.

"Ahem."

Chris's voice startled me out of my mini make-out session. My face and neck heated until my entire body was one giant ball of what my sister referred to as "man stink."

"Hi," I said to Jack again. In case he hadn't heard the first time or felt properly greeted by my tongue in his esophagus. "Hi. Um, I think I said that already. This is Chris Banks, and this is…"

"Jay Acosta," Jay said with a flirty smirk. "And you are delectable."

I was torn between pride and jealousy. "Yeah, so that's Jay, and this is Hannah, Alan, Sam, and Logan and Logan's sister Tara."

There was a woman standing between Hannah and Chris I'd never met before, so I added, "I'm sorry, I don't know your name…"

"This is Chelsea," Chris said, not giving her a chance to answer for herself. "She's with me."

I stared at him in numb shock. "Oh. Hi. I'm Teo, and this is Jack. Nice to meet you, Chelsea."

I turned to look at Jack, and the concern on his face nearly made me want to vomit. I tightened my teeth together and refused to be upset. After all, I'd brought someone too.

As if I needed reminding, Jack put his arm around me and pulled me tightly to his side, pressing a kiss to my temple and murmuring in my ear. "I missed you."

I turned and buried my face in his neck, wrapping him in another hug because I just needed it for a split second. Then I'd be fine.

He held me against him while he answered a question someone had asked about whether or not he was a Cubs fan. "Was Ron Santo at home on third base? Could Kerry Wood throw a baseball?"

When I pulled away, he didn't stop bantering with Logan and Tara about the Cubs, but he grabbed my hand and held it tight. We made our way through the gate and toward the private suite. I'd been with the Banks family many times before, but it never got old. I still felt like the luckiest kid alive when I passed through the gate and into the hallways to the private suites.

I remembered the first time Chris and his dad had invited me and my dad to join them at a game. The Cubs had crushed the Atlanta Braves. I'd watched Chipper Jones and Tom Glavine fill out baseball uniforms like the damned things had been made from spray paint.

When Glavine hiked up his knee and then stretched his chest out to pitch a ball... well, it had been pure heaven for a ten-year-old boy who didn't realize at the time why he was so obsessed with baseball players more than the game itself.

When we entered the suite, Chris went straight to the fridge and began to pull out cans of beer to pass around. Catering had set out food in silver chafing dishes, and I knew from experience and scent that there were amazing hot dogs inside at least one of them.

"This is amazing," Jack said, looking around. "Thanks for bringing me, Tee."

Chris handed him a beer. "You've never been in a box at Wrigley before?" he asked.

"Nah, man. I had box seats for *Hamilton* in New York once though. I went out with one of the dancers, and he hooked me up with them. It was amazing."

"For real?" Hannah asked. "God, I'm dying to see it. I need to find a dancer to hook up with. Who knew that was the shortcut?"

I watched Jack charm the pants off of my friends. He was confident and relaxed around new people, and I realized that being a commercial airline pilot would have put him in the position of having to make new friends almost every time he showed up for work. It seemed to be easy for him. He quickly turned the conversation around and began asking Hannah what other Broadway shows she'd seen and whether or not she'd ever been to New York. Logan joined in to ask Jack for some restaurant suggestions in Greenwich Village since he had a business trip coming up. The three of them made their way down into the stadium seats and continued talking.

As I poked around to see what food was in the covered dishes, I realized how comfortable he was around my friends right off the bat. There'd been no real reason to be nervous at all. I guessed I was projecting because I would have been way nervous if I was the one going into an established group of friends I didn't know.

I tried not to think about meeting Jack's family.

"What's up with you?" Chris asked. "You look like you just swallowed something nasty."

"What? Oh. I'm…" I let out a little nervous laugh. "I'm meeting Jack's family tomorrow night. I'm a little freaked-out I guess."

"That's awfully fast, don't you think?" Chris asked. "Is this thing serious between you two? I thought…"

Say it.

"I thought," he said again.

C'mon. Admit you thought it was supposed to be the two of us.

"Anyway, that's great. You'll do fine." Chris cleared his throat and took a sip of his beer. "And just think. It doesn't really matter anyway."

"What do you mean?"

"I thought you wanted to be with me long term," he said softly. His smile was affectionate and knowing. It pulled me in, the way it always did, but for the first time, I was reminded of that cheap-ass wooden paddle toy. The one with the hard rubber ball attached to it by the flimsiest elastic string ever. You had to yank back with all your might to get the ball to bounce against the paddle, but then it was off again, shooting out who-knew-how-far until it inevitably slammed you in the face and left a red mark smelling of nasty hard rubber.

"Well," I began, poking through the collection of hot dogs with the serving tongs. "I waited long enough, I think. So now I'm going to move on."

It wasn't the truth, of course. I didn't really want to move on. I still wanted him. I'd always wanted him. Wanting him was like brushing my teeth in the morning—it just was because it always had been. I didn't even need to think about it anymore. But I thought maybe a part of me wanted to try on the alternative to see how it would feel to begin the process of walking away.

Before Chris could answer, the crowd cheered suddenly, and we both turned to see what had happened. After that, the moment had passed, and I had to content myself with serving up a hot dog and covering it in all my favorite toppings. It didn't occur to me until after I took the first bite that a boyfriend might have made one for his significant other.

I walked over to stand behind Jack's chair before leaning down and murmuring, "You want a hot dog or something that looks like a chicken quesadilla?"

Jack reached his hand back and threaded his fingers through the back of my hair. "Hot dog with mustard and relish if they have it. Thanks, babe."

He pulled me closer to peck a kiss on my cheek before continuing whatever it was he'd been saying to Logan. I floated back over to the food to make my *boyfriend* a hot dog.

I could get used to this.

"He's goddamned adorable," Jay said in a hushed squeal. "Tell me everything. I can't stand it. Where'd you scoop him up, and if you say a hookup app, I'm going to have to punch you in the face."

I blinked at him. "A hookup app."

"No!" he said with a bold laugh. "What the hell? Why am I never that lucky? I mean, there's hot, and then there's that guy. He's like..." Jay looked back over at him. Jack was grinning from ear to ear at something Tara was saying. His one overly pointy canine tooth made me suck in a breath. I knew exactly how that tooth felt against my tongue and caught on my lip. And gently raking across the skin of my hip.

I shivered. "Yeah."

Jay wolf whistled and shook his head. "If you ever decide to toss that catch back, you let your friend Jay know, m'kay?"

"Mpfh." As if that was ever going to happen. Jay went through men like nurses went through sterile gloves.

I fixed up the relish dog and brought it to Jack. Just when Logan started to stand up to give me the seat next to Jack, Chris pulled me forward to the next row to sit next to him. Since Logan and Jack had been in the middle of a conversation, I didn't think much of it.

It took me about ten seconds to suspect that Chris had strategically placed me close enough to run interference between him and Chelsea.

She would not stop talking. She talked about anything and everything.

"So then I said I wouldn't work another hour even if they paid me triple time. I mean, not that I work hourly, because, Christ. Can you even imagine? But the point is the same. They're taking advantage." She took another swig of her beer before continuing. "I think I'm going to look for something else. My friend Lauren said she could get me in with one of the firms downtown, but I don't know. I told her I'd think about it, but what do you think?"

She looked at Chris expectantly. I knew for a fact he hadn't been paying attention to a word she'd said.

"Yeah," he said. "Sure."

"I should quit my job?"

He turned to her. "Wait, what?"

She rolled her eyes and leaned over him to get to me. "What do you think, Teo? Is it worth dealing with all the city bullshit? I mean, I'd either have to get a roommate or live like... south of the city in some... cheap-as-shit apartment."

"I live south of the city in some cheap-as-shit apartment," I told her with a smile. "And I've loved every damned minute of it. I wouldn't say I'd like to live in an apartment forever. I actually enjoy mowing my parents' lawn and planting veggies and kitchen herbs in the summer with my mom. I'd love to have my own house with a yard one day. But for now, while I've been in my twenties and not tied down? It's been amazing. The few train stops it takes me to get to the heart of the city are nothing compared to the long ride in from Carpentersville where we grew up."

"I grew up in Barrington," Chris mumbled, correcting me the way he always did. God forbid anyone think he came from the wrong side of the tracks.

"Fine, Barrington. Regardless, we both went to Barrington High. Chris and I met when we were like six. We were on the same Little League team."

"Awww, that's so sweet! So you two, like, love baseball together, and that's why we're here. Aww." She clapped her hands together and then lifted up her beer can in a mock toast. I glanced at Chris, who was pretending to be incredibly consumed by Jon Lester's lazy stroll to the mound.

"So, Chelsea... where did you and Chris meet?" I asked in an attempt to be friendly.

"Oh, so this is a great story," she began, sitting forward again so we could talk over Chris. "My work husband, not my real husband because gross, but anyway, my work husband is married to a doctor who, like, has him on all this soy milk and stuff, which means he can only get a decent coffee at the shop around the corner from work since we don't have any soy milk in our office. Which... now that I think about it... he could just buy some, I guess. But anyway..."

She continued telling me about a stranger's need for soy milk until even *I* was incredibly consumed by Jon Lester's lazy stroll to the mound.

"And that's where I met Christy," she finally said.

I looked at her after shooting a quick glance at Chris. He was 100 percent checked out. "Did you say Christy?" I asked. "With an *eee*?"

"Yeah. The girl who lives next door to Chris." She said it like it was obvious.

I stared at her until she shrugged. "So that's how we met," she finished. "I saw him in the hallway of his building."

I heard a low chuckle from behind me and turned to meet Jack's twinkling eyes. I shot him a *WTF* look, and he winked back at me.

Because I was an evil person and couldn't help myself, I turned back to her. "And when was this?"

18

JACK

"Yesterday," she said.

I reached out and squeezed Teo's shoulder to keep from laughing. He clasped my hand with his own and squeezed it until there was no blood circulation left.

"And we're so happy you've joined us," Teo said in his typical friendly voice. "Would you like another beer? I'm going to get some more food."

Chelsea nodded gratefully while Chris sank noticeably lower in his seat. What a jackass. But I was happy to see him affected by Teo's bringing me since that's what Teo had wanted out of all of this.

And if I was a little sick to my stomach... well, it was probably the relish. I excused myself from the conversation with Logan and his sister and stood up to meet Teo back by the counter where the food was set up inside the suite.

He walked right up to me and leaned his forehead on my shoulder. "Help," he whispered. "I think my ears are broken."

I put my arms around him and kissed the top of his hair, inhaling the lemony aftershave I remembered from the first time we got together. Everything about him lit up my senses.

"Hey, Tee," Chris called. "Will you grab me another beer too?"

We pulled apart so Teo could grab them some beers from the fridge. I poked through the rest of the food offerings, grabbing a few carrots and dip. I liked Teo's friends. With the exception of Chris himself, they all seemed friendly and fun. Jay flirted with me but didn't seem to mean anything by it. Logan was fascinated by my job and asked a ton of questions, and their friend Sam had made sure to offer me something to drink every time they got up to get anything.

As I stood there glancing out at the game and munching on carrot sticks, I suddenly realized that this was the exact point Millie had been trying to make to me for so long. Here I was, enjoying a baseball game on a gorgeous spring day with a welcoming group of interesting, friendly people. It was like having an actual social life outside of a hookup app or a quick dinner with a coworker on an overnight trip.

I pulled out my phone to text my sister.

Jack: *I'm at a Cubs game with Teo's friends. You were right. I've been missing out on having fun.*

Millie: *I'm sorry, who's this? I know it's not my ungrateful, know-it-all brother.*

Jack: *No, it's your reformed, you-told-me-so brother.*

Millie: *Send me pics of Kris Bryant and use your zoom lens.*

I laughed and moved to the front of the box to see if the third baseman was visible. He wasn't.

Jack: *Cubs at bat. Gimme a little while.*

Millie: *Mom is super excited to meet Teo.*

I did a double take on the text before frantically typing back.

Jack: *What?! How does she know anything about Teo? You said if I agreed to bring him, you wouldn't tell her.*

Millie: *I lied. You haven't dated anyone since Ty. It was too good to keep to myself.*

I looked up at Teo, who was in an animated conversation with his friend Hannah about her recent pet-sitting gig. He was so happy and alive. I'd forgotten what it was like to be somewhere with the person you were dating and be able to look across the crowd at them and feel that special something. It was like... like you had intimate knowledge of them and access to them in a way no one else in the room did. That feeling was like a warm little hearth fire in my chest, a feeling I hadn't had in years and didn't realize I was missing.

Teo caught my eye and stopped talking for a minute before lifting an eyebrow in an unspoken *Are you okay?* question. I smiled and winked at him before he resumed his conversation with a noticeably pinker face and neck. The hand that wasn't holding his beer flapped along with whatever he was saying to Hannah.

My stomach twisted again. He was such a good man. A sweet human being. He deserved the best. I looked at the back of Chris's head where he sat blatantly ignoring his chatty date. He certainly wasn't the best, and he for damned sure wasn't good enough for Teo Parisi.

I gritted my teeth. It was none of my fucking business.

But, god. I was starting to want it to be my business. And that was bad. The man was in love with someone else. It didn't matter if I wanted him. He wanted Chris.

And I'd promised to help Teo get him.

I wondered if it would make a difference if I chatted up Chelsea to get her attention away from Chris. Then maybe Teo could get his attention and spend some time with him.

After grabbing a couple bottles of water out of the bucket on the counter, I made my way over to the stadium seats and scooted past Chris and Chelsea to sit on Chelsea's other side. I offered her a water.

"It's warm out here. Nice to see spring finally springing," I said.

"Oh thank you," she said, taking the water and cracking it open. "Too much beer is going to go to my head, and I'm taking the LSAT in the morning."

"Are you? I heard you talking about changing jobs, but I didn't know you were considering law school."

She nodded. "I'm nervous. I can't stop thinking about it. My dad doesn't think I'm smart enough, but I'm tired of doing the work of an attorney and getting the pay of a PA. I figured I'd give it a shot. Besides, a friend of mine got help from Legal Aid one time and I thought they were awesome. Maybe…" She looked unsure. "Maybe if I make it through and actually get the degree, I can try to work there and really help people."

I thought back to what she'd said earlier and realized I'd totally misunderstood her complaints. I'd made assumptions based on my first impression of a bubbly, chatty woman. I was an asshole.

I reached out and put my hand on her arm before meeting her eyes. "You're going to do great. And I think my sister knows someone at Legal Aid, so let me get your number in case I can help at all."

After exchanging numbers, we continued to chat for a while about my experience moving to the Chicago area and what I liked and didn't like about it so far. I explained that I'd rented an apartment in an old house by McKinley Park and I enjoyed being able to run in the park and hop on the Orange Line to get to the airport or down-town Chicago.

"I live almost exactly halfway between the two," I said. "Twenty minutes west is Midway, and thirty minutes east is every restaurant, theater, and shop I could ever want. It's perfect."

"Maybe that's what I need," she said. "Someplace with a little bit of both. I wonder if I could come see where you live and check it out sometime?" she asked with a smile. "You could show off the park, or maybe we could go running together."

"Sure, that'd be great."

Chris leaned around her and shot me an incredulous look. "Seriously?"

I felt a warm hand squeeze my shoulder from behind, and then Teo's calm voice chimed in. "Jack, can we—"

"No, Teo," Chris said with annoyance. "You're not going to defend this guy—your *boyfriend*—hitting on my date."

I laughed until Teo's hand moved over my mouth. Then I wanted to lick it, but I refrained.

"Chris," Teo said with the patience of a saint. "In case this wasn't clear before, Jack is gay. Like, all the way gay. He's not trying to hit on Chelsea. There's such a thing as making new friends."

Chelsea chuckled. "I wasn't aware we were dating, Chris. But if you're looking for something serious, I'm game."

I could tell it was a test because clearly Chris wasn't the commitment type.

"We don't have to be dating for me to want you not to pick up other guys while we're out together."

I brought my hand to cover Teo's over my mouth and pressed a kiss to his palm before moving his hand down to my chest and holding it there. He leaned forward and wrapped his other arm around my neck too.

"Chris," Teo tried again, but Chelsea interrupted.

"It's fine. Actually, after talking about the LSAT, I think I'm just going to head home and make sure I get a good night's sleep." She turned to Chris. "Thank you for inviting me. If you want to try again sometime, give me a call. Otherwise, I encourage you to think about your own sexuality and what you really want." She looked over my shoulder at Teo.

Damn.

I felt Teo's grip tighten against my chest. Chris's nostrils flared.

"I'll walk you out," he mumbled before standing.

Once they were gone, I stood up to stretch and wander back to where the food was again. Teo and Jay stood up and joined me.

"Damn, boy," Jay said. "That was some drama right there. What the fuck is wrong with Chris tonight?"

Hannah stood up and joined us too. "He's finally having to

compete for Teo's affection," she said with a laugh. "Poor kid. He has no idea how to handle himself."

Jay looked back and forth between Hannah, Teo, and me. "What? What do you mean? Teo's brought guys around before. He's always got a boyfriend."

That was a surprise to me, and by the look on Teo's face, it was a surprise to him as well.

"No I haven't." He stepped closer to me. "Jack's the first man I've brought around. Ever." I reached over and ran my fingers through his hair, using it as an excuse to pull him even closer.

Jay continued to look between us, reality dawning as complete surprise and disappointment to him. "No way. For real? How is that..." He seemed to stop and think it through. "I remember telling Chris I was going to ask you out a while back, and he told me you were seeing someone. After that, every time I brought it up again, he told me you were involved and just didn't like to bring the guy around us for some reason. Why would Chris lie to me about that?"

Teo didn't say anything, but Hannah wasn't as circumspect. "Because Chris wants to have his cake and eat it too. Poor Tee has been carrying a torch for Chris for years," she said softly. "And Chris does just enough to keep him on the hook. Sorry, Teo, but it's true."

Jay frowned. "But Chris is straight."

Hannah snorted. "No. He's not. I have a friend who was at a sex party with him once and said Chris was just as into the hot dogs as he was the tacos. In fact, I think there were times he was enjoying both at the same time."

She glanced over at Teo with a wince. "Sorry, babe."

I looked down at Teo's poor face that was deep, blotchy red. I couldn't see his eyes since they were currently inspecting the carpet.

Jay still couldn't work it out. He was getting more upset by the minute, to the point I was starting to feel a tiny bit jealous. "So, wait. Are you saying—"

Just then Chris walked back into the suite and whistled. "Whew. Dodged a bullet there, I think. Sorry, guys."

Teo's chin came up. "You were so fucking rude to her!"

Everyone stood still in the awkward silence. Teo continued. His body seemed to be nearly vibrating next to me. "Why bring her if you're going to ignore her? Huh? Why? You acted like she was a complete waste of your time when all she wanted to do was be friendly with everyone. And then the minute someone actually gives her the time of day, you throw a hissy fit like some kind of..." He threw up his hands. "Whatever."

He turned back to me with a look of pleading in his face. "Can we go please?"

I nodded. My throat felt too thick to say anything, but I would have done anything he wanted in that moment. On our way out the door, I shot a look of disgust at Chris because I couldn't help myself.

"Wait," Chris called after a few beats. We were halfway out the door. Teo kept walking, so I followed him into the hallway. "Teo, wait," Chris repeated, following us into the quiet space. All the doors to the nearby suites were closed, and the noise of the game was hushed by the walls of the building around us.

Teo turned around and crossed his arms in front of his chest, defiant. "Don't you think I've waited long enough?"

Chris glanced at me. "Can you give us a minute please?" It was the nicest tone he'd used with me all day.

I looked at Teo, who nodded his head slightly, so I stepped forward and kissed his forehead. "I'll be in the bar at the end of the hallway. Take your time," I said softly.

When I got to the bar, I ordered a scotch on the rocks to keep me from turning back around and yanking Teo away from that user.

I repeated the same thing over and over to myself.

It was none of my business.

He wasn't mine.

19

Chris looked off-balance and unsure. It was unusual and off-putting.

"Look, Tee. I owe you an apology. I'm... I'm really sorry. I shouldn't have acted the way I did."

He combed his fingers through his hair and paced from side to side in the narrow hallway. "It's just... I don't like seeing you with that guy. He's... I... I don't understand why suddenly you're bringing a guy around. I thought you wanted to be with me."

I opened my mouth to speak, but he stopped pacing and held up his hand to forestall me. "No, wait. I know. I've been a complete ass. It's my fault. I told you I'd get my shit together if you came to work at Banks so we could spend more time together." He reached out and cupped the side of my neck. It was an intimate touch I wasn't expecting, so I kind of jumped a little when he did it.

Chris frowned. "You don't want me to touch you?"

"No, it's not that. You just startled me. You never touch me in public." As I spoke, Chris stepped closer to me, his eyes darting down to my lips and back up to my eyes and his hand tightening on my skin. For a split second, I stupidly thought he might have been thinking of kissing me. Instead, he stepped closer again and hugged me, holding me tight like a long-lost friend or lover.

I was neither.

"I'm sorry," he said softly into my hair. "Please don't give up on me. I love you."

I pulled back. "Then what the fuck are you doing bringing Chelsea around?"

He stepped back and threw up his hands. "I don't know. You told me about Jack and I just... ugh. I just didn't want to be some loser here without a date while you brought around your new 'boyfriend.' Can you blame me?" He used a snide voice and finger quotes on the word *boyfriend*. Like a fucking child.

"Yes, in fact, I can blame you. Because for fucking years you brought women around when I didn't have anyone. For years you've flaunted girlfriends around me when you knew I was in love with you. Like you didn't give one single thought about my feelings. Like it was all a fucking game to you! What about me, huh? What about my fucking feelings, Chris? Jesus fucking Christ. You're the most selfish person I fucking know!" My voice had gotten louder and louder until it was croaking, and my eyes felt like they were going to explode with tears like a cartoon.

I swiped at them angrily. "I wish I hated you. I wish I could tell you to go to hell. But I can't. Because I've loved you most of my life. And all I've gotten for it is absolutely nothing."

Chris's face was pale with shock. "Teo, I'm sorry. I didn't... I wasn't thinking. I never meant to hurt you. I thought... I thought we were too young. It was too soon. Jesus, Tee. We're only twenty-six. Are you really ready to—"

"For fuck's sake, don't you ever listen to me?" My shout echoed off the walls of the narrow hallway, surprising even me.

The sound of a grunt and something crashing came from the end of the corridor. Both of us turned to see Jack whip around the corner toward us. He looked pissed.

"What the fuck did you say to him?" he barked at Chris. Jack looked at me, and his face fell. "Baby, shit. Come here. Fuck." He reached for me and pulled me into his chest. "You're upset. What did he say to you?" He must have looked back up at Chris. "What the fuck did you say to him? Haven't you done enough? Jesus fuck. You know what? Never mind. We're leaving."

Out of the corner of my eye, I saw Jay, Sam, and Logan step out of the suite to see what was going on. My humiliation was complete now that everyone apparently knew I'd been holding on to a ridiculous fantasy all this time.

I tugged on Jack's shirt. "You're right, let's go," I said softly. "Please."

He clasped my face and studied me for a beat before using his thumbs to wipe off my tears. Then he pressed a long kiss to my cheek before clearing his throat and taking my hand. When we got to the end of the hallway, I saw a garbage can on its side with trash spilling out of it and a member of the janitorial staff working on putting it to rights.

Jack stopped and pulled out his wallet, passing the guy a wad of cash. "I'm so sorry, man. I turned the corner too fast and wiped it out."

The man's mouth turned up in a grin at the money. "Yeah, dude. No problem. Thanks."

I could tell Jack was angry, but I couldn't quite figure out if all of his anger was aimed at Chris or some of it at me for being such a pathetic loser. I was embarrassed and hurt. The reality of my unrequited love for Chris was finally bearing down on me, and it hurt like hell.

"I'm sorry," I whispered as he led me out through the doors and into the cool spring night. It seemed like everyone was staring at me.

Jack whipped around to face me. "No. No way. You have nothing to be sorry for, especially to me. You did nothing wrong."

The tears wanted to come again at his fierce defense of me. "But I shouldn't have—"

"No," he said again, reaching up to cup my face. I loved it when he did that. "He's the one who should be apologizing, not you. He's spent years stringing you along, saying just the right things to keep you on the hook, and god forbid you finally have someone for yourself. God forbid you want what he's had so many times over the years. I can't believe that selfish fucking bastard."

I blinked at him. "I'm such an idiot for not seeing it sooner. That's partly why I'm so upset. How could I have been so stupid? How could I have wasted so much fucking time? Who does that, Jack? Who waits a fucking *decade* for someone to follow through on a promise? And who holds someone to a promise they clearly have no interest in fulfilling? I feel sick. Just... why was I so naive?"

He pulled my face to his and slammed his lips on mine, right there outside of Wrigley Field. When Jack Snyder kissed me, he may as well be sucking out my brain in the process, because I instantly turned to derpy mush.

I clutched at his shirt front to keep from tipping over and stood up on tiptoes to get more, more, more. Finally, he pulled back and sucked in a breath. I stared at him.

"Your place or mine? Wait. Yours. You have Socrates and Waffles. Lead the way."

I stood on my toes to kiss him again, just a quick one to thank him for being so thoughtful and sweet, before threading my fingers through his and heading toward the station.

Walking hand in hand with him through the streets of Chicago was a dream come true. Even though it carried with it fear of people's negative reactions and possible bullying, it was still something I'd never been able to do before. Maybe it was a silly cliché, but it was little things like this I'd always wanted to do with Chris before.

I glanced up at Jack while we strode to the station. His jaw was still tight, but as soon as he caught me looking at him, his mouth broke into a wide smile. "What're you looking at, cutie?" he asked.

I grinned back at him. "I feel like I just got asked to the prom or something," I admitted. "I've never held anyone's hand in public like this. Isn't that crazy?"

He squeezed my hand. "Not crazy. Maybe a little overdue though." He yanked me closer and put his arm around my shoulder instead. I had to hop a little to try and get our strides synchronized so we didn't crash our hips together with every step.

"Nah," I said, stepping out from under his arm. "That's too awkward, or your legs are too long."

He took my hand again. "Do you want to talk about it?"

"Hell no," I said. "I want to tell you all about the rabbits that Hannah got to take care of last week. They sounded so adorable; I think I need a pet rabbit or twelve."

We made our way onto the train and across the city to the Fifty-Third Street station. I lived in a small studio apartment in Hyde Park. It was a great neighborhood with several large parks nearby and the University of Chicago's student population filling the shops and restaurants. I liked the energy of the area and had decided to stay after finishing my nursing degree.

I pointed things out to Jack as we walked the two and a half blocks to my building. "There are two Thai restaurants on this block. Don't ask me why because one of them should be condemned. No one ever goes there. Maybe it's a front for the mafia." I whispered the last word in a mock dramatic voice.

"You know how those mafia dons love their Panang," Jack teased.

"You hungry? We could grab something to take home. I think all I have in my apartment is the ingredients for pancakes."

He bumped my shoulder with his. "I love pancakes. But I'm not hungry after I ate my way through that hospitality suite."

"Yeah. Those dogs are good. I can't ever help myself when I'm there." I sighed. "There's just something about a hot dog and beer at a Cubs game."

I could feel the inane nervous chatter coming on the closer we got to my apartment. It was a sign I was nervous about being alone with him which was weird because I freaking loved being alone with him. Being alone with Jack meant naked and orgasming. And I loved orgasming. With Jack. Naked.

I let out a little squeak by accident.

"What's going on?"

"Nothing. I was talking about dogs. And cats. You're not allergic, are you? It's only... I have two cats, and I should have asked first.

Honestly, I should have reminded you about them, really. It was rude of me not to because I have... two cats."

Jack stopped and stared at me. I looked at the side of the building, the chipped piece of broken curb, the weeds on the nearby front steps, and anything else except Jack's eyes.

His finger lifted my chin up until I was forced to look at him. "I know about the cats. Take a breath. It's just me. You know me." His voice was low and soothing. "All I want to do is go into your place and meet your babies. Waffles used to be your neighbor's and has a tortoiseshell coat while Socrates is black with one white sock. And that's why people mistakenly call him Socks, and it drives you crazy since the real reason he was named Socrates was because you saw a stupid quote at a store and it made you laugh."

"It might as well have said Live, Laugh, Love," I said, throwing up my hands. "It was this giant parchment framed with like... shipwreck timber. And it said in bold script, 'Happiness is unrepentant plea-sure.' It was a Socrates quote, and all I could think was if Socrates had been standing right there at Anthropologie Barn or whatever the fuck the name of the place was, he would have keeled over laughing."

I led him up the stairs to my building and then looked back over my shoulder at him before unlocking the door. "The fact you remember that makes me feel... fizzy and light, like a can of fruity pop." I felt my face heat, so I turned back around quickly and unlocked the door. Jack's arms came around my front, and his deep voice slid into my ears.

"I feel like there's a joke to be made about popping open a fruity can—"

"Oh my god stop," I blurted with a laugh. "Gross."

"Babe, you seriously handed that one to me on a silver platter. A fruit platter."

I thought maybe my face was going to melt right off from embar-rassment. "I'm not a poet, okay? I just..."

As soon as we stepped into the tiled entryway of the building, Jack turned me around and pressed his lips to mine.

He tasted so sweet, I forgot all about my nerves and just enjoyed the fruity fizz.

When we finally separated long enough to make it to my apartment, I opened the door to discover a giant mess. Somehow, a bag of popcorn I had safely put away in a closed kitchen cabinet had been retrieved and scattered all over the studio apartment. I groaned and looked for the culprit. Waffles was nowhere to be found. Meanwhile Socrates was curled up in a tight ball on my neatly made bed as if nothing had happened.

Typical.

"Crap, I'm so sorry," I began, stooping to begin the cleanup. "She's such a jackass sometimes. I don't know how she does it, but Waffles is like... she's like goddamn Houdini or something, but only with snacks and toilet paper rolls."

Jack began picking up the spilled popcorn next to me, making a little *tsk* sound with his mouth periodically until Waffles, the jackass snacker, came slinking out from under my bed.

"C'mere, baby," Jack murmured, holding out a hand toward Waffles. For a split second, my stomach did that little flippy thing it always did when he spoke to me in that tender voice. But he wasn't talking to me, he was talking to the destroyer.

Waffles waddled her way over and sniffed Jack's hand before prancing a figure eight through Jack's legs and rubbing up against him like a slut.

I sighed. "Seriously? She's a menace." I continued cleaning while Jack sat down and made room for Waffles on his lap and continued to massage the cat like this was some kind of feline day spa.

After most of the popcorn was cleaned up, I realized I was staring at Jack's hands as he stroked his long fingers through Waffles's coat. Those hands had been all over my body. Those fingers had been inside of me. Just thinking about it ramped me up and made me want him again. In some ways, I felt like an adolescent who'd just discovered masturbation. Except... it was sex, and now I wanted it every minute of every day.

I wiggled my hips, trying to unkink my dick without making it obvious I needed to shift things around.

Jack's eyes met mine, and the corner of his mouth ticked up. "Whatcha looking at, cutie?"

"Nothing," I said stupidly. "Um, the cat."

My face flooded with heat. Why hadn't I just said, *You, you sexy fucker. Want to bang?*

Jack gently nudged Waffles out of his lap and stood up, reaching out a hand for me. "C'mere, baby." This time the words were meant for me. A knowing glint in his eye told me he knew exactly what he was doing. "Now would be an excellent time for your first advanced sex lesson."

"Um..."

"Take off your clothes, Teo."

"But, ah..." I looked around, wondering if I was ready for advanced moves. I'd barely gotten my basic competency on the regular moves.

"Get naked, or the first advanced move you're learning involves my palm leaving a nice pink mark on your ass."

20

———

JACK

Maybe it was a mistake to continue sleeping with Teo when I was clearly beginning to have more feelings for him than a simple hookup. He'd made it clear to me from the very beginning that he was in love with his best friend. Hell, it was the only reason we were even together today, to fool Chris into thinking Teo was seeing someone.

And it had worked. The fake-boyfriend thing had pulled out Chris's jealousy until he'd been forced to express his feelings for Teo. When I'd overheard Teo yelling at him in the hallway of the baseball complex, I'd lost it. All I'd wanted to do was get him out of there, get him away from the selfish prick who truly did want to have his cake and eat it too. The man was a user, and hearing Teo admit to still loving him had cracked something open in me. Envy, maybe. Perhaps I wanted to feel that way about someone too.

But now those feelings seemed to be directed at Teo, and that was the worst thing that could happen. I thought back to what Elaine Stickley had told me about wasting her life being in love with someone who was in love with someone else. At the time, I'd wondered why she hadn't just cut her losses and moved on, but now I was beginning to catch a glimpse of how that might not be as easy as it sounded.

As I watched Teo shuck his clothes off like they were on fire, I realized it didn't matter. For the next several hours, I was laying claim to the man regardless of whether or not he was mine. For the next several hours, he *was* mine, and I planned on taking advantage of every single second of our time together by licking, caressing, and teasing every single inch of his perfect body.

If I couldn't convince him to want me instead of Chris Banks, I would at least do my best to show him how he deserved to be treated by whoever he ended up with. He deserved the best. He deserved to be worshipped and pleasured until he could hardly think straight and his muscles and bones felt like a twist of overcooked noodles in the bed.

"I feel like the deer caught in the hunter's sights," Teo said with a nervous chuckle. He sat naked on the side of his perfectly made bed with his hands stretched behind him, propping him up. "I'm ready for the hunter to do a strip show before aiming his gun at me, if you don't mind."

I reached behind me to pull off my T-shirt. "This weapon has been pointed at you most of the day." I stepped closer after twisting open the button on my fly and lowering my zipper. "Hands and knees, Tee."

His bright eyes widened as he scrambled more fully onto the bed, scattering the cat and spreading his knees until I could see exactly what I wanted. His pale, round ass was smooth and full, lit up warmly from the bedside table lamp he'd turned on when he was undressing.

I stepped up and grabbed two handfuls, leaning down to suck up a mark on one creamy cheek before smacking it lightly and watching his ass jiggle. "Fuck, I want you."

Teo leaned over and stretched to open the bedside table drawer. I spotted multiple bottles of lube, a brand-new box of condoms, and at least two dildos in the drawer. He pulled out the condoms and a bottle of lube and tossed them on the bed next to me.

"You want me to pull out those toys?" I asked, leaning down to speak lowly into his ear. He shivered and shook his head.

"No. Just you. Want you. Please."

I ran my hand up his bare back and into his dark brown hair, feeling the thick strands through my fingers. I loved messing up his hair. It reminded me of how he looked after sex—debauched and well fucked. Glazed-over eyes, flushed skin, and hair everywhere. Just thinking about how he looked after sex was enough to make my dick hard as steel.

When I turned his head to the side, I noticed his lips were full and red, wet with his nervous licking and nibbling. I leaned over and took them into my mouth, tasting the surprising pineapple of one of my Hawaii candies on his tongue. I cupped the back of his head and held him close, seeking more of the pineapple sweetness. Teo made little whimpers and moans and seemed to melt further into the mattress.

My heart thundered with an odd kind of anxiety I hadn't felt before, like a mixture of fear and excitement all rolled into one. The feeling was heavy with promise but dangerous too, like I was messing with something completely out of my depth.

I kissed his bare shoulder and down his warm skin to the sharp angle of his shoulder blade. I could taste salt and sunshine on his skin as I moved the kisses down his spine. Teo looked over his shoulder at me, his eyes already a little dazed. The forest-green ring around his irises was stark against the lighter green center, and his pupils were dark and wide. He really was stunningly beautiful, and it boggled my mind that he was still single, that neither Chris nor any other man had managed to grab him up for their very own.

He was one of the kindest men I'd ever met. Even in the short time I'd known him, I'd seen how gentle he was as a caregiver, how sweet he was as a friend, and how vulnerable he was in a world that seemed harsher than he deserved. As my hands moved across miles of his skin and my lips mapped his body, I thought about what I could do to make his life better... *easier*.

For one, I could stop being an asshole about his best friend.

Maybe he knew things about Chris that somehow excused or at least explained his bad behavior. Or maybe it was none of my fucking business anyway. Regardless, if Teo wanted Chris, then I would help him get him. Because what I realized I wanted more than anything was for Teo to be happy and have everything his heart desired.

And I was going to start by giving him the best orgasm of his life.

I reached for the lube and wet my fingers before sliding them one at a time into his body while reaching around to grasp his cock with my other hand.

"Jack," he whimpered. "Fuck. Fuck. Please... *fuck.*"

"Your vocabulary gets noticeably less varied the harder your dick becomes," I teased in a low voice.

"I can't... fuck," he breathed again. I swiped my finger over his gland, and he moaned. His entire body tightened up in pleasure, and his dick jumped in my hand.

"That's it. Feel good?"

Teo's only answer was more unintelligible noises. I continued fingering his ass and stretching him with one hand while reaching for the condom with the other. Finally, I had to give up and use both hands to get the damned box open and the condom on, but as soon as I was ready, I leaned over his back and pressed my cock to his hole, feeling the heat of his body and the tight clench of his muscles through the thin latex.

Now it was my turn to groan. "Christ, Tee. Fuck, you feel good."

He reached back and grabbed my hip with one hand, letting his chest fall to the mattress. Sliding into his body was coming home after a string of back-to-back trips. The relief was so overwhelming, I felt my throat tighten. I tucked my face into the side of his neck and began to slide in and out of him slowly, relishing every noise and squeeze of his body.

"Jack." His voice was breathy and broken, begging for me.

"You feel so good." I knew I'd said it already, but I didn't know what other words to use to describe how incredible it felt to be inside him, to be with him like this while he was at his most vulnerable and beautiful.

The words weren't there, but the feelings were. They reached up and squeezed my throat, banging the final nail in the coffin of my desire for him. This was so much more than a hookup, more than fake anything, and yet I hadn't wanted this. I hadn't been looking for anything like it. In fact, I'd deliberately set out to avoid falling for someone again.

I closed my eyes and concentrated on the moment. How many times did I need to remind myself to simply enjoy this time with him?

"Harder," he begged. "Faster. It feels… it…" His breathing was fast, and his hand clenched on the skin of my hip. "Too much. I need… Jack, please."

I sped up and pounded into him harder, ignoring my desire to flip him over so I could look into his eyes as I pushed him over the edge. If I did that, if I made the connection between us even more intimate, I might ruin everything. I didn't want to lose him completely, and I knew that if I told him how I was feeling, I'd be crossing a line we'd never recover from.

I knelt up and pressed a hand flat between his shoulder blades, holding him down firmly against the bed as I drove into him. With my teeth clenched against words I couldn't say, I silently begged for him to come. He stroked himself with one hand, whimpering and crying out when I thrust into him.

Just as I felt my own release bearing down on me, I heard him scream my name and felt his body tense as he came. Watching, hearing, and feeling him come was enough to bring my own release on swift and hard. He was so hot, writhing and crying beneath me, that it ripped my own orgasm out of me with shocking force.

I groaned until I gasped for breath. My arms shook as I tried to keep from collapsing on top of him and crushing his smaller body into the bed. After dropping small kisses across his neck and shoulder and murmuring words to him about how beautiful he was, how incredibly sexy he was, I gently pulled out and turned to find the bathroom. I returned to the bed with a damp towel to help clean him up and then moved him under the covers so we could lie together and catch our breaths for a little while.

Teo rested his head on my chest and lazily ran his fingers across my skin while my own found their way into the messy waves of his hair. I half expected him to fall asleep on me. He'd had a long week trying to balance looking after Mr. Banks with also finishing up some of his consulting work. But after a few minutes, he surprised me.

"I was trying to think of what to make to bring to your sister's tomorrow night, and I realized they're probably going to have birthday cake, right? So I shouldn't do dessert. What do you think about a big greek salad? I put olives and pepperoncini in it. Sometimes I put little strips of salami in it too, but I don't have to do that if there will be vegetarians there."

He tilted his head back to look up at me with those gorgeous eyes.

I ran a thumb across one of his dark eyebrows. "You don't need to bring anything."

"Jack, I'm Italian. We bring food. It's kind of a requirement. Normally I'd bring cannoli or these tiramisu cupcake things my mom always made for bake sales. But if there's going to be a birthday cake, I should bring something else. Oh! I could put together an antipasti tray. Like cheeses and meats, olives and stuff. Would that be better?"

He settled his head back on my chest. "I don't want to show up empty-handed."

"The salad sounds great. I know my mom especially would love it since she never likes to eat heavy things at a family get-together like this."

"Oh good. Then we'll have to go to the market in the morning and pick up what I need. I already have a big plastic bowl with a lid we can take it in, but I might need to find something to put the dressing in."

"Doesn't it come in a bottle?"

He leaned up again to meet my eye. "It's homemade. For shame, Jack Snyder. For *shame*."

I laughed and kissed the top of his head. "Sorry. Mine has always come in a bottle. I thought that's how dressing was made."

Teo chuckled. "It's plucked from the bottle tree just like that."

"Exactly."

A comfortable silence descended as we continued sharing soft touches and enjoying the quiet together. Socrates had jumped up and made a new nest on a side table in front of the window, burrowing down into one of Teo's T-shirts that had been left there. There was no sign of the other cat.

"Jack?"

"Mm-hm."

When he spoke, Teo's voice sounded surprisingly dejected. "When do you know it's time to walk away from someone you love?"

21

TEO

I hadn't really wanted to ask Jack's advice on relationships, but he was the only person I knew with enough history to maybe know the answer to my question. My friend Jay never really dated anyone seriously, Hannah kept her love life private, my sister was... ugh, I wasn't even going there. So that left Jack.

His hand was in my hair as usual, and it made me want to purr like Socrates during a good scratching session.

"Well, that's a tough one. It's different for everyone." Jack shifted me off him until we were lying on our sides facing each other. "One of the things you might consider is making a list of the things you want in a relationship, and then make a list of the ways in which being with Chris would match up with those needs."

I thought about it. "I want to settle down." It was one of the reasons I knew better than to fantasize about a relationship with Jack himself. He'd broken up with his last boyfriend for that exact reason. "And I want someone to take care of. I know that sounds stupid, but—"

"Doesn't sound stupid," Jack said in a gruff voice. "Sounds nice. You're a natural caregiver, Tee. It makes sense you want to find someone to care for."

"And I like to cook. Maybe I learned it from my mom, but cooking for people is kind of a way of loving them, you know? Chris loves it when I cook for him. So I already know that matches up."

"What are some other things you need in a relationship?"

I thought about it for a minute. "I like spending time with family. I like visiting his great-aunt and his grandpa and my own family. If I have an off weekend with nothing else going on, sometimes I'll go home just to catch up with my mom or my sister or help my dad with stuff around the house."

"Does Chris like to spend time with his family too?"

"Well, it's different for him because he works with his family all day. So on the weekend, he usually wants a break. He's more of a partier than I am, but sometimes he'll come home with me and visit his mom while I visit my family."

"What about hobbies and things? What else do you enjoy doing besides cooking and visiting family? And what does he like doing in his free time?"

"I like running. I know you told Chelsea that was one reason you settled where you did. Same with me here by the shore. Here, I've got Washington Park and Jackson Park. It's tough to motivate in winter, but the rest of the year I love it. I like seeing shows when I can afford it. Funky music offerings and trying different types of restaurants. Things like that. In the summer, I grow tomatoes and herbs out on my little balcony, and I help my mom with her kitchen garden at home."

I felt like I was boring as fuck.

"One of my clients recommended the *Taming of the Shrew* production going on right now at the Shakespeare Theater. I have a friend I used to fly with who can usually get me last-minute deals on tickets if you're interested in—"

"Yes!" I blurted. "Yes, I would love that. I never have anyone to go with. That..." I tried to take a breath and not sound like such a desperate freak. "That would be amazing. Thank you."

Jack's eyes were wide, but his lips were quirked up in a smile wide enough to show off the pointy canine that made my dick hard.

"If only you were the one I'd met all those years ago," I murmured without thought, leaning in to kiss that silly vampire tooth. Jack's arms wrapped around me as he pulled me on top of him.

I could have sworn I heard him mutter *No shit* under his breath. But then again, I'd always been a dreamer.

HANDS DOWN, the best part of having a fake boyfriend was waking up in his arms on a Saturday morning. I stretched against him and grinned like a lunatic. Yes, I'd woken up with him in Goose Bay, but this was different. He was in my bed in my apartment with my cat curled up on top of his head.

"You look maniacal," Jack mumbled. "And why is there a Waffles paw on my forehead?"

"She's petting you. Waffles is very snuggly in the morning. I like to think of it as her mea culpa for all the bullshit she gets up to during the day."

"Mpfh."

He dozed again for a few minutes until I couldn't keep my hands off him and began touching things. I started by tweaking his nipple just a little bit. Then I ran a finger down the center of his chest to his happy trail. God, he was sexy as fuck. I still couldn't believe he'd rather be in my bed than literally anyone else's.

"You could be on the cover of Hot Pilot magazine," I mused out loud. "Or Hot Thirty-Somethings. Or Hot Chicagoans. Or Hot—"

He grabbed my hand and put it on his dick which was already hard as iron. "I sense a theme with these fictional magazines of yours."

I stroked him slowly, enjoying the feel of the smooth heat of his skin. "Fine. We'll stick with Hot Pilot."

"Never heard of it, but I'd like a subscription. Maybe you can get that for me with the money you make from your Hot Nurse cover shoot."

His voice was rumbly with sleep, and his face had a pillow wrinkle on it. How was this my life?

I leaned in and pressed a firm kiss to his prickly cheek, noticing my pillow smelled like his cologne now. I was never, ever washing that pillowcase. He was so delicious, I felt like if I didn't hop up now, I'd never get out of bed.

"Come on," I said, throwing back the covers and scaring the pants off Waffles. "We have to go to the market, remember?"

A strong hand shot out and grabbed my wrist, and before I knew what was happening, I was facedown on the bed with Jack's morning wood pressed hard between my ass cheeks.

"Or this," I squeaked. "This is a good alternative."

His morning stubble scraped its way across my tender skin as his lips trailed kisses down my back. By the time he got to my ass, I was humping the bed, and when those spiky whiskers made their way between my cheeks, I lost it completely.

By the time he reached for a condom and slid inside me, I was incoherent. The orgasm that rocketed through me a little while later made me rethink all of my plans for getting up and starting the day. Maybe Jack's diabolical sex plan was the better idea.

Within seconds after shooting all over the bed beneath me, I was dead asleep again. When I finally awoke sometime later, I heard Jack talking to someone in a low voice. It took me a minute to make out his words.

"I don't know which of these you guys prefer. Ocean mix or tender chicken entree? No. Not that one. That's coffee for me and your dad. Let's go with ocean mix. Socrates, you look like a fish lover."

I lifted my head and saw him standing in my tiny kitchen area in his boxer briefs. Socrates was doing figure eights through his legs while Waffles sat on the counter like a bastard, trying to swat everything Jack laid out onto the floor.

I watched him for a few minutes while he continued talking to them about manners and admonished them to keep the meows down so "Dad" could sleep. My entire fucking dream was standing right there in my kitchen, and the realization hit me in the gut like a two-by-four.

Here was the whole package: someone I admired and liked, someone sexy as hell who also treated me like I was special, accepted my oddities, encouraged me, and was a superstar in bed. A man who cared about spending time with family, so much so that he changed jobs to be closer to them. Someone who was so selfless, he'd volunteered for three extra flights next week because the client felt more comfortable with him than the other pilots.

This wasn't the way it was supposed to be. If there was one thing guaranteed with falling in love so early on with my best friend, it was the joy of knowing I'd be able to avoid wanting someone I couldn't have. Now here I was, unable to have Chris because he wasn't ready and unable to have Jack because he wasn't interested in long-term relationships and settling down.

You're only twenty-six. Calm the fuck down. I tried talking myself off the ledge, but deep down it still hurt like hell. I didn't care how old or young I was, I knew what I wanted. I wanted someone to spend my life with. I didn't need marriage or a lifetime commitment. Honestly, I just wanted someone to spend a nice Saturday with.

You have that. He's standing right there arguing with your cats.

I watched Jack move around the space, helping himself to the coffee mugs in the cabinet and the creamer in the fridge. With every move he made, his muscled ass flexed in his white boxer briefs, and his hairy legs flashed through a strip of sunlight cutting across the room from the window. The wide expanse of his bare back had a red mark in one spot that reminded me of the moment I reached back and clawed at him last night when I was begging to come.

My phone buzzed on the side table, drawing Jack's attention. He turned toward me with mugs in both hands. "Morning." He handed me one of the mugs and crawled back into bed with the other while I reached for my phone. It was a text from my sister.

Fia: *Stronzo!*

Teo: *You barely speak Italian, and stop calling me an asshole.*

Fia: *You start dating a man after a million years of bupkis and don't tell your own sister?*

I stared at the screen before realizing I was going to need to down several gulps of coffee before proceeding.

"What's up?" Jack asked. "Everything okay?"

I tilted the phone away from him as inconspicuously as I could so he couldn't see my family drama. "Oh, fine. Just my sister."

Teo: *What, now you speak Yiddish? Who told you I was dating a man?*

Fia: *You going to pretend you're not gay now?*

It was too early for this.

Teo: *What? I'm gay. I've always been gay and out. What are you talking about?*

Fia: *BOYFRIEND. Tell me everything.*

Teo: *What did you hear? From whom?*

Fia: *My friend Noreen scored tickets to a Cubs game and swears she saw you getting cozy with some guy. Is that true?*

Teo: *Kind of?*

Fia: *And it's not Chris?*

Teo: *No.*

Fia: *Don't make me come to the city and beat you. Give me details.*

I clicked through some of the sneaky pics I'd taken of Jack in

Goose Bay and at the game last night. When I found the best one, I attached it to a text and sent it to her. It was from the game. His face was bright with laughter at something Sam had told him.

Fia: *Oh. My. God.*

Teo: *Don't get too excited. It's not serious.*

Fia: *Do you have any other pics?*

I started to click through until I realized why she was asking.

Teo: *Stop perving on my pilot.*

Fia: *He's a PILOT?!*

I couldn't stop a laugh from bubbling out.

"What're you laughing at over there?" Jack asked.

My face heated. "My sister heard that I had a boyfriend. She's giving me hell about you. Asking for photos like you're some piece of meat."

Jack grabbed my phone and clicked on the camera app before leaning in and kissing my cheek. He snapped a selfie of the kiss and then tossed the phone in my lap and sat back to finish his coffee.

I stared at him before scrambling to look at the photo.

We were clearly in bed together, sleep ruffled and topless. Jack's dark stubble was like something out of a porn video, and for some reason my eyes were closed in a comical expression of ecstasy. My heart frolicked around my chest like My Little Pony on speed. I now had proof I'd had this glorious man in my bed.

I sent it to her and tried not to mentally strut around like some kind of boyfriend master.

My phone rang immediately. I was terrified to answer it and have Jack hear her screech, so I hit the button to decline the call.

Jack chuckled next to me. "You're adorable."

"Shut up. She's going to embarrass me. It's bad enough you know the truth."

His forehead crinkled in confusion. "What truth?"

"That I've never had a boyfriend or whatever," I muttered, hiding behind a big sip of coffee.

He reached out and took my coffee mug, sat it on the table next to me, and then pulled me into his lap until I was straddling him. Since I was still naked and he had on underwear, I felt a little exposed. I tried sneaking the sheet over my junk.

"Stop that," he muttered, grabbing the fistful of cotton out of my hand. "I've seen you naked a thousand times by now. I like seeing you naked. Seeing you naked is my new favorite thing."

He leaned in and kissed my neck. "So is this." He ran both of his hands into my hair. "And this."

We were never going to make it to the market, and I was a thousand percent okay with that.

My phone rang again.

"Fuck."

Jack laughed and picked it up, answering the call from Fia.

"Buongiorno, Teo's sister," he said with a smile and a wink at me. "This is Jack."

The screech could have probably been heard from the middle of Lake Michigan. I fell backward onto the bed and pulled the sheet over my face with a groan.

Jack put the call on speaker and then pulled the sheet off me again and yanked me back up into his lap.

"... and wait till I tell our mother because she is going to want to meet you yesterday. I hope you and—"

"Fia!" I cried, cutting her off. "Fia, please. You're embarrassing me."

"Don't be ridiculous. Jack sounds like a perfectly understanding man, isn't that right, Jack?"

His smirk was legendary. "Absolutely. And seeing bright red flags of mortification on Teo's cheeks is pretty fun too."

"Oh god," I groaned, leaning in to hide my face in his chest. His deliciously hairy chest. He smelled so good, but I felt like maybe I'd already noted that a thousand times or more in my mind. This wasn't the time for brainless Jack licking.

"Bring him around, Teodor. Or I will invite him directly, and Mom and Dad can ask him a few simple questions like how much money he makes per year and whether or not he understands the lifestyle demands of someone who loves cats more than football and who still to this day insists on all crusts being cut off his—"

I scrambled for the phone and hit the red button to end the call before shoving the phone under the bed and accidentally scaring the skin off poor Socrates.

The phone rang again. And then again. I ignored all her attempts to call back. Instead, I tried distracting Jack with coffee-flavored kisses. Finally, it was his phone that rang.

"Hello?"

He glanced at me with a frown before saying, "Yeah, he's right here. Hang on," and handing me the phone. Since I knew there was no way Fia had Jack's number, I wondered who it could possibly be.

"Hello?"

"Tee, oh thank god. I need you." Chris's voice sounded croaky with emotion which shot my heart rate up immediately. Chris rarely got upset about anything. The last time I'd heard him cry was when he'd slammed his hand in the door of his dad's truck our senior year in high school.

"What's wrong? What happened?"

"It's Grandpa. He's had a severe stroke. They say he's not going to make it through the day."

22

JACK

When Teo had gotten the news about Mr. Banks's stroke, it was like a set of steel shutters had come down between us. He'd been in shock at first, and then it had quickly morphed into guilt.

"I should have been there," he'd said over and over while he'd scrambled to get dressed. Chris had asked him to pick up Mr. Banks's sister, Hattie, from the senior care facility where she lived and bring her to the hospital to say goodbye.

"You have been there," I'd reminded him. "You've been with him practically around the clock since returning from Canada."

"I shouldn't have gone to the game. I shouldn't have been so fucking selfish! What if I could have—"

"Stop," I'd said, reaching to pull him into a hug. I'd intended to remind him strokes weren't something he could have prevented, but he'd yanked himself out of my grip and swatted my hands away.

He'd barely looked at me before leaving me standing out on the sidewalk in front of his building. I'd watched him walk away, knowing in my mind that he was simply upset and distracted by the terrible news. But that hadn't stopped my heart from sinking.

When I'd found my way to the train station to make my way home, my phone had buzzed with a text.

Teo: *Please apologize to your family for me about tonight. I'm sorry.*

Jack: *They will understand. Do you want me to meet you at the hospital?*

I hadn't gotten an answer. Later that evening, I'd texted to ask how he was doing and again, got no response.

Finally at one in the morning, when I was just finishing up the dishes at my sister's house, the text had come in saying only, *He's gone.*

At that point, I'd finally had to accept the fact I wasn't his person in this situation. I'd tried to be there for him, but he hadn't needed me. It hurt worse than it should have. Not the rejection as much as the knowledge that he was there, with the Banks family, hurting so badly and presumably not getting the comfort and care I knew he needed.

"You've been staring at that phone screen for five minutes," Millie said softly, leaning in the doorway of her quaint little kitchen. "What's going on?"

I looked up at her, and whatever she saw in my face made her own face fall. "Oh shit, Jack. You've gone and fallen in love with him, haven't you?"

My chest tightened uncomfortably. "What? No, god no. Of course not. I've barely known him long enough to even..." I took a deep breath and rubbed at my chest. "It's just... Mr. Banks died, and Teo... he takes responsibility of people he cares about, especially people who've been his patients. He had this one patient at the home where he used to work. Her name is Dolores Johnson, but everyone calls her Mrs. J. And when he worked at the senior home, he used to bring Mrs. J. a scratch-off lottery ticket every Wednesday because her husband used to do that for her, and Teo thought it was the sweetest thing ever. He's a romantic like you wouldn't believe. Anyway, he changed jobs months ago, but every Wednesday he still takes his lunch break early so he can take Mrs. J. her scratch-off before she takes her lunch and lies down for a nap."

Millie put her hands over her heart. "What a sweet man."

I nodded. "The sweetest. The woman who worked the front desk at the hotel in Goose Bay had a cast on her hand and arm, so she had trouble writing. Teo asked me to take him to the dollar store so he could find a foam ball and a cheap pen. He stabbed the pen through the foam ball and gave it to her, showing her how to use it to write while she had the cast on."

Millie shot me a tender, knowing smile. "You're in love with him."

"I'm not," I snapped. "He's just such a good fucking man. And the person he wants is an idiot."

My jaw tightened the way it always did when I thought of Chris Banks. Maybe I should have been more kind or understanding considering the poor man had just lost his grandfather, but I couldn't bring myself to be so reasonable.

Millie didn't look surprised at my revelation. "I knew there was a catch. Tell me."

I shook my head, furious that I'd landed myself in exactly the kind of situation I'd sworn off, simply because I'd answered a damned hookup request. If I hadn't had such a crazy flight that day, maybe I wouldn't have been so tempted by the thought of a silent hookup.

Liar.

I knew the truth was more complicated than that. Something about his need to be treated special had called to me. I hadn't been able to deny my desire to play happy couple for one night, to make love to a man as if he belonged to me and hold him in my arms all night without feeling the heavy burden of his expectations on me.

But now here we were, a stark reminder that there was a flip side to the burden of expectations, and that was the joy of being able to provide comfort and care to someone who needed it.

"He's in love with his best friend," I admitted. "He's using me to make him jealous." Millie's face turned red, but before she could spout off, I preempted her. "Not like that. It was a plan the two of us came up with together. Actually, I think it was my idea. And I probably subconsciously or not-so-subconsciously came up with it as an excuse to spend more time with him."

Her angry face dissolved back into the pity face. I wasn't quite sure which was worse.

"Are you going to the funeral at least?"

I shrugged. "The man just died. I have no idea what any funeral plans would be, and the way things are going right now... Teo isn't really telling me much. I'm sure he's grieving and also trying to be there for Chris and his family. Plus, I have an insane week. One of my clients is a motivational speaker, and he has me scheduled for three trips already."

Millie walked over to where I stood leaning my ass against the counter by the sink. She slid her arms around me and hugged me tight. Her salon-blond hair was twisted up in a messy bun on top of her head, and I smelled the familiar scent of the honey hand cream she always kept on the counter by her purse. She wasn't pregnant enough to have a baby bump yet, but I was still careful with her in case she wasn't feeling 100 percent.

"You're a good fucking man too, Jack. And Teo would be lucky to have you."

I hugged her back but didn't trust myself to speak.

"Even if all you can be for him right now is a friend, be the best damned friend the man has ever had," she said before pulling back and standing on tiptoes to kiss my cheek. "Now, go to bed. It's late."

Thankfully, I slept hard because when I woke up the next morning, the work calls started coming in. Not only did I have the flights already scheduled for Rourke, but now I had requests to help cover some of the Banks Consulting flights to pick up friends and family from around the country to bring them to Chicago for the services at the end of the week.

Despite several texts letting Teo know I was thinking about him, I continued not getting any response from him for the next several days. When I finally heard from him on Thursday evening, it was short and sweet.

Teo: *Thank you for your messages. I'm too tired to say more than thank you. For everything.*

I was in Miami at the time, doing preflight checks for our return flight to Chicago. I stared at the screen unsure of how to respond.

"Bad news?" Rourke asked from his chair at the front of the passenger cabin.

I glanced up at him. "Remember the friend I told you about who lost his surrogate grandfather?"

Rourke nodded.

"He finally got back to me. Sounds like he's exhausted and overwhelmed." I slid the phone back into my pocket without responding. I'd think through what I wanted to say while we were in the air in hopes of avoiding coming off as some obsessive stalker with an immediate response. I already felt like I was overwhelming him since I'd messaged him so many more times than he'd messaged me.

"Poor guy," Rourke said. "When we lost our grandmother last year, it was awful. Even when you expect it, it's hard."

I made a sound of agreement and returned to making sure everything was closed and stowed properly and Rourke was strapped in. Sometimes he liked to sit in the copilot's seat during flight, but today he said he had work to do on his laptop. It was probably for the best. I enjoyed talking to him during the flight when he sat up front with me, but the last couple of times I'd gotten the feeling he was flirting with me. Normally, I would have flirted back, but I was so twisted up inside about Teo, I didn't have much energy for that lately.

"Are you going to the funeral?" Rourke asked, sounding like my sister.

"It's on Saturday," I said. Today was Thursday. I was scheduled to fly Rourke to San Diego Saturday morning for a conference where he was delivering the keynote address that evening.

"Shit, Jack. I can request another pilot. Take the day off and go be with your friend."

"Not sure he wants me there, honestly," I admitted, talking over my shoulder as I climbed into the pilot's seat. "It's complicated."

"Ahh. One of those. I see." He was quiet for a few moments while I continued getting us ready to taxi out. After another couple of minutes, he asked, "Are you two seeing each other?"

"No," I said firmly. "Definitely not. He's in a relationship already." Which was technically true, even though the type of relationship might have been up in the air. After Chris's display at the baseball game, I had no doubt he had true feelings for Teo. His jealousy and anger were proof enough of that.

"And what about you? Are you seeing anyone?"

I turned around to see if this was just his usual flirtation, but his face was serious.

"No," I said. "If you'd asked me six months ago, I would have told you I wasn't interested in settling down. Now... now, I'm not so sure. But it's tough with this job, you know?"

He smiled and nodded in understanding. "Believe me, I know exactly what you mean," he said with a chuckle before returning to whatever he'd been doing on his phone.

Rourke was a handsome man. His smile was dimpled, and his warm brown eyes twinkled. From living life in a wheelchair, he had big, strong shoulders and muscular arms as well as a stacked chest. He was well respected among his peers, and we'd shared several meals together while traveling. I wondered what his love-life story was, whether his physical challenges played a role in his being single or whether it was more by choice or job circumstances. At one point, he'd mentioned enjoying the freedom to travel without having to answer to a partner, but I knew from personal experience now there could come a time where that balance tipped the other direction.

Maybe it wasn't "answering to a partner" as much as "having someone to miss you when you were gone."

When I got home to my empty apartment, the feeling became even more pronounced. Since I'd jumped straight into my new job after moving in several months ago, there were still boxes half unpacked and there was nothing on the walls making the place look even remotely lived in. I thought about Teo's little studio apartment where he had photos of his niece in her soccer uniform and pictures of his parents on their retirement cruise hanging on the wall. He had several little pottery knickknacks on a shelf by his bed that had been made for him by some of his patients at the senior home. His cats' toys were scattered here and there on the floor, the mug I'd had my coffee in had said "World's Okayest Nurse" on it, and one of his coat hooks had several colorful 5k and half-marathon medals hanging from it.

Teo's tiny studio was more of a home than my spacious two-bedroom apartment probably ever would be. And even if my place was fully put together and homey, I'd still probably rather spend my time at the smaller studio.

Because that's where Teo was.

I stripped my clothes off and stepped into a hot shower to wash away the travel grime. Millie had texted a few times this week to check up on me and ask if I wanted her to come into the city to stay with me for a few days. I'd also gotten a call from Chelsea asking if I wanted to go running in the park one day this weekend. I'd politely dismissed both of them, but now I wondered if I shouldn't plan some things outside of work to keep my mind off Teo.

Oh, who was I kidding? I needed to plan some things to help me *get over* Teo.

It was early, but I hadn't been sleeping well all week. Maybe I needed to get some rest. Once I got into bed, I pulled my phone out and scrolled through Grindr, wondering not for the first time if a hookup with someone else would help erase the fresh memory of my time with Teo. As soon as my gut began twisting with thoughts of cheating, I tossed the phone down in a huff.

"We're not dating," I reminded myself out loud. "He is not my boyfriend. And even if he was, we wouldn't be exclusive."

In order to prove the point to myself, I thought about what would happen if Chris finally decided to get together with Teo. Wouldn't Teo jump at the chance to be with Chris? Wouldn't he go ahead with it without sparing me a single thought?

I groaned and pulled a pillow over my face. The very image of Chris and Teo fucking made me want to throw something against the wall.

This uncertainty, this up and down of emotions was exactly what

I'd hoped to avoid. *You never fucking wanted this. You never wanted the boyfriend and domestic thing. Jesus, Jack.*

After spending the next hour tossing and turning—arguing with myself and making the case for why I really did, in fact, want the domestic thing—I finally gave up and decided to show up at Teo's apartment. If nothing else, maybe he'd let me play pretend boyfriend for the night and hold him while we slept.

23

———————

TEO

I read a book one time about a teenage girl who'd lost her father in a tragic drunk-driving accident. The author had described the girl's grief like walking through the ocean against a strong tide in loose sand. I couldn't even begin to imagine what losing my father would be like, but I knew that losing Grandpa Banks gutted me in a way I hadn't expected.

My own grandparents had died long ago without my ever having really known them well. Losing Grandpa Banks was the first time I'd experienced the death of a loved one, and the emotional upheaval it caused was made considerably more confusing by my feelings of not being quite family.

Gordon had always treated me like family, but Mike and Deb never had. Chris and his great-aunt Hattie had treated me like family, but none of the other aunts, uncles, and cousins had. The Banks family had so much money that I'd always felt a little bit like the poor semi-relation people didn't talk much about. And that was fine. But it made the week after Gordon's death very strange.

On the one hand, Chris clung to me like I was his second skin.

The minute I'd arrived at the hospital with Hattie in tow, Chris had grabbed me and held me tight, sobbing into my neck like one of us had just been released by terrorist kidnappers.

"Is he gone?" I'd asked him, assuming his breakdown was due to Gordon's passing.

"Not yet. He wants to see Hattie. And you." Chris had pulled back and swiped at his eyes with the heels of his hands. "Sorry, Tee. I just... I think I didn't take it seriously before. He's always been larger than life, you know? I didn't think... And you tried to tell me."

I'd pulled him in for another hug. "I know. It's hard to imagine losing someone so important."

After Hattie had taken her turn saying goodbye, I'd snuck into Gordon's room. Mike had been standing in the corner talking softly on his phone, and Chris's mom had been standing by the window looking out into the spring sunshine. It had struck me at the time how odd it was to face the death of someone dear while the sun continued to shine and the world kept spinning. I'd always imagined it needed to be a dreary, dark, and rainy day when death came to take someone away, but of course I knew better. I'd worked at Wilton long enough to have seen many sweet patients pass away on days as nice as this one. And, hell... maybe it was a good thing. Maybe the sun was a symbol of optimism or something, reminding the rest of us to buck up and enjoy the life we still had.

Gordon had looked awful. His skin was mottled, and his breathing was already slowing down. I knew that after the addition of the heart disease diagnosis, he'd decided to sign a Do Not Resuscitate order in case he had another heart attack or stroke. After watching his wife go through several strokes before her death, he'd been afraid of putting his family through the same turmoil. I'd understood and respected his decision, but it had still hurt like hell to watch him dying when I knew doctors could have kept him alive longer.

But I also knew from experience that wasn't always the right decision, and recovering from a massive stroke at his age with complicating medical factors would have been exhausting and overwhelming.

"Hi," I'd whispered, taking his chilled hand in mine. His fingers had curled a little when I'd held it. "I'm so sorry I wasn't with you when it happened. I hope they took good care of you." I'd swiped tears off my face and taken a deep breath. "Thank you for raising Mike so he could have Chris so I could meet your family. Thank you for everything you've ever done for me. I love you."

His hand had moved again in mine, and I'd squeezed a little more firmly. He'd probably been heavily sedated for comfort, and there'd been no telling what his comprehension ability would have been had he even been conscious. Still, I'd wanted him to know how much he'd meant to me.

When I'd finally kissed his cheek and left the room, I'd found Chris again and fallen into his arms. We'd spent the rest of the day leaning against each other on a sofa in the family waiting room. Chris had taken several more visits into Gordon's room until he'd finally passed away.

Leaving Gordon at the hospital had been harder than I'd anticipated. I'd thought maybe it was a good thing I'd had this experience so I could better empathize with my own patients' families. Dealing with this had been so much worse than I'd thought it would be.

After a somber dinner with Chris's parents, we'd gone home to Chris's apartment near Union Station where I'd assumed I'd spend the night on the sofa the way I always did when I stayed over. But Chris had taken my hand and led me into his bedroom, pulling me into another hug and rubbing his hands up and down my back. When he'd pulled away, he'd pressed a long kiss to my cheek. "Stay with me in here tonight? Please?"

I'd nodded in surprise and stripped down to my T-shirt and boxer briefs before climbing into the luxurious queen-sized bed with its fancy sheets and fluffy pillows. There I'd been in one of my lifelong fantasies of climbing into Chris Banks' bed, yet I'd been so tired, I'd fallen right to sleep before he'd even crawled in beside me.

But this morning, I'd jolted awake when I began to snuggle into the hard body and harder dick pressed against me before realizing it was *not* Jack Snyder.

I slapped a hand over my mouth to keep from yelping at the same time my brain provided the explanation by reminding me I'd shared a bed with Chris the night before.

Chris's arms tightened around me and pulled me closer to him. "Mm, you feel good," he murmured, pushing a leg between mine. I felt the brush of his hard-on against my ass, and it caused me to leap out of bed for an "emergency" visit to the bathroom.

Shit. Shit. Shit.

What had just happened, and how did I feel about it?

I used the toilet and washed my hands before rifling through his cabinet in search of a spare toothbrush. As I brushed the hell out of my teeth, I lectured myself.

This is not how this is going to go down. You will not take advantage of someone going through grief.

My heart thundered. None of this felt right, and that was enough to remind me to put the brakes on it. Besides, he'd practically still been asleep. He hadn't meant anything by it. Had he? No.

I finished up and made my way back to the bedroom as nonchalantly as possible, expecting an awkward encounter in which I'd be forced to decline his advances and explain that he was under a tremendous amount of emotional stress at the moment.

He was snoring.

I sighed and made my way out to the kitchen to put on some coffee. When he finally came shuffling out of the bedroom an hour later, there was no acknowledgement of either his snuggle hold or the semi-rutting. Fine. Good. That was good.

But, after a long day of dealing with family and funeral details, Chris asked me to stay over again. And the rutting and snuggling happened again.

And again the next night.

I would have been confused by the mixed messages except they weren't mixed. During the day, Chris was just as affectionate as he was in bed. He reached for my hand when crossing the street or making a hard decision, he leaned his head on my shoulder when he was overwhelmed, and he'd even kissed me on the cheek a few times. One of those times, I could have sworn he was aiming for my lips, but my phone buzzed at the last minute, causing me to turn my head before I realized what he was doing.

It was like... suddenly we were more than just friends, but I didn't know what the hell we were.

Meanwhile, Jack kept checking in on me making sure I was okay. He asked if I was remembering to eat and getting enough sleep. When he texted on Thursday to see if he could arrange to have dinner delivered to me that night, I burst into tears.

I was at Wilton Manor checking in on Hattie when I received the text. I'd just come out of helping her put a necklace back in her little jewelry box when the words she'd said hit me full force.

"I should give this to Chris to give to his wife one day."

I remembered all the times Chris's mother had talked about Chris's "future wife" and how that phrase had always been like a knife to the heart. This time it was too much.

"What in the world?" my friend Trinity said under her breath, coming out from behind the nurses' station to pull me down the hall and into the break room. "You poor thing. You must be worn full out. Sit down."

She'd always been the "mom" of the shift when I'd worked there, so I let her fuss over me. It felt good to finally be the one receiving comfort rather than giving it.

"There's this guy," I said stupidly. My voice was cracked and pathetic.

She tsk'd. "Mm. There always is."

"And—" I sniffed and took the tissue she handed me. "—and he's the nicest person in the entire world."

She sat down across the break table from me and took one of my hands in hers. "That is not the direction I thought this was gonna go in."

My words were broken up with sniffs and hiccups as I tried to explain my problem. "He... he... he cares about me, Trinity. He's... been looking out for me like... I can't even tell you. He asks if I've eaten, if I've slept. He even asked if I needed him to dry-clean my suit for the funeral service. This man..." When she let go to grab the tissue box from the counter behind her, I folded my arms on the table and buried my face in them. The tears came even harder when I replayed Jack's text over and over in my mind.

She rubbed my back and shushed me in that wonderful caring way some of the best nurses do, but the empathy only made me feel more emotional.

"Sorry, Trin. I'm just tired, you know? It's been a long week."

I used more of the tissues to dry my face, and I tried to concentrate on slowing down my breathing. She sat down next to me and continued rubbing my back with one hand while leaning her head on the other with her elbow on the table.

"Tell me this. Since when is Chris the kind of guy who looks after you this way?"

She didn't really say it in a bitchy way, more like... she was surprised and confused.

"It's not Chris," I admitted in a whisper, as if somehow the Fates would hear me and fuck everything up even more than they'd already done. Not that it was anyone else's fault than mine. Now that Chris was finally coming around, my fickle heart was having second thoughts.

I wasn't sure what I was expecting Trinity's reaction to be, but it certainly wasn't laughter. She cackled like a madwoman.

"Oh, honey." She laughed some more even though she was trying to hide it behind her hand. "Sorry. It's just... you spent years pining for that boy. I'm so happy you found someone else."

I stared at her. "Really? Are you kidding me right now?"

"What? Don't act like everyone here didn't know what a hard-on you had for Hattie's grandson. That boy was like fancy damned chocolate coming up in here right when you were dying for something sweet."

"He's her great-nephew," I corrected under my breath. As if it mattered. "Besides, I don't even like chocolate."

"Liar. Every damned time you pulled a double night-shift weekend, you snuck a giant box of Milk Duds in here. I know this because I used to swipe one or twelve of them when you did it."

I let out a breath. "I like the caramel."

"Yeah, well, who doesn't? The point is, it's a good thing you moved on to greener pastures. That Banks kid wasn't ever good enough for you."

I thought of the man who'd been holding me every night in bed this week, the boy who'd shown up first at the hospital the night I'd sprained my ankle slipping on ice in a parking lot in high school. The friend who'd screamed with excitement when I'd told him I'd gotten into nursing school, and the person who'd bought me my first official drink when I'd turned twenty-one. Chris had been there for so many important moments in my life that his love for me in the past was hard to pick apart from the potential of his love in the future.

"That's not true. He has been by my side for twenty years. He was the one who encouraged me to move to the city to finish my degree at the university. He helped me get the job at Wilton. Chris held me while I listened to my sister's screams in childbirth." Defending him only made me more tired. I felt like I could crawl into Trinity's ample lap and fall asleep on her crisp, clean scrubs while her long fake nails scored soft lines up and down my back.

"In all those situations, could you swap out Chris for your sister and have it still make sense?" I lifted an eyebrow at her, and she rolled her eyes. "Except the childbirth one. Don't be a smartass."

"What's your point?"

"Point is, there's a difference between someone who's loved you all your life as family or friend and someone who wants to be your beloved, someone you want to... you know what? I just realized I'm having the exact same conversation I've been having with my girl-friends since seventh grade."

I was having a hard time following her. "How so?"

She took my hands again. "Hon, there is a difference between loving someone and being *in* love with them. So you've gotta think about which one you have with Chris and which one you have with new guy."

"New guy doesn't want a serious relationship. What if Chris is the one who actually wants to be with me now?"

"A bird in the hand is worth two in the bush," Trinity said thoughtfully.

I hadn't expected her to side with Chris. "Exactly."

Her smile was sympathetic. "Unless the one in your hand is lameass chicken and the two in the bush are the most beautiful, multicolored peacocks you've dreamed about your whole life."

I tried to laugh. "I feel like there's a gay joke in there somewhere, but I'm too tired to make it happen."

Trinity held my hands between hers and patted them. Her skin was warm and soft, comforting. "Regardless of which bird is best, it's clear this is not the week to make that kind of decision. I prescribe bed rest and lots of it. Maybe take a break from trying to be there for your friend, and instead take a little time for yourself."

She was right. I was so keyed up from second-guessing what was going on with Chris in addition to checking in on Hattie and running interference at the office while Mike and Chris were out, that I barely knew which way was up. When I finally hugged everyone at Wilton goodbye and made my way to the station, I texted Chris.

Teo: *I'm heading home to my apartment for the night.*

I didn't get a response, but I figured he was busy with all of the family that had been gathering in town. He may have even headed out to his family's big house in Barrington since that's where the service would be held on Saturday. His mother was already inundated with houseguests and had been begging him to come help entertain everyone.

I realized I'd never responded to Jack after he'd offered to order me dinner earlier in the day. There were so many things I wanted to say to him, but I at least needed to start with some gratitude for how thoughtful he'd been this week. Maybe after I ate and rested, I'd have some better words.

Teo: *Thank you for your messages. I'm too tired to say more than thank you. For everything.*

On the way home, I took my time, wandering around the neighborhood picking up an iced coffee, a few groceries for dinner, and a couple of boxes of Thank You cards so I could help Chris's mom thank everyone for the flowers and food I was sure they were sending. While I was in the stationery store, I saw a set of paperclips shaped like little airplanes. Maybe it was silly of me, but I went ahead and bought them in hopes I'd see Jack again sometime soon and could give them to him as a little thank-you for thinking of me so much this week.

By the time I made it back to my apartment, I was already on my way toward feeling more relaxed. Trinity had been right. I'd needed some time alone to take a breath and recenter myself. It was only Thursday, but it had been a long week. Gordon had died on Saturday night, and every day since had felt like it had lasted fifty hours instead of twenty-four. But getting away from Chris and Hattie and all of the arrangements for the funeral service had been just the boost I'd needed.

I breathed easier and could see a light at the end of the tunnel. I was sad to have lost Gordon, but I also knew that life went on and he would want us to be happy. As I entered my building and walked up the stairs, I thought about how different my job would be now that I didn't have Gordon to look after. I'd be back to the consulting side full-time. Office work and phone calls. Time on the computer analyzing project plans and putting together suggested best practice protocols. The realization depressed me which wasn't surprising.

What was surprising was the new perspective I had. Life was too short to stay in a job that depressed me. While I'd been at Wilton, I'd popped my head in and visited with at least ten of my favorite patients. I'd played a game of chess with Mrs. Varma and helped fix a botched fingernail painting job by Mrs. Chisolm. I'd heard all about Mr. Kramer's new great-granddaughter and caught up on Mrs. Gresham's telenovela updates. Being back there had energized me and made me feel more myself than I had in a long time. Maybe that was part of what had contributed to my outburst with poor Trinity.

I knew I wouldn't be able to leave Banks Consulting anytime soon

—I wouldn't do that to Mike and Chris right now—but I also knew I couldn't stay there forever. Regardless of what happened between Chris and me, I needed to work directly with patients. I knew that now, and knowing it with such confidence calmed something in me.

When I entered my apartment, I was shocked to see Chris in my bed. He was leaning against the headboard, scrolling through his phone.

"What are you doing here?" I asked.

"You said we were staying over here tonight, so I came straight from the office. I picked up your favorite tikka masala. It's in the microwave so the cats will stop messing with it." He went back to looking at his phone like it was perfectly normal for him to be there. Despite having given him a spare key back when I'd first moved in, I could have counted on one hand the number of times he'd visited my place. It wasn't that he didn't like it, it was simply that my place was out of the center of the city and his was right in the middle of everything. His place had always been more convenient.

I set my things down and checked my own phone to reread the text I'd sent him.

Teo: *I'm heading home to my apartment for the night.*

Why was I annoyed?

I opened my mouth to say something about how I'd intended to spend the evening alone, but of course I couldn't get the words out. That would be rude.

Socrates meowed up at me from the floor, demanding attention.

"The black one has been bitching like that ever since I got here. I think it's hungry," Chris said without looking up from his phone.

I fed the cats first and then put the groceries away. Finally, I pulled the Indian food out of the microwave and made myself a plate. "You want me to make you a plate too? There's plenty here to share."

He flapped a hand. "No, I already had mine. I was starving."

I sat down at my little table and dug in, reaching down to give the cats scratches as they rubbed up against my leg.

Chris tossed his phone down and reached for the remote to my television. "Want to watch the Cubs game?"

I finished the last bite of dinner before standing up to clean my plate at the sink. "Sure. Going to grab a shower first though."

It was all very normal... *domestic*. But not in the way I'd always imagined. Something was missing. I thought back to the night Jack had stayed over, the night before Gordon's stroke. The morning after... when he'd made me coffee and fed the cats.

I stripped down and stepped into the shower. Memories of that night and morning washed over me with the hot water. I also thought back to the showers we'd taken together in Goose Bay where the sight of his large hands soaping up my body had made me hard as steel.

It was no surprise just the thought of Jack's hands on me made me hard again. I stroked myself with the soap under the guise of washing. There was no way I was jacking off with Chris right on the other side of the door, especially if the man I was fantasizing about was my casual hookup and not Chris himself.

But fuck it felt good to feel myself and remember the way it had felt in Jack's arms. The way he'd shoved me face-first into the shower wall one time and squatted down to rim me. I'd screeched in shock, but then the sound had quickly changed to moans and pleas for more.

I closed my eyes and remembered.

Suddenly, there was a draft in the shower. I opened my eyes to see a completely naked Chris opening my shower door with the clear intent of joining me. Before I realized it, I was screaming bloody murder and jumping out of my skin, grabbing onto the faucet to keep from slipping and falling. I accidentally turned the hot water off which left me under a spray of pure icy hell.

"Fucking hell! What are you doing in here?" I cried, throwing my hand in front of my rapidly deflating dick while at the same time trying to turn the hot water back on.

"Jesus, Tee. I was going to join you in the shower."

What the hell was he talking about? "Since when?"

"Since you're my boyfriend. Since I've been trying to make a fucking move on you all week."

The B-word got my attention. I wasn't sure it was possible to be more surprised and freaked-out at the moment. "Get out," I said through my chattering teeth. "I can't deal with this right now. Please get out and close the door."

He looked hurt, but he did as I asked without complaint. Once I was left in the bathroom by myself and I finally had the water at a decent temperature again, I stared at the closed door that separated me from Chris.

What the hell had just happened?

And how the hell did I feel about it?

24

JACK

I was nervous. I couldn't even remember the last time I'd been so nervous. Once I'd made the decision to drop in on him, I'd only stopped long enough to grab his favorite chocolate.

When I got to the building, two women were just leaving and held the door open for me. Maybe I looked trustworthy or something, but I was grateful nonetheless.

I knocked on Teo's apartment door and waited.

A minute later, Chris Banks answered wearing nothing but a towel. I blinked at him.

"Ah... hi... Chris. I'm so sorry to hear about your grandfather," I began. "I only met him twice, but he was very kind both times. I hope your parents are doing all right."

Why was he only wearing a towel? Why was he at Teo's apartment at ten o'clock at night?

Chris gave me a cursory smile. "Thanks. I appreciate that. They're hanging in there."

Awkward silence filled the space between us. I tried glancing past Chris into the apartment in hopes of spotting Teo, but there was no sign of him. Waffles, on the other hand, shot out of the apartment and reached her front claws up my legs in a full-body stretch.

"Shit," I blurted, reaching down to extract her carefully. "Waffles, Christ, those talons are sharp."

I picked her up and cradled her, scratching the side of her face the way she liked. When Chris didn't call for Teo or invite me in, I glanced past him again. "Is Teo around?"

"He's in the shower. I was just about to join him. Do you want me to give him a message?"

My stomach dropped. I might have thought he was joking if I hadn't heard the shower running and seen the man standing there in nothing but a towel.

"Yeah, uh…" I pulled the box of Milk Duds out of my pocket and handed them to him. "Give him these?"

Chris's eyebrows dipped in confusion as he took the box from me. "Okay… was he expecting you or something?"

"No. Not at all. I just wanted to let him know I was thinking about him. I know he cared about your grandfather quite a bit." I swallowed and leaned past him just enough to set Waffles down in the kitchen. Socrates stared at me from the center of Teo's bed. An unmade bed Chris's clothes were currently piled on. "So, anyway. Take care."

I turned and fled like the floor was a thin layer of ice over a raging river and a crack had just started at Teo's door. My feet barely touched the ground until I was outside. It was a good thing I'd worn shorts and running shoes because I shot down his street and ran. I didn't slow down until I saw signs for Pershing Road, and even then, I only stopped long enough to make sure it was the same Pershing that ran by my neighborhood. Once I turned left, I ran the final three miles at a slower pace. It was a warm enough evening that I was drenched in sweat by the time I approached my apartment building. My legs felt like jelly, and it reminded me of how much less I'd been running lately since starting my new job.

The good news was, as soon as I took another shower—this time a quick cool one—I fell into a deep, dreamless sleep where, for seven solid hours I didn't have to imagine Chris Banks's hands on my sweet Teo's naked body.

And when I woke up the next day, ready to fly to Springfield,

Missouri, to pick up several members of the extended Banks family in the Gulfstream with Nate, I tried my best to shut Teo completely out of my mind. I had a job to do. Besides, Teo had never been anything but completely honest with me about his feelings for Chris. He'd been in love with the man for years, and they had so much shared history, it wasn't something I could have ever competed with anyway.

In fact, I should have been happy for Tee, but I wasn't that good of a person.

I kept my head down during the trip, speaking to Nate only when necessary. I was sure he knew something was up with me, but I didn't have the emotional energy to even make up an excuse. By the time we landed back in Chicago, I'd sent a message to my dispatcher to confirm I was still able to fly Rourke to Newark first thing in the morning. I hadn't heard back from Teo after dropping by his place, so I was fairly sure there was no reason for me to think he'd want or need me at the funeral.

It made sense that a death in the family had finally brought them together. Stressful times often made people realize that life was too short to play silly games. Hopefully, that's what had happened with Chris. Maybe losing his grandfather had reminded him what was really important.

He was a lucky bastard.

Since we were back in Chicago before midafternoon, I rented a car and drove to my sister's place in La Porte for the night. Part of me felt like if I went back to my shitty empty apartment alone, I'd run the six miles all over again to make *sure* Teo didn't want me. If I was at Millie's, safely in Indiana, I couldn't do something stupid in the middle of the night again.

"Jack, what the hell?" she said when she opened the door. I walked right into her and wrapped my arms around her waist. My throat was tight, and I didn't want to talk about it. If I even had to open my mouth, it was going to be really ugly.

"Oh, babe," she whispered as she held me tight. Kirk's old dog, Weezer, came sauntering out of the kitchen wagging his tail slowly.

After giving my sister another squeeze, I sat down on the floor and opened my arms up for the sweet old mutt. Millie knew me well enough to leave me alone with Weezer for a while. I heard her talking to Kirk in hushed tones in the kitchen but chose to ignore it, concentrating on massaging Weezer's soft body instead. He was in heaven, rolling over on his back and begging for chest and belly scratches. I lay next to him for a long time and raked my fingers through his coat until both of us were half-asleep. Since I couldn't get shitfaced drunk the night before a morning flight, it was the closest I could come to comforting myself for the time being.

I thought about Socrates and Waffles and how I'd hoped they'd been keeping Teo company since Mr. Banks's death so he had someone to cuddle. It turned out not to be necessary since he'd had Chris for that.

Maybe I needed to go for another run.

I ignored the stupid thought and continued stroking Weezer's fur until Millie came over and reached a hand down to me. "Come on. There's a glass of wine with your name on it in the kitchen. I have some leftover grilled chicken if you're hungry."

I scraped myself off the ground and followed her into the kitchen. At least having one glass of wine was acceptable, and maybe it would help me at least be able to sleep.

Kirk looked up from a stack of mail he was sorting through. "Hey, bud. Good to see you." He reached out a hand to shake. "Millie said you've been working hard this week flying Rourke Wagner around. That guy's amazing. I heard him speak at—"

"Dammit, Kirk," Millie said with a laugh, fake-slapping him on the back of his head. "You weren't supposed to repeat that."

"It's fine. Rourke doesn't mind," I told them. "His travel schedule is public, and he's Instagrammed photos of me and the plane before. But yeah, he's amazing. Doesn't travel with any help if he can avoid it. He's super self-sufficient."

"And handsome," Millie added with a raised eyebrow.

I rolled my eyes as Kirk groaned. "Yes. He's handsome," I agreed. "And smart and funny and successful. Do you want his number?"

"Sorry," she said, rubbing my arm. "That was in poor taste. I only meant to imply there are other fish in the sea. But I know that doesn't help make you feel any better."

I shrugged. "It kind of does, and you're right. There are other men out there who would be fun to get to know better and spend time with. Rourke actually asked me to a show tomorrow night in New York. He wants to see *The Play That Goes Wrong*, but he doesn't want to go by himself."

Millie got a lovesick look on her face. "Aww, he's just saying that to cheer you up. What a nice man."

"He doesn't know I need cheering up." That wasn't exactly true, but the idea he was trying to snap me out of my funk was a little too thoughtful and sweet for me right now. I had enough tenderheartedness toward Teo. I certainly didn't need more toward another man altogether.

"You should go," she said.

"I think I will. He's not actually speaking until Monday morning, but he wanted to fly up tomorrow morning to do some shopping first. So I have to be out of here by like seven. Sorry to turn up so late."

Kirk flapped his hand. "It's fine. You saved me from having to watch that new Sabrina with your sister."

"He's scared of it," Millie stage-whispered.

It was comforting to be here listening to their usual banter and hearing the familiar snores of Weezer on the floor by Kirk's feet. My parent's old cuckoo clock hung on the wall by the breakfast table ticking its loud obnoxious seconds off one at a time. Millie had begged the thing off my parents back when they did a renovation several years ago. She'd claimed it was a critical relic from her childhood memories since the bird always came out to tell us when to race out to the school bus in the morning. As annoying as the sound had always been, tonight it was a familiar presence that I appreciated. This was exactly what I'd needed.

Suddenly, I was exhausted. "I think I'm going to head to bed if you don't mind. Thank you for letting me crash."

Millie came over to give me another hug. "I'm so glad you showed up. This was exactly what I was hoping for when you moved back. I love being only an hour away from you now."

"Well, you know you two can come use my place if you want a night in the city. It's why I got a two-bedroom in the first place."

After saying good night to both of them, I made my way to the guest room. It was nice and cool from the central air and the crisp, white sheets on the bed reminded me of a hotel room. Some of the framed photos on the wall were shots Kirk and Millie had taken on a camping trip to the Upper Peninsula a few years ago. They'd invited me to join them, but I'd been too busy with work. As I got ready for bed, I thought about whether or not they'd want to take another trip like that before the baby came. This time I'd make it a priority to go with them. I could even help with the heavy lifting so Millie wouldn't have to do any of the work.

Instead of sliding into bed, I walked back out to the kitchen to float the idea to them. After all, if there was one thing I could use right now, it was a vacation to look forward to. Maybe the planning itself would distract me in the meantime.

I'd changed jobs for a reason, dammit. And that was to get a life. That didn't mean I had to have a boyfriend. It meant I needed there to be more to life than my work. I'd start by planning this trip. Then I'd take Rourke up on his offer to go to the play. And when I returned to the city next week, I'd call Chelsea to schedule a jog in the park.

I was fine. And now I had a plan.

25

———————

TEO

When I finally got up the nerve to come out of the bathroom after my shower, Chris was lying back in my bed in his underwear flicking through his phone as if nothing had just happened between us.

I went straight to my dresser and found a clean T-shirt and pair of sleep pants, sliding them on under my towel like a prude.

"Dude, I've seen you naked a thousand times, including ten minutes ago in the shower," Chris said, not looking up from his phone.

I hung my damp towel on the bathroom doorknob. "It's different now."

He finally put the phone down and looked up at me. "Yes. It is different now. That's what I was trying to acknowledge between us in the bathroom, Tee. But you freaked out."

"Yeah, I freaked out. Of course I freaked out. We're just friends for years and suddenly you call me your boyfriend out of the blue while you're hopping in the shower with me? What the hell?" I was angrier than I thought. All the times I'd wished for him to claim me, all the times I'd wanted nothing more than to be his boyfriend, and *that's* how it was going to happen? No conversation? No asking me out on a date or leaning in for a sweet kiss first?

My jaw tightened so hard, I heard my teeth squeak. So many words fought to escape my mouth all at the same time, but something held me back.

This isn't the time to scream and yell at him. He just lost his grandfather.

"Teo," he said softly, reaching out for me with one hand. "I thought this was what you wanted?"

He was right. Kind of.

"Yeah, but not right now. Not like this." I slid into bed next to him and leaned over to turn off the bedside table light on my side. "It's too much right now, Chris. I think we just need to get through the service, get back into a routine at work, and then revisit this when things feel more steady."

Chris turned off the light on his side after shooing Socrates off the foot of the bed where he'd been curled into a little ball. A mean voice in my head made a snarky comment about how he had more right to that spot than Chris did, but I ignored my pettiness. As much as I'd been looking forward to being alone tonight, I really didn't mind having someone to hold me all night. After spending several nights with Jack in Canada, I'd discovered just how much I enjoyed not being alone in bed.

It wasn't the same with Chris, but I chalked that up to the fact we weren't having sex together. Surely, if we were fucking, things would be as good as they'd been with Jack, right?

"You do still want this, right?" Chris asked after a few minutes of silence. "Want *me*?"

"Of course I do," I said automatically. Was he crazy? I'd wanted him forever.

"What about Jack?" Chris's voice sounded genuinely unsure.

Jack wasn't up for a relationship, but I didn't want to admit that to Chris. It would make it sound like that was the only reason I'd pick Chris over Jack, and it wasn't.

Was it?

"I don't want to talk about Jack tonight. Can we just go to sleep please?"

After a few more beats of silence, he started talking again. "Remember when we found that twenty-dollar bill in the field by the lake?"

I thought back to middle school. "Yeah. You wanted to save up for a Wii, but I wanted to…" I tried to remember. It was geeky, that's all I could recall.

Chris snorted. "Write a letter to some space organization to petition them to let Pluto remain a planet."

I groaned and put my hands over my face. "It has moons, for god's sake. And, for the record, it's still a planet, it's just a dwarf planet."

Chris reached over and ruffled my hair. I batted his hand away. It didn't feel good when he did that. It felt like he thought I was his kid brother, a feeling I'd had on and off the entire time we'd known each other.

"Oh my god, that reminds me," Chris said, moving to his side to face me. "Guess who I ran into the other day? Rachel Bell."

"Your girlfriend from college? That Rachel?"

"Yeah. The one who shot me down when I brought up the subject of marriage. Broke my fucking heart. Anyway, she's living my dream right now. Staying in some high-end executive penthouse downtown, traveling internationally all the fucking time, and earning gangster money at…"

His words were drowned out by the sudden clicking together of puzzle pieces I'd been carrying around in my pocket for years. As I lay there, his words finally, finally sank in. His dream was nothing like mine. Mine involved a little house in the suburbs with a garden out back and maybe a sunroom for the cats. Mine involved meaningful work with patients during the day and returning home to a loving husband at night. Mine involved game nights with family and friends on the weekends and maybe, if I was lucky, little league games—or figure skating or library story time or anything else fun like that— with my kids one day.

And none of that, *none* of that, was what Chris had ever wanted.

A hysterical giggle escaped before I could clap my hand over my mouth. Chris froze.

"I'm sorry. I... I forgot I hadn't told you that." He looked guilty.

"Told me what?"

"About asking Rachel to marry me. Well, I didn't actually propose, so it didn't really count, did it? You can't be mad at me."

Yeah, that part had hurt like a bitch. But I'd already known it. Rachel herself had come to me to ask about the best way to let him down easy. I'd told her to tell him the truth, that she had huge corporate ambitions that didn't gel with being married young. And then I'd returned to my apartment and cried like a baby for five straight days.

It was good to hear she was living her dream.

"First of all, I can, indeed, be mad at you," I said, ticking the point off with a finger. "Because you'd promised me a committed future. You sat there in the bed of your uncle's pickup truck that night by the lake and asked me to wait for you so that someday we could build a life together just the two of us. So, yes. I can be mad as fuck at you for stringing me along." I felt the anger of so many years of disappointment and heartbreak building up. It needed to come out, but it was going to ruin everything.

"Secondly," I continued, "I already knew about it. And third, good for her for not letting someone else change the path she wanted for herself. It reminds me of something I've been meaning to talk to you about."

He looked worried now. "You knew? All this time you knew that I'd talked to Rachel about marriage?"

"I'm quitting Banks. I'm going to try and get my job at Wilton back."

He opened his eyes wider. "What? No. You can't. We need you there. *I* need you there. I love being with you like that every day. Don't you?"

I reached for his hand and held it between us. "No. I hate it. I hate working behind a desk. I hate working on compliance protocols, rules, and best-practices handbooks. I want my patients back. I want someone to care for."

"You can care for me," he said softly.

I shook my head. "No. I'm done with that too. For so long, I tried fitting you into this cardboard cutout of the perfect boyfriend. But that's not you. It never was you. You have aspirations that don't fit with mine. And they're great. I love how much you love your job and how dedicated you are to growing the family business. It suits you. And I can see you enjoying your jet-set life with more travel and more exciting sales deals. But that's not me."

"What are you saying? That you don't want to be with me?" His confusion seemed to morph to anger right before my eyes. "After all this fucking time of expecting me to change, I finally do exactly what you want and now forget it? You've changed your fucking mind?"

His voice had raised enough to worry me a little. I'd never known him to get physical or violent, but it was also rare for him to get this upset.

"Is this about Jack? Are you seriously dumping me for a glorified bus driver? The week of my grandfather's fucking funeral?"

"I'm not dumping you. We aren't together," I reminded him.

"Could have fooled me," he snapped, whipping the covers off and scaring both cats into hiding. "I'm going home."

I stared in disbelief as he threw on his clothes and stomped into his shoes. When he finally headed toward the door, he grabbed something off the kitchen counter and threw it at me before storming out of the apartment and slamming the door.

I looked down at the yellowish-orange box in my hands.

Milk Duds.

Now I felt like a total ass.

I glanced back up at the closed door. Had he really been making a serious attempt to start something between us, or was this the comfort seeking I'd originally thought it was? This box of candy was one of the most thoughtful things he'd ever done for me, and I'd ruined it.

26

———

JACK

The trip to New York with Rourke had kept me sufficiently distracted, although I couldn't stop myself from sending Teo a quick text the morning of the funeral just to let him know I was thinking about him. Predictably, he didn't message me back, which was fine.

Okay, it wasn't fine. But that was something I just had to get over. I'd had a surprisingly nice time in Rourke's company in New York and was even scheduled to meet him for a dinner theater experience in a few nights. We'd discovered a mutual love for unique theatrical experiences and had spent lots of time talking about the productions we'd seen in our respective travels.

It had been fun being out with him in a way because he was a recognizable public figure and people swarmed to him. He wasn't so famous that we weren't able to eat our dinner in peace, but he was popular enough from a TED Talk he'd done that he was approached several times during our time together. The fans gushed over him, and the best part was watching him come alive under the attention. No matter how tired he was from traveling, speaking, or simply making his way around the city in a wheelchair, he always perked up when fans appeared.

Despite having a great time in his company, I wasn't tempted to try for more with Rourke. He was sexy as hell, and if I hadn't met Teo, I would have probably tried desperately to get him into bed with me, but I had met Teo. And meeting Tee had moved the bar so high up, I worried another man may never reach it again.

So I tried to take it as a sign that this wasn't the season of my life that needed to be filled with sex. It was the season I needed to spend on figuring out what else I enjoyed spending my time doing. An unexpected project popped up just at the right time when Millie and Kirk mentioned wishing the one large rec room in their house was a guest bedroom and bath instead. Up till now, it had been a giant catchall-type room with a guest bed and also a desk for when Millie and Kirk needed to catch up on bookkeeping and admin from home for their small business.

Since money was tight right now due to the unexpected departure of Kirk's business partner, they couldn't afford to hire contractors to do the work. My dad had volunteered the two of us to do it as a baby gift to them. We'd done similar work on my parents' house when I was in high school. I was looking forward to spending some time with my dad, and I thought working together to create a guest suite where I could come for lots of baby visits was a great idea.

Two weeks after the funeral for Gordon Banks, I was finally buying into my own attitude adjustment. I'd been running twice with Chelsea, been out to the interesting dinner theater with Rourke, and had even met a couple of old high school friends in the city for beer one night. My dad and I had planned to meet up on Saturday to make a game plan for the renovation and start ordering supplies.

I was doing well. Totally fine. Excellent, in fact. My life was right on track.

And then Teo's messy brown hair and vibrant green eyes flashed up on my phone screen just as I was walking away from Rourke's Cessna after a quick day trip to Minneapolis. My finger pressed the green button to accept the call before I even processed what was happening.

"Hey," I said, suddenly breathless.

"Oh my god, it's so good to hear your voice," he said with a nervous laugh. "I didn't know if you'd be flying or—"

"No, I just got back from a trip. This is good. Perfect. I mean, it's a good time. How have you been?"

My hands were shaking. What the hell was wrong with me?

"Not great, honestly. I'm really kind of... confused. And... well, I was wondering if we could get together and do something? I..." He let out a breath. "I could really use a friend right now."

"Absolutely. Are you feeling like a night out? A night in? I'm up for whatever you want to do." I picked up my pace so I could get home and showered as quickly as possible.

"You remember how we watched that old teen movie in Goose Bay and we both really liked it?"

I couldn't help but laugh. "*The Breakfast Club*?"

"Yeah, don't laugh at me." I could hear the smile in his voice. "I thought maybe we could watch some of the others like it. I never saw them. Like *Sixteen Candles* and stuff?"

"You are a newborn baby. But yes, I'd love that. Want me to come to you, or do you want to come to my place? Either is fine with me."

After a little bit of back-and-forth, we decided to meet at his place since he had Socrates and Waffles. I hopped on the train and willed it to go faster. Once at my place, I quickly showered, shaved, and changed into comfortable shorts and a T-shirt. Then I tamped down my enthusiasm when I realized I was "getting ready for a date." Whatever that meant. I switched out my nice designer T-shirt for a shitty Pride one and tried washing off the cologne I'd sprayed on. To hell with it. I was a lost cause.

I forced myself not to stop for flowers, wine, more Milk Duds, or anything else I could think of that would show him I cared. Instead, I tried to play it cool. He needed a friend. He didn't need a pushy asshole. I was going to go in there and be his friend.

Then he opened the door.

And he looked so fucking beautiful, I clenched my teeth against the dreamy sigh that was on the tip of my tongue.

I expected an awkward, foot-shuffling moment where we both

sort of grunted *Hi* to each other, but after half a second of eye contact, Teo launched himself at me and hugged me like it had been years instead of weeks. He felt so damned good in my arms. Holding Teo in my arms gave me the same feeling of happiness and relief I got sliding into my own bed after a long trip away from home. I lifted him up until his legs wrapped around my waist, and then I cupped the back of his head to keep his nose tucked into my neck.

"Fuck, you feel good," I said into his hair. My voice sounded weird, like it wasn't my own.

I felt one of the cats brushing against my legs, so I was careful stepping forward to make room to close the apartment door.

"I missed you." His words were muffled against my skin, and I felt the warmth from his breath there.

Maybe I couldn't do this. Maybe I was so far gone for him that being around him and not being able to have my hands all over him was going to literally kill me. Because while I had him there in my arms, I remembered Chris standing in that exact same spot in nothing but a towel.

I gently set him down on the floor and pressed a kiss to his cheek, taking that moment to inhale the lemony scent of him.

After clearing my throat, I plastered on a smile. "It's good to see you."

That sounded ridiculous.

When I finally got up the nerve to look him in the eye, I noticed they were red-rimmed and damp. I held out a hand to swipe the moisture away with my thumb.

"Hey, what's going on?" I asked as gently as I could. "Are you still upset about Gordon? It must be hard going back to the office without him there."

Teo shook his head and turned away. "No, that's not it. I just have a lot on my mind. Do you want a beer or a glass of wine?"

"Just some ice water, if you don't mind." I let him busy himself making a couple of glasses of water. In the meantime, I reached down and scratched Waffles's chin before stroking down her back. Socrates was conspicuously absent, but I assumed he was curled up under

Teo's bed or somewhere else out of sight. "How's work? Any more travel coming up?"

It was throwaway talk, the kind you do when you're warming back up to someone after an absence, so he surprised me when he laughed and said, "I quit."

I stood back up and leaned a hip against the counter, reaching out to take the glass from him when he handed it to me. "Did you?"

He nodded and took a sip of his water before setting it down. "I hated it. It was stupid of me to think I could do a desk job like that. I don't like to sit still. I like to help people."

"Good for you."

Teo laughed. "You look like a psycho with that giant grin on your face. Clearly you think I did the right thing."

I nodded. "Do you need reassurance? Are you doubting your decision?"

"No, not for one single minute. I know I did the right thing. Unfortunately, Wilton couldn't take me back on full-time. So I'm working part-time right now until they have a spot for me."

"How's Hattie?"

His eyes widened. "You remembered. She's okay. Her dementia's gotten worse which is awful, but it's at least protecting her from some of the grief."

I swallowed my pride and asked the next polite question. "How is Chris?"

Teo looked down into his glass of water. "I don't know... That's kind of what I wanted to talk about. I need some advice."

I took a seat at his small kitchen table and stretched out my legs. Waffles decided my shoelaces were her new favorite thing. "Tell me what's going on."

He made his way into the seat opposite mine and held his glass between both hands on the table in front of him. I could hear the rattling hum of his air-conditioning unit and the muffled honking noises of the city outside the window.

When his eyes flicked up from studying his glass, I could see how unsure he was about what he was getting ready to say.

"First of all, I'm an ungrateful ass. I know that. But I don't think that wanting something for a long time should mean I'm required to choose it because what happens if things change or if things are different than you thought they were, and maybe they were always different? Like, you thought things were one way but they never really were and it took getting it before you realized it wasn't what you thought it was, and then even if you knew you *should* want something, it was a different thing than what you thought, or at least dif—"

I reached across and took his hand. "Shh, take a breath. Slow down."

He shook his head quickly, his eyes wide with worry. "I can't. I can't slow down. I'm a terrible person, and I just need someone to tell me it's okay for me to be selfish." Teo's chin quivered as he spoke, and it seemed he was on the verge of tears again.

"Sweetheart, you're not a terrible person. And I can't imagine you ever being selfish. Tell me what happened." Although I had a pretty good idea.

"Chris wanted to date me. He... he thought it was time, or... he kind of thought we were already dating. Or something. I think... I think the stress of losing his grandfather maybe brought up some feelings, and suddenly..." He glanced up at me and back down at our joined hands. "Suddenly, he thought we were dating."

"And how did you feel about that?"

He glanced up at me again, clearly not all that comfortable talking to me about it. His cheeks were pink, and his eyelashes fluttered nervously. "Surprised, at first. Shocked, really. He came into the bathroom when I was in the shower, and I kind of flipped out."

"Are you kidding?" I barked. Teo jumped in his seat in surprise. "Sorry, fuck. I didn't mean to scare you. I just... can't believe that asshole. That's not okay."

"He's my best friend," he said defiantly.

And he's a selfish, entitled prick.

I kept my thoughts to myself, but then I realized something. "Was this a couple of nights before the funeral?"

He tilted his head. "How did you know?"

"I..." I hesitated, unsure of whether or not to mention having stopped by. Surely he already knew. Surely Chris wouldn't have been that deceptive. "You said—"

He made a choking sound. "The Milk Duds."

We stared at each other. His face crumpled, and he turned away, standing up to move to the bed where he flopped face-first into the pillows. Socrates appeared from out of nowhere and sniffed at Teo's ear.

I wasn't sure what to do, so I just sat there, frozen, until Teo reached a hand out to me and made a grabby motion. I moved over and lay next to him, carefully putting my arm around him and pulling him against me in a kind of spooning hug. It wasn't sexual at all, although I wanted him. I always wanted him. But right now he needed a friend. He needed comfort.

After a while, his voice came out low, almost a whisper. "Did you bring those Milk Duds? Was that you?"

"Yeah."

"What... what happened? I mean... why didn't you come in?"

His body was tense, as if he suspected the real reason and was anticipating the blow from me putting it into words.

"Chris answered the door in a towel. He didn't invite me in. You were in the shower."

"Fuck. That motherfucker." His words were angry, but his tone was hurt. "Thanks. That actually helps, believe it or not. I told him no that night, but he didn't take it well. Then I had to tell him no several more times after the funeral. I still don't think he's gotten the message."

"Why don't you want to be with him now?" I had a pretty good idea, but I still wanted to hear him say it.

"He's my past. He's comfort and familiarity. But... I was blind to the fact he isn't the right person for my future. And I feel so stupid looking back on how much I tried forcing it based on a childhood ideal and a teenage promise. I was a fool."

"You were a romantic."

"I was an idiot."

"You were lonely," I said as gently as I could.

"Yes. So fucking lonely. But there are other ways to solve that than clinging onto the wrong person. It's taken a lot of soul-searching and some long conversations with one of my friends at work, but I finally see it much clearer. I would have made him miserable. And he for damned sure would have made me the same."

"It's good to recognize that now, I guess."

"Yeah, but it still hurts like a bitch. Losing the idea of him, the future I had planned with him, is like grieving."

It made sense, and my heart ached for him. I knew how much stock he'd put in his picture-perfect future with Chris.

I nudged Teo back onto his front and slid my hand under his shirt to run my fingernails lightly over his back. It was a soothing gesture my mother had always done on me when I was little.

"That feels good," he murmured into the pillow.

"My family calls it chicken scratch," I explained. "It's my mom's specialty. If you're feeling sick or upset about anything, this'll do the trick or at least lull you into a stupor and make you stop caring about it."

"Mmm."

He let me tickle his back for a while before he said, "I'm sorry."

"For what?"

Teo turned his head so he could look at me. "For not messaging you back. For not being here when you came by. For..."

"Stop. You don't need to apologize to me. You don't owe me anything. We're friends. You were going through a tough time."

His body seemed to let go of some tension at my words. "Thanks, Jack. I don't really know how to navigate this. I've spent so much time and energy focusing on Chris and how to get him to finally start building a life with me that I've neglected focusing on myself and others. And that's what pisses me off the most about this."

I stopped rubbing his back and sat up against the headboard. He followed suit.

"Listen," I began. "I understand what you're saying, but I disagree with part of it. You've never stopped focusing on others. You've devoted yourself to the care of others, not only in your career but also your personal life. You've been there for your sister when she and Bella needed you. You told me how much you babysat for Bella in those early years while you were still trying to get good enough grades at the community college to get into nursing school. *And* you were working full-time. I also know from talking to Sam at the game that you volunteer at the center on Halstead together. So cut that shit out and stop making yourself out to be selfish when you're the furthest thing from it."

His eyes widened as I spoke. "Okay, fine. But I haven't spent enough time being me on my own, pursuing my own interests and expanding my own horizons. I was waiting for someone—Chris—to come take care of me, and that's bullshit."

I reached out to flick a wayward curl over his ear. "It's okay to want to be taken care of. But I get what you're saying. You want some time to focus on Teo now. I think that's a good thing. Healthy. So what does Teo want to do that he's not already doing?"

He crisscrossed his legs and rubbed his hands together. "I've been thinking about it. I definitely love the work I do at the center, and obviously I've already made the job change too. But I want to take a knitting class to learn how to do cables so I can try to knit a fisherman's sweater one day. And I also want to go on a boat. I've never been on one."

I laughed. "What kind of boat? A sailboat or just any kind?"

"It doesn't matter. There's an architecture cruise on the Chicago river that I've always wanted to take. I know it's kind of touristy, but who cares? So I booked it for next weekend. Hannah's going to do it with me."

"That's great, Tee." I loved seeing him excited about pursing his own interests. It was about time he looked out for himself.

"There's a speedboat one on the lake that looks cool too. Maybe I'll try that before the end of summer. Or there are probably tours on sailboats too."

We talked for a while about all the things he wanted to do now that he was going to focus on himself a little more. Teo questioned

me at length about my own plans which included the renovation at
Millie's, the runs with Chelsea, and the horseback riding lessons I'd
signed up for after I'd had one too many glasses of wine with Rourke.
It was appealing to share my plans with someone who was genuinely
interested and seemed to hang on my every word.

"Oooh! Can I go too?"

I stared at Teo. "Go where?"

"Horseback riding."

"I thought you were intimidated by large animals. I asked if you'd
taken your niece to the zoo and you looked at me like I was nuts."

"Well, yeah. But isn't that the point? I want to get out of my
comfort zone, try new things. I want to have a freaking life that's more
than just going to work and coming home to my two cats." He
reached out a hand to pet Socrates, who was curled into a ball
between us. "No offense, baby."

"I don't see why not. I'm going with Rourke Wagner. It's on his
bucket list, and he talked me into going with him. He found a special
place outside the city that can accommodate him."

Teo's face, which had been open and happy, suddenly morphed
into an odd kind of fake smile.

"Oh. No, that's okay. I can find someone else to go with."

And suddenly things were awkward between us again.

27

TEO

Rourke. Beautiful, successful, rich as hell Rourke.

It wasn't like I wanted to date Jack. Of course I didn't. I was on a new path, the independent Teo path. I didn't need a boyfriend to make me feel whole. I was out to embrace and celebrate my singleness.

Ahem.

I tried to sound cool and calm. As if the idea of Jack dating the gorgeous Rourke Wagner was A-Okay with me. None of my business. "I don't want to be a third wheel."

Jack looked at me with a twinkle of knowing in his eyes. "What makes you think you'd be a third wheel?"

I concentrated on the spot where Socrates's white paw met the inky black fur of his leg. The fur there was smooth and silky, so I ran a fingertip across it. "It's fine. I mean, maybe horseback riding is a bridge too far for me after all." I pushed out a laugh. "Can you even imagine me, of all people, galloping across a field?"

"I think if a man who's paralyzed from the hips down can do it, you certainly can."

Fuck. He had a point. "Yeah, but he's known for being brave.

That's like... his entire persona. He's just one of those guys who's a badass at everything he does."

"Not true. Did you know that he got kicked off a wheelchair basketball team because he kept tipping over?"

"They have special chairs to help you not tip when you're doing those kinds of sports," I said. "Surely he can afford one. The guy owns his own plane."

"He had one," Jack said with a laugh. "But he still kept tipping over, and it was dangerous to the other players. You should hear him talk about it. I thought I was going to piss myself. He ended up admitting that in eight months of practicing with that group, he'd never made one basket."

I chuckled. "Ah, the real reason they kicked him off."

"Exactly."

"I was jealous of a paralyzed man," I admitted. "Someone who has to work ten times harder than I do just going about his normal day. I'm an ass."

Jack cupped my cheek and shot me a smirk. "Jealous how?"

I flapped my hand dismissively. "I don't want a boyfriend, and you don't either, so it doesn't matter." I crawled over and straddled him, sliding my arms around his neck and bringing my face close to his. "Can we still have sex, even though we're just friends and neither one of us wants more?"

"Oh hell yes," Jack breathed on a sigh of relief. The sound hit me low in the belly, making my dick plump up. His hands moved down to cup my ass and pull me tighter into him until our dicks ground together. I groaned.

"Maybe the talking can be over for a little while."

Jack leaned in and kissed me on the lips, taking his time tasting me and nipping first my top lip, then my bottom one. He tasted sweet and familiar. The faint scent of his cologne filled my nose. I wanted his body all over mine. I wanted him to roll that scent around in my bed until it was a permanent fixture.

"Get this off," he muttered, pulling up my T-shirt. "Get all of it off."

I stood over him on the bed and stripped as fast as I could while he peeled his own shirt off. My excitement reminded me of walking into Bert's Candy Emporium on a family vacation to Wisconsin when I was nine. The store had been wall-to-wall bins of every candy you could imagine. I'd been so overwhelmed with a feeling of wanting it all and having no idea where to even start, that I'd burst into tears.

Jack's eyes stayed on mine as he pulled his own clothes off. By the time we were both naked, all I could picture was my cum on his stomach. Or in his mouth. Or spattered on his inner thigh. The mental pictures were enough to make me whimper and breathe faster.

"Orgasm," I said stupidly. "Please," I added for decorum's sake.

Jack reached for my wrist and yanked me down on top of him. His body was broad and firm and warm. I licked the side of his neck and then followed my hungry tongue down his chest to his stomach. It was leaner than before and more defined. I wondered if he'd been doing more than running, but I didn't slow down enough to ask. I had a destination in mind.

He was hard as fuck which made me irrationally proud, like he wouldn't have been nearly as hard with some other naked man on top of him. But still, it made me feel like a boner-making rock star because there wasn't some other naked man on top of him. There was me.

And I celebrated that fact by shamelessly humping his leg while drooling on his cock.

"Shit. Fuck. Suck it. *Please.* Fuck." His voice was rough and deep. Listening to him lose his poise was pretty damned sweet. I licked up and down his dick before sucking on the head. The sound he made lit me up, but when he put his hand in my hair, I almost lost it completely.

"God, fuck. Tee, shit." He was grunting, the tendons straining in his neck like he was going to blow, but just when I thought he was going to lose it, he yanked me away and scrambled up, tossing me underneath him. "Want to fuck you so bad. Need to be inside that tight body."

I wasn't even sure he realized he was talking out loud, but I didn't care. There was a slight buzzing sound in my ears from my jacked-up heart rate. I wondered if this man had spoiled me for every future sex encounter because I couldn't imagine a single scenario in which I could possibly be more turned on.

He fumbled through my bedside table, spilling things out and grabbing what he wanted, all the while mumbling hot as shit nonsense about my body, what he wanted to do to me, and how much I turned him on.

"You make me fuckin' crazy," he muttered under his breath, shoving my knees up to my ears and leaning down to lick a stripe across my ass. I said a prayer of thanks to the gods of evening showers and reached back for the headboard to keep from banging into it.

Jack licked and sucked at me until I was making embarrassing whimpering noises. His fingers joined in, stretching and lubing me until I was dizzy with desperation. Finally, *finally*, he gloved up and began pushing in. I squeezed my eyes closed and tried to memorize every sensation. The burning stretch, the clench of his fingers on the backs of my thighs, the heavenly scented mixture of his cologne with his sweat, the sound of his jagged breathing. It was so fucking good—so fucking perfect—and I wanted to burn it onto my brain for all time so I could never forget what this incredible experience was like.

Because I was terrified I'd never get to do it again.

28

———

JACK

I'd known deep down it was a mistake.

The minute I slid inside of him, all of my insistence that a "friends with benefits" scenario between us would work fine went out the damned window. I didn't want to just be his friend.

"Ohhh." I groaned with a combination of pleasure and relief. He was mine. He was *mine*. I... I couldn't imagine not having him like this in the future. That there could be a day where someone else got to experience this feeling, this intimacy with him was just... incomprehensible. Unacceptable.

I leaned in and kissed him sweetly on the mouth, teasing his lips and tongue while his body took a minute to accept me. Part of me wanted to rail him into the mattress, and the other part of me wanted to slow it way down and edge him tenderly until he cried.

Instead, I pulled almost all the way out and held there until he grabbed for me, pulling at my hips with his greedy fingers. The noises he was making were like tranquilizer darts aimed right at my chest, making it warm and tight. I thrust into him again and again, watching and listening for every reaction. I wanted to remember Teo like this, flushed and willing beneath me, chasing his orgasm while I was joined as closely with him as possible.

"So beautiful," I murmured, brushing the dark wild hair from his forehead. "So fucking sweet."

"Don't stop." His voice was breathy, and his eyes were half-lidded. The kiwi color turned darker like a four-leaf clover. "Jack…"

I didn't stop. I cupped the top of his head as I moved in and out of his body, relishing in the feel of his tight squeeze around my cock. "Tee, fuck." His lips were full and red, spit-slick and open in a gasp. I leaned in and took them, kissing him hard as I sped up my thrusting. I reached down for his cock, but the minute I squeezed it in my grasp, Tee threw his head back with a cry and came.

It was so sudden and he was so hot like that, my body chased his over the edge with one last slam inside of him.

I shoved my face into the pillow next to his head and screamed through my release. Tee was still making little gasps and sounds as he came down from his high. When I caught my breath, I leaned back up to kiss him some more, slow gentle presses of my lips against his.

His hands came up to hold my face so I didn't pull away. As if I'd ever pull away when he was in the middle of gifting me with those full lips.

"You spoil me," he said softly against my lips.

"Mm, other way around, I'm afraid."

I eventually had to pull out of him to dispose of the condom and clean us both up, but then I climbed into bed with him and pulled him into his spot against my side. Or what I always thought of as his spot anyway. I *wanted* it to be his spot.

I was pathetic. But I was pathetic *and* happy at the moment so it was fine.

"You still want to stay and watch movies?" Teo sounded insecure all of a sudden.

I kissed the top of his head and reached for the remote on the bedside table. "Of course. Which one first? I think you might like *Pretty in Pink* because of the clothes in it." I handed him the remote and then reached out for Socrates, who'd hopped up now that the vigorous bed activity was over. He sniffed hesitantly at my shoulder before stepping across my chest and curling up above Teo's head on my pillow.

Waffles was on the floor messing with stuff. I could hear her batting something around and letting out a periodic *mrrt* when her play didn't go according to plan. The sounds of the city provided dim background noise to the opening credits of the movie. I glanced around Teo's tiny studio apartment and thought about how comfortable and relaxed I felt there. I'd noticed the feeling before, but it came back in a rush. The personalized photos, the unique colorful touches of items he'd deliberately chosen or was given to make his little apartment his nest, and all the various special mementos of his life.

In addition to his things, he'd also strung twinkle lights over the triple window and had hung some shelving here and there to hold healthy green plants. Some of them hung down from their shelves with draping leafy stems and some spiked up in fat, colorful pots. I remembered him telling me how much he liked to garden. I wondered if he realized this was a prime example of the fact he'd always at least partly followed his own path. This apartment was nothing like the Chris Banks I'd met, but it was everything like Teo Parisi. He had his own unique style and the ability to make it into a cozy home I didn't really want to leave.

"Can I stay the night?" I asked in a voice that already sounded half-asleep.

"Duh." He reached for a sip of his ice water. I'd fetched our glasses when I'd gotten up to go to the bathroom. If I knew Teo, there would inevitably be snacks at some point. But for now, I was content to doze against him while he enjoyed watching Andie and Duckie banter back and forth.

At some point I woke up to Teo's soft sniffles. The credits were rolling on the movie which was fine since I'd seen it a million times. "Why are you crying?"

"She should have picked Duckie."

I wondered if he was caught up in the emotions since he, too, had been in love with his best friend. "But she and Duckie didn't have the spark."

"Yes they did. Don't be ridiculous." He stood up and made his way to the bathroom across from the bed. My eyes went straight to his adorable pale butt, and I kept my eyes riveted on the bathroom door like a perv waiting for the front view.

Within moments, I got what I was waiting for. His soft dick hung down from a dark nest of curls. His slender thigh muscles moved under his skin as he walked back toward the bed, and his stomach was flatter than I remembered.

I glanced up at his face and caught him smirking at me. He winked. "Want me to twirl so you can get the whole view?"

"Have you been eating enough?" I asked. His face fell. "I don't mean it like that. You're hot as shit, Tee. I just mean you look thinner. I wanted to make sure you're taking care of yourself."

He made a big point of opening a kitchen cabinet and pulling out a jar of peanuts. "I've been eating nuts every chance I get," he said with a return of the smirk. He wiggled his sexy hips on his way back to the bed.

I was glad to see he'd gotten over his Molly Ringwald angst, at least temporarily. I didn't like to think of him still being torn up over whether or not he should be with Chris.

"You know..." he began, looking up at me shyly after he'd gotten back in bed. "I helped build my neighbor a chicken coop once. I'm not the handiest man you'll ever meet, but if you and your dad want help at Millie's house..."

I pictured him shirtless and sweaty with a worn leather tool belt hanging off his hips. "Yes, please."

He laughed and set the peanuts on the table before snuggling back against me. "What's next?"

What 1980s teen film didn't have a love triangle in it? "*Gleaming the Cube*," I said, reaching for the remote. "Christian Slater on a skateboard, mm-hm."

Both of us fell asleep during that one and woke up to real life. I had an annual physical scheduled for work, and Teo had a shift at

Wilton starting fairly early as well. We shared a quick shower and a rushed goodbye kiss before I was out the door.

It only took twelve hours for my chest to feel strangely tight with longing and my fingers itching to text him. He'd made it clear we were friends with benefits, but I had the emotions of a clingy stalker right now. I forced myself to turn my phone off long enough to go to the gym and pick up some sushi. When I returned to my quiet apartment, I shoved the phone in the kitchen drawer for another solid hour.

But then my brain played tricks on me. What if Millie had trouble with her pregnancy? What if one of my parents slipped and fell while watering the lawn? What if...?

I turned the phone back on to a barrage of texts. Most of them were from the automatic scheduling system at work, but one was from Tee.

Teo: *I meant what I said about the DIY stuff at your sister's. I'd love to help.*

My heart kicked up a beat.

Jack: *I'm heading there for the weekend. Think you can leave the boys that long?*

Teo: *My neighbor can watch them. You sure you don't mind the company?*

Jack: *You owe me a fake boyfriend visit to my fam, remember?*

Teo: *I'm in. I get off work at 3pm Friday. That okay?*

Jack: *I land around noon from a quick trip to Nashville. Pick you up at 4pm? It's a little over an hour drive.*

One of my coworkers had helped me find a good deal on a used

SUV that was low mileage but beat up enough to haul lumber in without worrying too much about it. It cost me an arm and a leg to park it at a nearby garage, but it was worth it for the ability to drive out to La Porte whenever I wanted.

When Friday finally arrived, I was both excited and nervous to pick Teo up. Obviously I was excited to spend an entire weekend with him, but I was also nervous about introducing him to my family. I didn't want to lie to them, but not only had I already implied several weeks before that we were dating, my sister knew I had real feelings for him. It wasn't like I could introduce him as only a friend and still expect to be able to share a bedroom and touch him all weekend. But if I introduced him as my boyfriend, my family would get excited for something that was more of a pipe dream than a reality.

The difference now was... there might be a possibility of something in the future. If he truly was getting over Chris, and I was finally ready to consider a serious relationship again, didn't that mean we could potentially end up together down the road?

I groaned. *Stop fantasizing.* He probably imagined a big "Banks" life with penthouses, private jets, and box seats to Cubs games. All I had to offer was the same kind of middle-class lifestyle he had on his own as a nurse. I'd taken a big pay cut to go private. I could always go back to the large airline, but I was actually enjoying flying corporate jets. It was more personable, more flexible, and less of a hassle than I'd had to deal with at the airline.

Teo doesn't care about wealth and status.

No, but he deserved the best. He deserved a comfortable life.

You can give him a comfortable life.

I shook my head and tried shoving those stupid thoughts out of my mind. I needed to slow down and enjoy what I had for the moment. And I had a full weekend ahead of me with all of my absolute favorite people under the same roof.

When I pulled up to the curb in front of Teo's apartment, he was waiting for me on the sidewalk with a duffle bag over his shoulder and some kind of wooden pallet box in his arms. I hopped out to help him load his stuff into the SUV.

"What's this?" I asked, taking it from him. There were bags of soil and packets of seeds inside the wooden tray, along with an empty mason jar.

"I hope they like it. I found it at the farmer's market. It's a little salad garden kit, kind of like an EarthBox. I can fix it up for Millie and Kirk this weekend while we're there, and then all they'll need to do is water it. By the end of July, they should have the fixings for a good salad. I brought the recipe for my mom's dressing too."

After settling the items in the back and hopping back in the driver's seat, I glanced over at him. "They're going to love it. Thank you. You didn't have to bring anything." I leaned in and kissed him without thinking. I'd intended it to be a quick peck of hello, but then I stayed for more.

"Mm, should have brought you something too," he murmured against my lips.

"You did. These sexy lips," I said before pressing another kiss to his mouth and forcing myself off him so I could pull into afternoon traffic.

While we battled our way out of the city, Teo caught me up on Wilton gossip. He was happy and chatty which was nice to see, and it was clear he was back where he belonged.

"Oh! You'll never guess who I met this morning at work," he said with excitement.

I tried to think of famous Chicagoans old enough to be at Wilton. "Harrison Ford? Bob Newhart?"

"Pretty sure those guys would hire in-home care at their mansions. So, no. Also, don't imply Harrison Ford needs senior care. He's... shit."

"Almost eighty?"

"Never mind. But you're on the right track. It's a celebrity. But you're never going to guess."

"I like guessing. Give me another chance. Was it..."

His laugh was light and sweet. "Hush. You don't watch YouTube anyway. This guy is a YouTube star. His name is Ryan Fae and he has, like, twenty million subscribers. He's kind of like a beauty blogger. He does tons of makeup tutorials and drag queen makeovers, stuff like that. But he also does the most amazing special-effects makeup. So like... sci-fi aliens and horror movie monsters. It's so cool."

"It's true," I admitted with a smirk. "I don't watch makeup tutorials on YouTube."

Teo smacked my shoulder. "Shut up. This guy is fucking gorgeous. If you met him, you'd drool like an idiot and want to get into his pants. Anyway, apparently his grandmother is one of my patients, and I had no idea. You remember me telling you about Coral, the lady who sings?"

I remembered the night in Goose Bay when I'd caught him singing a song in the shower from the 1950s. He'd said it was Ritchie Valens's "We Belong Together" and he'd learned it from one of his patients who had the voice of an angel. He'd just told me about his crush on Chris, and I remembered thinking he should have been singing "The Great Pretender" instead.

"Yes, I remember. The wannabe crooner."

He smiled and lay back in his seat, stretching his legs out in the late-afternoon sun coming through the window. "She always wanted to be a Chordette or Shirelle. She's got the vocal chops for it. Too bad she was the daughter of a blue-blood politician. The woman was never getting out of the country club scene regardless of how well she sang."

"So now she has a grandson who makes a living entertaining others. That's something anyway. I take it she's good to him? Accepting?"

"Oh yeah. That woman brags about Ryan to anyone who will listen. I'd always heard about her talented grandson Ryan, I just never made the connection it was Ryan Fae."

I glanced over at him. His dark hair was stylishly messy as usual, and his skin had a healthy summer glow already. He looked stunning as usual. "So you got to meet a real-life celebrity crush. That's exciting." I teased him just to see him blush.

"He says he doesn't leave the house much. That's why I hadn't met him before. But he's trying to do better. It sounded like he has some fears. I talked to him about my fear of flying and how I'd only just begun to realize how much it was holding me back."

I reached over and grasped his hand, threading our fingers together. "You know if you want to fly somewhere, I can probably find a way to take you, right? Or I still have connections at United and can get you some passes."

He looked away from me out the window. I felt his hand twitch a little. "Thanks, but, um... I think money's going to be tight for a little while until I get the full-time placement at Wilton. Right now I'm—"

"Yeah, of course," I said quickly, cutting him off. "I forgot about that. Well, it's there when you get more settled and want to make plans."

He squeezed my hand. "Thanks. I kind of daydream about taking Fia and Bella to Disney someday."

We talked the rest of the drive about dream trips we'd each wanted to take. When he mentioned a place I'd been, I told him what I knew about it. The drive went quickly, and before I knew it, we were pulling into Millie and Kirk's driveway.

And there, on the front porch, stood Kirk's brother, Ty.

My ex.

29

At first, I assumed the beautiful man on the front porch was Jack's brother-in-law, Kirk.

"You didn't tell me Millie was married to a hottie," I teased as Jack parked the truck. When he didn't answer, I looked over at him. Jack's jaw was tight, and his entire body was tense right along with it.

Jack took a deep breath and turned to me. "Listen—"

Whatever he was going to say was interrupted by a happy screech and the slightly pregnant woman from the front porch came rushing out to greet us.

"She looks like you," I said, noticing they shared the same shiny dirty-blond hair and angular chin. Millie's nose was slightly more turned up at the end which made her look younger instead of the two years older I knew her to be. Jack and I had talked at length about our sisters when we'd spent too much time together in Goose Bay. In a way, I felt like I already knew Millie because Jack absolutely adored her and talked about her often.

She ripped open the door to the SUV and yanked me out, engulfing me in a hug I hadn't been expecting.

"Oh my god, you're fucking adorable," she said. Then she lowered her voice so only I could hear her. "He thinks the world of you, just so you know."

My face pretty much self-combusted right there on the spot. Part of me wanted to tell her that I thought the world of him as well, but then I remembered that she was a meddling sister who thought the two of us were dating. Of course she was going to push us together regardless of Jack's true feelings.

Also, I was single by choice. It was my new identity, and I was trying to wear it like a rainbow T-shirt, out and proud. When, in reality, it was tight and itchy and I was desperate to rip it off.

"It's nice to meet you," I said when she released me from her clutches. "I'm Teo."

"We're so happy you're here! Come inside and meet my husband. He's opening some wine."

I glanced at the man I'd assumed was Kirk. He was busy hugging the shit out of Jack. "Oh," I said stupidly.

Millie glanced at the pair and froze. "Right. That's, ah... my brother-in-law. Ty. He decided to surprise us this weekend."

Oh. Ty the ex. Ty, the drop-dead gorgeous ex. Ty, the man who was still in love with Jack when Jack walked away. Perfect.

"Oh," I said again. Jack turned and shot me a searching glance. I tried smiling, but it felt like I'd just set all my teeth out on the front lawn for polishing. "Great. How wonderful for you. For us. For all of us. Many hands make quick work... is what... someone always said. Not sure who. But it's true though. I've always found that—"

Jack saved me from more stupid word vomit by calling out my name and reaching out a hand for me with an encouraging smile. "Ty, this is my boyfriend, Teo Parisi. Tee, this is Tyler Nosen, Kirk's brother."

I reached out a hand to shake. Ty's face was surprised but friendly. He looked me up and down but not in a creepy way, more curiosity than anything else. "Nice to meet you, Teo. I didn't realize Jack was in a relationship." He said the word relationship in a deliberate way that made me want to melt into the grass and slither away. Jack's hand tightened around mine as if he could read my mind.

I opened my mouth to say, *Me neither*, as a joke, but then closed it abruptly. Better safe than sorry.

Millie grabbed my elbow and pulled me toward the door, saying something about needing to meet Kirk to get the wine flowing ASAP. She wasn't wrong. If there was one thing this awkward as hell shindig needed, it was alcohol to really loosen tongues.

I shot Ty an apologetic look as if without bossy Millie, I'd stand there and become his bestie with hours of clever chatter. As soon as we crossed the threshold, Millie turned to me and began apologizing.

"Shit, I'm so sorry. We did not know he was coming, I promise you."

"It's fine."

"No, god. It's not fine. Jack finally brings someone else home and his ex shows up. Argh, why is Murphy's Law such a bitch? Kirk! I hope you bought multiple boxes. We're going to need it."

Sure enough, when we entered the kitchen, Millie's husband was struggling to pull the tap out of a box of wine. I absolutely loved the fact they weren't trying to impress anyone with something fancy. "I love Black Box. My mom buys it at Costco all the time."

"Yeah, sorry. We're kind of on a budget these days. Kirk's business partner ditched us a few months ago, and we've been scrambling to keep the business afloat."

"Don't apologize at all. I meant what I said, I love this stuff. I didn't mean to make you feel—"

Kirk interrupted me with a handshake. "Ignore her, she just feels bad because usually we'd go all out to welcome Jack's new man. Kirk Nosen. Welcome to La Porte, the tiny Indiana town best known for its foot doctor."

"Not true," Millie said with a laugh. "In addition to Dr. Scholl, we also have bragging rights to one of Indiana's most notorious serial killers, *and* she was a woman. Let that be a warning to you fellas."

I heard Jack's familiar rumble of laughter, and a second later his arms came around me from behind. "I'm so sorry," he whispered in my ear. "I didn't know."

I nodded since I was afraid of my voice cracking if I tried to say anything. And it truly was fine. He seemed like a nice enough guy, and I certainly didn't have a claim on Jack or anything.

I reached for the wine.

Eventually, we all made our way onto the back patio where a sweet old dog was laid out dead asleep on its back. The weather was beautiful, and Kirk began to get the grill ready for burgers. I leaned over to Jack and asked in a low voice if I should get the container garden out of the car or leave it for tomorrow. He grabbed my hand and pulled me up. "Let's go get it now."

As soon as we walked around the house to the front, Jack pulled me into a tight hug and apologized again. "It's fine," I said, gesturing between the two of us. "We're not even... I mean it's not..."

Jack's nostrils flared like I'd said something wrong or bad, but then he leaned down and kissed me to keep me from finishing my thought. We kissed long enough for me to completely forget what I'd been thinking anyway. When he finally pulled away with a shit-eating grin, I narrowed my eyes at him.

"Why do I feel like I've just been played?"

Jack blushed a little which I had to admit was cute. "I used the flower box as an excuse to get you alone so I could kiss you and squeeze your ass."

I hadn't realized his hands were on my ass since it felt so normal. Suddenly I was aware of whatever neighbors might be watching. I had to imagine small-town Indiana wasn't the most rainbow-colored place for two men to grope each other in public.

I stepped back and pushed him away gently. "Yeah, not sure La Porte needs to see my dick get hard at the backyard barbecue."

After moving past Jack to get to the rear hatch of his SUV, I felt him move beside me and put a large hand on my lower back. "Let me get this. You grab the..." His voice trailed off as he spotted something at the base of a nearby tree.

A For Sale sign.

"What the hell?" He stormed over to look more closely. Sure enough, there was a For Sale sign in Kirk and Millie's yard.

"I thought we were here to do a renovation?" I asked without thinking. "Is it to get the house ready to sell?"

"No. It's not." I hadn't seen him angry before like this. He yanked the little metal sign out of the yard and stomped back around the house. I left the SUV and followed him.

"What the hell is going on?" he asked his sister, shaking the sign in the air. Her face fell and she looked at Kirk.

"You said you were going to put that away until we told him."

"Sorry, babe," he said with a face full of remorse. "When Ty showed up, I forgot all about it."

Jack threw the sign down. "And when were you going to tell me? You love this fucking house. The two of you worked your asses off for the down payment. You spent hundreds of hours repainting the walls and refinishing the floor. You—"

I grabbed his arm to stop him because with every impassioned word, he was causing Millie to get more and more upset.

"We can't afford to keep it," she finally cried. "We've done every-thing we can think of, Jack. It's not working. The business needs—"

"I'll help," Jack said. "I have savings, and I'll go back to the airline. I can probably get a Chicago-based position with them so I'm still close by. And—"

It was Kirk's turn to pipe up. "Hell no."

"I have an idea." Ty's voice was so much calmer than the rest, but I could tell from the look on his face, he was as upset as everyone else. I felt like I was intruding on a family moment.

I whispered to Jack. "Do you want me to—"

"No," he said, sliding his arm up my grip until he was holding my hand. "Please stay with me."

Millie gave me a watery smile to let me know I was welcome. I moved Jack to sit back in our chairs at the six-person patio table and slid his wineglass closer to him as a hint. He took a sip.

Ty cleared his throat. "This wasn't exactly how I wanted to announce it, but... I got a job here."

Kirk's face lightened into a genuine smile. He moved to hug his brother. "Hell yeah. Congrats, man. That's the best news ever. Tell us about the job."

Ty accepted the hug and then sat back down, glancing over at Jack before looking at his brother again. "It's working for the LaPorte County Convention & Visitors Bureau as their tourism manager. The job is actually in Michigan City, but it's only like twenty minutes from here." His eyes bounced over to Jack again before returning to Kirk and Millie. "I thought maybe I could stay here for a while and pay rent. That way you'll have help with the mortgage, help with the baby, and it will give me time to decide where I want to settle."

Everyone was quiet while the idea sank in.

"Or not," Ty added quickly. "If it's too weird or you don't want to—"

"Oh please!" Millie cried at Kirk. I jumped in my seat which made Jack chuckle. "Kirk, this is perfect."

"Babe, I can't charge my own brother rent." He looked at Ty. "Sorry, bud."

Ty leaned forward. "Paying you for a room will be much cheaper than throwing my money away on an apartment I won't spend much time in. Face it, I'm either going to be working overtime proving myself at the new job, or I'm going to be over here lying on your couch and eating your food anyway."

Kirk rolled his eyes, but I could see the corner of his mouth tick up. "He's not lying," he muttered good-naturedly. "And I could put you to work in the garden."

"I have a black thumb, but I'm willing to kill anything you want."

The tension seemed to resolve for now. I assumed there'd have to be more detailed conversations about the plan later, but I was curious if there was also a way to help boost their skydiving business to help them get over the financial burden of having to buy their partner out of his share unexpectedly. I made a mental note to brainstorm ideas later in case I could think of anything that would help. It was one of the closest skydiving locations to Chicago, so they had the entire metro area to advertise to. They were planning a big jump event for the three-day weekend, and I wondered if I could somehow help spread the word to boost attendance.

Ty told Kirk he was hoping to go for a dive while he was in town this weekend, and the two of them began making plans to go up before Ty had to fly back to New York.

"Will you go with them?" I asked Jack.

His eyes widened, but before he could answer, Ty answered for him with a laugh. "Jack doesn't jump out of perfectly good planes."

He said it like it was a phrase Jack used often. I turned to Jack in surprise. "Really? You're scared of something involving aviation?"

Jack ran his fingers through my hair. "Bailing out doesn't have anything to do with aviation," he said. "Pilots are meant to stay *inside* the plane."

Kirk laughed at him. "Believe me, Teo, we've tried. The man's a chicken, through and through."

I smiled at Jack. That was the best news I'd heard all day. It made me feel less weird about my own fears. "I'm with you. I think you'd have to shoot me up with hard-core street drugs just to get my fingernails out of the fuselage."

Jack pulled my head forward and kissed me on the forehead. "I knew there was a reason I l-liked you." It was odd to hear him trip over the word "like," as if even admitting he liked me in front of his family and his ex was tricky. It left me feeling unexpectedly flat. I already felt like an odd fifth wheel, and now I was fighting the urge to claim a sudden stomach problem and beg to be shown to my room for the night.

But that shrinking violet was the old Teo, the one who felt like he was waiting for his life to begin. That's not who I wanted to be anymore. I wanted to be brave, embrace my natural love for social situations, and enjoy getting to know the person Jack thought so highly of.

"Millie, when are you due?" I asked when the subject turned toward whether or not the nursery room needed renovations too.

"Halloween," she said, her hands automatically going to her small bump. Her smile was radiant, and it reminded me of the few times I'd caught Jack with a similar expression.

An older woman's voice came from behind me. "Is someone talking about my first and only grandchild?"

I turned to see an older couple approaching from around the side of the house. I stood up to greet the people I assumed were Mr. and Mrs. Snyder, Jack's parents. Despite my new resolution to be brave, my hands were trembling.

"Mom, Dad, this is Teo Parisi," Jack said. His hand was once again on my back as a kind of steady reassurance. I appreciated it more than I expected, because I was ten times more nervous than I expected. I'd never met anyone's parents before like this, and even though we weren't actually dating, Jack was extremely important to me. I hoped to be in his life for a long time, even if friendship was the most we'd ever be to one another.

"It's so nice to meet you," I said, reaching out a hand first to Mrs. Snyder. "You raised a very good man. I'm honored to know him."

Millie put both hands in front of her mouth and turned soft eyes on Kirk. Mrs. Snyder stopped extending her hand to me and yanked me into a hug instead.

"Oh, aren't you the sweetest thing," she said, squeezing me tight against her soft body. She smelled like Gold Bond hand cream, the kind one of my patients at Wilton swore by. "And so handsome. Hank, look at these green eyes. I want grandchildren with these eyes."

"Mom!" Millie cried with a laugh while Jack groaned.

"What? He looks like a model. Oh hi, Tyler. I didn't know you were coming this weekend. It's great to see you, hon."

"Mrs. Snyder," he said. "Mr. Snyder."

Mr. Snyder spoke up. "It's Keith and Lori. You know that. Good to see you." He shook Ty's hand. "And it's very nice to meet you, Teo. Jack has been like a Chatty Cathy ever since he met you."

After shaking his hand, I glanced up at Jack, whose ears had turned crimson. "Whatever," he muttered. "Don't listen to them." He moved forward to give his parents a hug.

We made room around the table for Keith and Lori while Kirk and Jack got to work on the grill. Everyone, including Ty, was very welcoming and friendly. I wanted to hate him so much, but I couldn't. He was cute and humble in addition to being very attentive to Millie.

He made sure his sister-in-law was comfortable and didn't lift anything. It was actually very sweet.

Dammit.

But I did notice his periodic wistful glances at Jack. It was clear to me he still had feelings for his ex, and who could blame him, really? Jack was everything.

While I was busy ruminating on how perfect Jack was, Ty had moved to the seat next to mine. "Jack tells me you're a nurse in a senior home. I have a good friend in New York who works with hospice, and she loves it. I think it takes someone with a big heart and lots of patience to work with the elderly."

Just when I was trying to decide whether or not to be annoyed by his words, he continued. "It's hard for some of us to slow down enough to listen to the incredible stories the older generations have. I remember my great-grandfather, when I was little, telling stories about rationing during the war and how he had a neighbor lady who traded for extra butter because one of her sons had asked for just butter for Christmas." He chuckled. "The kid ate the entire thing if you can believe it."

"Ugh, why not have it made into a cake or cookies?" I asked with a groan and a laugh. "I can't imagine what that butter did to that poor kid's stomach."

Jack looked over at the two of us laughing together with a comical expression on his face. I ignored him and began to ask Ty questions about his new job. Apparently, it was the right subject change because the man's face lit up. He told me all about Michigan City's location on the shore and its famous lighthouse, how couples loved to plan weddings in the area, and how he hoped to make La Porte County a corporate events destination for Chicago companies looking for a little more space and nature. We talked for a long time about how to market La Porte County to Chicagoans, and he asked me lots of questions about growing up in the Chicago area.

By the time the food was ready, I felt... not exactly thrilled he was there, of course, but at least I felt less intimidated by him than I had when I'd first realized who he was. I even had the random thought that if Jack and Ty ended up together, that wouldn't be so bad for Jack. Ty was kind and interesting, clearly smart and successful at what he did, and he already had the family connection as Kirk's brother. If the only thing holding Jack back from committing to Ty was his disinterest in settling down with *anyone*, that meant the minute Jack was ready to settle down, he still had the option for it to be with Ty.

Those thoughts took me down a dark path that unsettled my stomach.

"You okay?" Jack asked, whispering low in my ear. His hand was resting on my thigh under the table, and his touch had helped up until this stupid train of thought about Ty and Jack and their perfect house in La Porte together.

"I..." I looked around at Millie, who was teasing Ty about his ideas for the baby's nursery. Keith was busy asking Kirk about work, and Lori was gathering up dirty plates from the table. I stood to help her. "My head's starting to hurt," I said quietly to Jack. "I might need to beg off early." It wasn't really a lie. The stress of meeting Jack's whole family in addition to his beautiful and perfect ex was getting to me with a low throb behind my forehead. I wanted some time to myself in a dark room to just be still.

Jack's brows furrowed. He reached out to brush the hair back from my face in a tender gesture that made a lump form in my throat. "Okay, let's go up to bed, then."

My heart thundered erratically. The affectionate look in his eyes, the gentle caress of his hand... his assumption that if I needed to go to bed, then he was coming too. It all hit me at once.

I was in love with him.

"No!" I blurted, suddenly frantic. If he came with me, I'd say it. I'd say it out loud like a stupid jackass and ruin everything. I didn't want to lose him, lose what we had now. Friendship was better than nothing, and I sure as shit didn't want nothing with him.

Jack's expression froze in surprise, and then he pasted on a fake smile. "Okay, let me show you where we're sleeping, and I'll leave you to it."

I wasn't sure what I'd expected, really. Bringing Teo to meet my family would have been stressful enough as it was, but then adding in the unexpected appearance of my ex, and it was excruciating.

All I wanted was to get him into the guest bed and snuggle the shit out of him. Or maybe suck his dick until his brain went offline. Either way, what I did *not* want to do was leave him. But he seemed to be in need of some alone time, so I did anyway.

"He okay?" Millie asked as I returned to the patio. It was a nice early summer night, and I appreciated the chance to sit outside.

"Headache. He's been working odd shifts, so his sleeping is off. I'm worried he's been skipping meals because of it too."

I took a seat again at the table next to my mom, who patted my arm. "He's a real cutie, Jack."

My dad nodded, but I noticed Ty look down at his glass of wine.

"He's a sweetheart," I added softly. "I'm glad you all got a chance to finally meet him."

The sound of summer nights floated around us, crickets and neighbors having their own backyard barbecue a few houses away.

"I like him too." Ty's voice was hesitant. "He reminds me a little bit of Pat Farrow. Remember him? Tina's friend who we met at that party in Chelsea?"

I thought back to the man with the bright green eyes who was trying to make a living as a professional figure skater. "It's the eyes," I said with a laugh.

"And the dark hair, and the dimple. But also, he just has that nurturing vibe, you know? He's nice, Jack." He met my eyes. There was sadness and regret there, but I could see he meant what he said. "It's good to see you with someone. I hate thinking of you being alone."

"I..." I'd started to say I wasn't *with* anyone, but I couldn't exactly admit that when I'd brought Teo here for the weekend. "It's not serious," I said instead.

Every single person sitting at the table burst out laughing.

"Sure it's not," Millie said through tears.

"Yeah, right," Kirk added.

Even my dad was chuckling. "Son, you've got a screw loose if you think there's nothing serious between you two. I'm not sure if..." He glanced at Ty.

My mom wasn't as hesitant. "What your father's trying to say is, maybe you're downplaying it for Ty's sake, but we can all see you're in love with the boy. And Ty's a grown-up. Respect him enough to be able to handle it."

In love. Hardly.

I turned to my ex. Poor Ty looked like he wanted to crawl under the table and slink off into the woods. "She's not wrong," he muttered. "I'm not exactly still crying into my pillowcase every night. We've been broken up for years, Jack."

"Are you seeing anyone?" I asked gently.

He shook his head. "I was, but it wasn't serious. He'd never been out of New York and had no interest in travel or adventure. I may be ready to settle down, but I'm not ready to stop traveling and trying new things. Plus, I knew I was getting more serious about moving here, so I didn't pursue it."

Millie clapped her hands which was never a good sign. "We'll take you to South Bend and show you the gay bars."

"Um, no," I said. "I'll take you to Chicago and show you the gay bars."

Ty's face lit up. "That sounds much better."

Eventually the topic changed to the renovation, and my dad grabbed the yellow legal pad he always kept somewhere in his truck. We sketched out some ideas and used the measurements Kirk had already taken. By the time my parents left, we had a general plan of what we wanted to do the following day. I'd forgotten to mention to Teo that doing construction in the room where we were staying meant we'd be sleeping in a construction zone the following night. But moving to the sofa bed in the living room wasn't an option since I assumed Ty would be crashing there.

When I finally joined him in the large room upstairs, Tee was curled into a tiny ball under the thin cotton blanket. Only some of his messy dark hair peeked above the stark white bedding, and I wondered if he was cold. When I approached him to pull up a second blanket, I noticed he was wearing a T-shirt out of my own duffle. It was the same old, supersoft NYC Pride tee I'd had on when I'd come over to his place earlier in the week. I'd tossed it in my bag with some of my other dirty clothes so I could do laundry while I was here. It was huge on him, but, god, did he look sexy in my clothes.

I brushed my teeth before slipping into bed and pulling him against my chest. "Love you," he murmured in his sleep.

The words lit up everything inside of me even though I knew they weren't intentional. What if there came a day when he truly did love me? I started to have my usual panic at the idea of something serious, but then my brain quickly reminded me this was Teo we were talking about. What if Teo loved me one day?

My heart skittered around in my chest like a mouse in a maze who was desperate to know the quickest way to the cheese.

I would be the luckiest motherfucker alive.

It took me a long time to fall asleep after that. I felt my life's plan shifting under me, changing everything. Maybe walking away from

Tyler hadn't been about me not being ready to settle down. Maybe it'd been because I hadn't been ready to settle down with him.

As I inhaled the lemony scent of Tee mixed with the smoke from the grill, I realized I had everything I hadn't known I'd wanted: Teo in my arms, Millie and Kirk creating an exciting new niece or nephew, and friends like Rourke, Chelsea, and Ty, who were slowly but surely teaching me that there was a difference between settling down and living a dull life.

Leaving Newark and the airline had been a risk that was paying off. Without the change, I wouldn't have met any of the new people in my life, including Teo. So I finally fell asleep with warm thoughts toward Jefferson Plenty and his friend at Douglas Aviation.

I WOKE up to a phone call in the middle of the night summoning me in to work.

Fuck Douglas Aviation.

"Tee, baby," I said, pressing a kiss to his ear. "I have to go to work. They need me on a trip."

"Huh?"

"I'm going to leave you the SUV so you can drive yourself back. The Gulfstream is picking me up at the airport here in La Porte."

"What?" He was still half-asleep and confused as hell. He tried sitting up and rubbing his eyes. "I don't understand."

I kissed his sleep-warmed cheek. "A client requested me for a last-minute trip to Europe. I'm still the newest hire, so I can't say no. I'll be gone a week. I'm so sorry. Will you be okay driving back by yourself to the city? If not—"

"Yeah, yeah, that's fine. I'm just..." He finally seemed to process what was happening. "I'm just going to miss you."

The words were on the tip of my tongue, that I wanted more, that I wanted all of it with him. Even if he wasn't ready, I would wait. But I couldn't open up an entire conversation that I didn't have time for right now.

"When I get back, we'll—"

He nodded and kissed me hard on the lips, cutting me off and throwing his arms around my neck to squeeze tightly.

After he ended the kiss, I pressed more kisses to his cheeks and his forehead. "Please be safe," I begged. "I need you to... I need... I need you to be here when I get back, okay?"

"Here?" he asked in confusion.

I messed with his hair. "Not *here*, here. Just..."

He threw himself at me again for another kiss and hug. "Okay. I'll be here." His shy grin was adorable. I kissed the tip of his nose and bit my tongue against three words that would change everything.

When the plane landed to pick me up, I was shocked to see it was Banks Consulting's Gulfstream. Chris was the first person I saw when I boarded the airplane. He narrowed his eyes at me for a microsecond before continuing whatever conversation he was having with the two men sitting next to him. They all had Starbucks cups in their hands and slick laptops spread out over the table between them. Somehow, it didn't surprise me that he refused to acknowledge knowing me in front of his dude bros from work.

It wasn't until we were at cruising altitude that I put two and two together that someone at Banks had specifically requested me on this trip the same weekend I just so happened to have been out of town with Teo. Was Chris really that possessive? And how would Teo feel if he found out about it?

I decided not to tell him regardless. I didn't want to be the person who wrecked his view of his best friend even more than had already happened.

So I sat back and flew half a world away from the man I was falling in love with, leaving him at the mercy of my family and my ex-boyfriend while I played chauffeur to his own quasi ex.

It was going to be a long week, and being in close proximity with Chris Banks without losing my patience and my job was going to be an awfully tall order.

31

TEO

When I finally woke up for the day and realized Jack wasn't there, I felt awkward. Would they still want me to stay the weekend? Did they still need my help with the renovation? Would it be weird with Ty there?

But as soon as I walked into the kitchen, Millie threw herself in my arms. "Oh my god, I'm so glad you're here. Ty and Kirk are going skydiving all day, and my dad threw his back out somehow while taking the trash out this morning. So, I was hoping..." She drew the word out with a pleading tone. "That you would come with me to the hangar to help me organize some of the decorations for next weekend's jump fest."

Even if I didn't like her as much as I did, I wouldn't have been able to say no to the adorable pregnant lady. "Okay."

She flashed me a smile and turned to the fridge to pull out a large insulated tumbler. "I made you an iced coffee. Jack said it's your favorite. We don't have a great coffee shop close by, so I hope homemade is okay."

I stared at it before reaching for the glorious chalice of heavenly blessings. "You made me an iced coffee?"

She snickered. "Well, to be fair, Jack said it was our best chance at getting the most productivity out of you first thing in the morning."

"He's not wrong," I muttered into the drinking spout on the lid. It was delicious, and I told her so. "I want you to be my sister. My actual sister would never do something so kind and benevolent for me."

"Siblings are assholes. Anyway, I also got a gift card to the local baby boutique from one of my mom's friends. I thought maybe we could stop by there on the way to work and see what they have. Are you up for a little baby shopping?" She bit her lip as if worrying she was asking too much of me.

"Millie," I said as seriously as I could. "There are two types of gays. Those who enjoy shopping and those who don't."

Her face started to fall.

"You're in luck," I continued. "I happen to be a shopping gay. Pretty sure your brother is a non-shopping gay."

"I can attest to that," Ty said, shuffling toward the coffee maker. "I once dragged him to the big Macy's in New York because I needed new clothes for a work thing. He lasted fifteen minutes, tops, before he suddenly had an urge for pastrami on rye. We'd eaten lunch an hour before."

The reminder of their life together sat hard on my gut, but I brushed it off, forcing myself to resist the temptation not to try and one-up him. I had absolutely no leg to stand on in a contest of which one of us knew him better. Hands down, it was the better-looking man in the room.

"Do you want to come with us?" I asked instead.

"Oh, no, thank you. I promised Kirk I'd help run some jumps today."

"Are you a pilot?" I wasn't sure how the skydiving business worked exactly.

"No. I'm a tandem instructor though. Kirk and I started skydiving as soon as we turned eighteen. He fell in love with it big-time and forced me to get certified with him so we could work summers in college at a skydive center. We grew up and went to school in Arizona so we could skydive year round." He must have seen confusion on my face, because he tried explaining more. "A newbie gets strapped to my front so they don't have to worry about any of the technical things like pulling the chute open. That's called jumping tandem."

"Oh. Still sounds terrifying," I said with a nervous chuckle. I was low-key anxious even *going* to a place where planes and skydiving was happening. The idea of actually going up in one and jumping out of it were vomit-inducing.

Millie set a toasted bagel on a plate in front of me and handed me a tub of cream cheese. "Eat this so we can get going. Ty, you'd better get your ass to the drop zone before they go up without you."

Clearly the lady was ready to start her day.

And it was a great day. Millie and I had similar reactions to the items at the fancy baby boutique. Everything was to die for mostly because it was tiny. She ended up selecting a few super-soft sleeper suits and a little wall art for the nursery that had a gorgeous colorful patchwork unicorn on it with the phrase *Just Be You* written above it. We both squealed as soon as we saw it because it was perfect.

Throughout the morning together, I felt more comfortable with Millie and began to regret running out early last night. What kind of message had my actions sent Jack? Did he think I didn't like his family? Would he think that meant I didn't like *him* or want to be with him?

Because I did want to be with him. Of course I did. I was fooling myself if I thought I could keep from telling him my feelings.

"We should totally go back for that uncle T-shirt set," Millie said, reaching for the radio station dial.

"They didn't have one big enough for Jack. I checked." I batted her hand away before she could change it to a country music station. Again.

"They had it in your size, silly," she said, shoving my hand away and trying again.

It took a second for the words to sink in. "Me?" I squeaked. "Why me?" The poor woman had fallen too hard for our fake relationship.

"Don't bullshit me, Teo. You're it for my brother, and I can see he's it for you too. I'm thrilled. Kirk and I stayed up late talking about it and making plans."

"W-what are you talking about? We... we're just..."

"Faking it? Yeah, nice try. Jack told me how you were pretending to be a fake couple, but he has never, ever, *ever* talked about a man like he talks about you. He's never looked at a man like he looks at you. Teo, I know what Jack looks like when he's faking it. Believe me, this isn't it. It's one of the reasons I'm convinced this is serious for him." She turned in her seat to face me more fully. "But the biggest clue he's batshit crazy over you? He cried when he thought he'd lost you."

I wondered if I should pull off the road to keep from sideswiping the curb. My hands were shaking from nervous anticipation. "Huh? What... what are you saying? When?"

She waited until I pulled into the parking lot under the Nose Dive sign and put the SUV into park before answering me. "He showed up here late one night during the week looking like dog shit. The minute I opened the door, I knew it was about you. He was devastated."

"When? When was this?" My voice was croaky and weird, but I had to know. I couldn't even imagine Jack being that upset over me. Surely he was upset about something else.

"The night after he found Chris at your apartment and ran six miles home. He was afraid if he didn't come here for the night, he'd go back to your apartment again."

My stomach fell, but at the same time, my heart soared. He cared about me. This wasn't one-sided like I'd feared. But that didn't mean he was ready for a relationship. Did it?

"How do you know all of this?"

She reached over and squeezed my forearm. "I finally weaseled it out of him piece by piece. It was like pulling teeth."

I turned to look out the driver's-side window so I wouldn't have to look at her hopeful expression. I felt ripped wide open, like my guts were on display. "Why didn't he tell *me*?"

"Oh, Teo. He's fucking terrified. It's so much easier to keep himself walled off from people. That way he doesn't get hurt or hurt anyone else."

I turned to face her again. "What do you mean hurt anyone else?"

She let out a sigh. "He stayed with Ty too long. I didn't realize it at the time because I wanted it too much, but they were never really suited. It had just worked so perfectly with the four of us hanging out together. By trying to make it fun for me, he ended up hurting Ty. Then when he finally broke up with Ty, he was afraid he'd hurt not only Ty, but also me."

"Why do you say they weren't suited? Ty's great."

Okay, so maybe I was fishing.

"He is great. But Ty... Ty has an ambitious streak that Jack doesn't really have. Jack *thinks* he's ambitious because he's pursued his flying career so doggedly, but the truth is, he just loves to fly planes. It's why he was willing to take a big pay cut to go private. It's more fun to fly the small planes. Ty needs someone... who has the same focus on career. Also, I kind of think Jack wants to have kids, and that's not really something Ty has ever expressed an interest in. He's more likely to want to keep a perfectly decorated house that never gets messed up. I'm actually shocked he's moving here. I think Kirk is going to need to talk to him to make sure he's not moving here with some secret motivation to help us with the business. Kirk would freak if Ty saw him as a charity case."

Even more reason I wanted to help them succeed. I would start by being the best decorator organizer I could be.

"Then let's get to work," I said, opening the door to the SUV. "Don't forget to grab your smoothie before it melts."

Because apparently pregnant women had to have certain things. Before he'd left the house this morning, Kirk had warned me not to question the desires of the belly.

Once we got to the side of the hangar where the action was, things got a little out of hand. I was so distracted by everything going on around me, I was useless helping organize the decorations. I'd had no idea it was as big of an operation as it was. In addition to four airplanes and an enormous hangar, they had the entire runway to themselves. I couldn't stop gawping at everything. It was a truly impressive operation.

During the day there, I learned more about what had happened with the dud business partner. He'd been in charge of the office side of things while Kirk was in charge of the actual instructions and jumps. When they discovered Dave hadn't actually been booking marketing or paying half the bills, they'd confronted him, and he'd demanded they liquidate the company to get his investment back out.

In order to be able to buy him out of his share, Millie and Kirk had already had to refinance their house, sell one of their cars, and make some tough decisions. But realizing the full impact of none of the marketing being done during the off-season had meant also dealing with a lower amount of sales and income. They needed help getting some exposure and stat. A low summer season could put them out of business even after all of their hard work.

Thinking through possible solutions was one of the things that kept me so distracted during the day. That evening, when Millie and Kirk were in their bedroom "taking a rest for a minute," Ty and I started brainstorming with a pad and paper at the kitchen table.

"It's too bad we don't know any celebrities we could get to come jump," Ty mused, taking a sip from an icy cold beer bottle. Remnants of the pizza we'd picked up for dinner lay scattered at the other end of the heavy wooden table. "Does Jack fly anyone famous now that he's private?"

"He's flown Seth Meyers, but I don't think he'd feel comfortable approaching him. It would need to be a client he has a comfortable relationship with." I thought of Rourke. "He flies Rourke Wagner, but Rourke is in a wheelchair."

"He flies Rourke Wagner?" Ty asked. Clearly he was both impressed and excited. "That guy is amazing. Have you heard him speak?"

"Yeah. Not in person, but I've seen his TED Talk on the internet."

Ty looked past me at the wall. "God he's gorgeous. And smart too. Did you know he went to Yale on a full scholarship and then worked full-time at a nonprofit while he was there? He grew up with nothing.

He qualified for full need-based scholarships, but he went on merit-based ones. He busted his ass on the phones advocating for people with functional limitations, and he even helped convince government agencies like the Illinois Department of Children and Family Services to increase oversight to foster families with disabled children. He—"

Ty stopped and stared at me, realizing he'd gone off on a little tangent there. I sensed a celebrity crush in our midst.

"Sorry," he said with a laugh.

"No, go on. Keep telling me about the beautiful perfect man who spends so much time trapped in a shiny metal tube with my boyfriend. It's awesome," I teased, blushing when I heard myself call Jack my boyfriend.

He laughed harder. "You don't think...? No. I can't see the two of them together. Rourke needs someone who..." He stopped and glanced at me. "Someone more like you. A caretaker. He works too hard and travels too much. He needs someone to ground him."

"You're either trying to set me up to get me away from your ex, or you've actually met Rourke in person."

He held up his hands and grinned. "The latter. I swear, it's the latter. I don't have designs on Jack, I swear."

Ty was kind of cute when he got flustered. "Tell me about meeting him." I stood up to get us each another beer while Ty described a speech Rourke had given to his company a year ago at the annual sales kickoff event. I listened with half an ear. I had to admit, the more Ty talked about Rourke's attractive qualities, the more I second-guessed myself and began to feel insecure. I thought of all the times Jack had said *Rourke thinks this* and *Rourke said that*. Maybe I was naive and Jack really did have feelings for the successful businessman.

"Well, I'm not sure he wants to jump out of a perfectly good airplane," I said eventually, feeling warm and fuzzy when I heard Jack's gripe come out of my own mouth. "Besides, Jack is in Europe this week, so we have no way to get in touch with Rourke."

Ty gave me the deeply skeptical look this statement deserved.

So, yes, fine, I was being a wee bit jealous and ridiculous, but I didn't need the amazing and talented Rourke to be the one to save the day. I waved my hand dismissively and said, "Ahem. So. Who else can we ask?"

Ty's lips twitched, but he didn't say a word. More proof he was a decent man. I wasn't sure if the fact Jack was surrounded by so many good men in his life made me angry or happy. Either way, I appreciated Ty not calling me on my shit.

"Too bad we don't have an in with a social media influencer. They'd know how to get a post to go viral in a short period of time."

As soon as the words were out of his mouth, I remembered meeting Ryan Fae this week at Wilton. We'd totally hit it off and had even exchanged phone numbers.

The only problem was, Ryan Fae rarely left his house. But it was worth a phone call at least. Wasn't it?

The following day, I called Ryan on my way back to the city in Jack's SUV. My original plan was to ask if he knew any other celebrity types who might be willing to do a public jump that we could film and publicize to get exposure for Nose Dive.

"I'll do it," he said, shocking the hell out of me. "On one condition."

I blew out a sigh of relief. This was going to be huge. I couldn't wait to tell Millie and Kirk. "Anything," I said.

That turned out to be a mistake.

32

JACK

"He's doing *what*?" I shouted into the phone. I'd just finally fucking landed at Midway after a hellish trip to Frankfurt and Florence with Chris and his jackass friends when Millie called with her big exciting news.

"Skydiving. Duh."

When her news rendered me speechless, she continued. "Teo didn't tell you? Haven't you talked to him?"

"I've talked to him every day! And I know exactly why he didn't tell me, because I would have flown home and tied his insane, do-gooder ass to a chair."

"Well, it's too late for that. He jumps in less than an hour. Where are you?"

"I'm in Chicago, at Midway airport, for god's sake. Tell him not to do it. Please. You know how I feel about this. Millie, he's terrified of flying. He can't… just please tell him not to get on that plane. Tell him to wait for me." I hung up the phone to try and call his number.

The thought of the man I cared about jumping out of an airplane into free fall was too terrifying to contemplate. My hands were already shaking with a combination of nerves and fear.

"Jack?" I glanced up to see Rourke wheeling his way out of the lobby with Nate. "They said you were on another trip. Sorry to miss you." He seemed to notice my expression because he stopped and frowned. "You okay?"

"No. I need to get to La Porte to stop Teo from doing something stupid," I muttered, trying Tee and hearing the call go straight to voicemail.

"What's going on?"

I gave him the short version. "Apparently, he's roped some celebrity into skydiving to help my sister and brother-in-law's skydiving business get some exposure. But the guy is forcing Tee to go with him, and he's terrified of planes."

"Damn," Nate muttered. "I can't imagine he'll actually make it out the bay door though."

"He's a stubborn asshole," I said. "And he'll do anything to help a friend. That's how he'll see this. He'll get to the open door and convince himself to jump out of fear of letting us all down if he doesn't."

Rourke wheeled closer and gripped my arm. "Then I guess we're headed to La Porte. I've always wanted to try skydiving. Think they make accommodations?"

I glanced up at Nate, who was grinning before I looked back down at Rourke. "You're joking."

Rourke shook his head. "Nope. Never. You know how much I love a good adventure. Don't deny me my skydiving chance now that you've brought it up."

I made a half-hearted attempt to argue, but I knew he was telling the truth when he mentioned loving adventure. Within twenty minutes we were taking off on the short hop to Kirk's landing strip. Rourke's Cessna was plenty small enough to land there with no problems, and it was strange to sit in the copilot seat for once since Nate was the captain on this trip.

I radioed Kirk. "Don't let him jump."

"Dude, chill out. He'll be fine."

"He's terrified of flying, Kirk. He's going to piss himself when he has to jump out of that plane. He's only doing it to help us."

"I know that, and I'm grateful as hell. If I thought he was in any danger, I wouldn't let him do it. Trust me."

"Fuck." I would have punched something if everything in arm's reach hadn't been critical to flight control.

Nate was awfully smiley today. "Never thought our emergency landing in Goose Bay would find you a boyfriend."

"Ugh," I groaned. "This is why I don't do relationships! My hands are sweating, and I feel like I'm going to need CPR pretty soon. What the fuck is he thinking?"

Rourke's voice came over the headset from the seat behind us. "He's thinking he's in love with you, and he knows how much your family means to you."

I glanced over at him, ready to tell him he was full of shit. But I knew he wasn't. The only thing that would get Teo Parisi up in a damned skydiving rig was love.

"Ready to land," Nate warned Rourke. "Belt on and all that." As soon as we were on the ground and taxied to a stop off to the side of the apron, Nate gave me the go-ahead to exit the plane and find Millie.

Instead of bolting, I took the time to help Rourke into his chair and down the lift until both of us were racing toward the drop zone which was off the side of the runway about halfway down the tarmac.

Tons of people were already there. Video cameras, photographers, tourists, staff, and my family all stood happily off to the side anticipating the jumpers' descent. Millie yelped and threw herself at me with excitement when she saw me, but I shrugged her off.

"How could you let him do this?" I was even angrier than before. I knew any minute he'd be forcing himself out the door of that plane, and I wasn't there to encourage him.

"How could I not? He was so happy to help. Jack, he's a grown man."

Someone yelled, "There they are!" We all looked up. At this point I was shaking so hard, I was having trouble standing. My stomach was ten seconds away from revolting, and sweat was pouring down the center of my back making my pilot's uniform shirt stick to me like clingfilm.

Rourke tried reaching for my hand, but I yanked it away with a muttered apology. I couldn't stand still. I couldn't look. What if something happened to him? What if he hit the ground wrong or got tangled in the gear? What if—

"He's under the yellow canopy. His friend is the purple one," Millie said into my ear. She was pointing to the colors in the sky.

My entire fucking heart, my entire goddamned *world* was hanging by two straps and a sheet of thin nylon. He had to be so damned scared. And he was doing it without any support. Hell, he barely knew any of these people including whoever the hell this blogger celebrity guy was.

"Oh god." *Please, please let him land softly.*

"He'll be fine," Millie said with a chuckle. "Kirk does this like ten times a day."

I snapped at her. "Yeah, and Kirk once got a compound fracture of his tibia for his troubles!"

My brain knew that skydiving wasn't dangerous, but my gut had never been able to overcome my intellect on this one. Skydiving had always scared the hell out of me. I'd tried to keep my fear suppressed so as not to offend Kirk and subsequently my own sister, but I was not a fan.

I paced back and forth across the freshly mown grass with my eyes riveted on the tandem bodies beneath the yellow canopy.

He'd better be strapped to Kirk himself.

My back teeth hurt from clenching and grinding. Finally, finally, they landed. It looked soft and smooth at first, but then Teo's foot got caught under them and the pair went tumbling across the drop zone.

My heart dropped, and I went running.

33

TEO

I did it!

The exhilaration I felt was jacked up by the relief of finally being safe on the ground. Had it been breathtaking and freeing? Yes. Would I ever do it again? Hell fucking no. I felt like I was going to puke and my ears hurt. The harness was too tight, and my face was cold. My body was shaking with the effects of an adrenaline response.

But I'd done it. And seeing all of the cameras recording Ryan Fae's landing was all the reassurance I needed that my jump had been worth doing. I only wished Jack hadn't been away on a trip so I could have surprised him with it in person.

"You asshole!"

I looked up from the mess I'd made of the landing to see the subject of my thoughts storming at me across the green grass of the drop zone. He was here. I grinned at him wildly. How was he here?

"How could you do this? Are you fucking crazy? Do you have any idea how fucking..." He seemed to realize where he was, that there were cameras rolling. He grabbed his short hair with both hands and turned his back on me. "Fuck!"

I felt the jostling of Kirk unbuckling me from himself and then my own harness. When I was free to move, I stumbled forward but went down hard when my ankle didn't hold. "*Oof.*" Kirk hurried over, but Jack didn't seem to notice.

"Shit. Did you twist it?" Kirk reached down to palpate it gently.

I tested it. "No, I think it's fine. Just tweaked it." I stood again and took a gingerly step. This time it supported me and only felt a little weak. I kept my eyes on Jack, who was pacing and muttering under his breath off to the side, near where Millie stood watching me with a worried expression. I tried giving her a smile of reassurance, but I wasn't feeling it.

After all that, after what I'd just accomplished, Jack was mad at me. I didn't understand.

"Why is he so upset?" I asked Kirk. My heart was in my throat at the thought I'd disappointed him or done something to upset him. "I thought he'd be proud of me for facing my fear. I kind of thought he'd be happy."

Kirk chuckled softly. "Teo, he's terrified of skydiving and fiercely protective of the people he loves. So the idea of you jumping out of an airplane scared the shit out of him. He'll get over it now that you're safely down."

People he loves?

That couldn't be it, and the more I watched him throw a tantrum, the more annoyed I became. I marched over to him and shoved his shoulder to get his attention. "What the hell is your problem?"

He turned on me, batting my hand away angrily. "My problem? What the fuck is your problem? Are you insane? Why would you do this when you're scared of flying? Why would you put yourself at risk like this? What in the world were you thinking when you decided to jump out of a perfectly—"

"Good airplane," I finished with him in a mocking voice. "Did it ever occur to you I wanted to help your family? It wasn't my plan to jump out of a fucking airplane, Jack! But when I finally found someone who could help Nose Dive, there was a catch. And the catch was, I had to jump too."

"You didn't have to say yes! Millie and Kirk could have found another way." His face was flushed with anger. "Why do you have to keep fucking setting yourself on fire to keep everyone else warm? Why can't you just let people solve their own problems sometimes instead of—"

I held up my hand to stop his ridiculous rant. And then I turned and walked away without another word.

"Teo!" he yelled at my back. "Don't walk away from me, dammit."

"Why not?" I snapped over my shoulder as I continued walking. "Give me one good reason to stay here and take this bullshit nonsense."

I heard Millie's soft voice saying, "Tell him, you idiot."

But he didn't say anything. The silence lasted long enough for me to turn around and look at him.

He was on his knees with his hands clasped in front of his forehead. "Because I love you." His voice cracked and broke. He looked up at me with such anguish, dropping his hands onto his thighs. "And I don't ever want you to be scared. And the idea of you sacrificing your happiness to help my family is... is... overwhelming. What if something had happened to you? What if you'd been hurt? I can't lose you, because I love you. So much. So fucking much."

I stared at him with my mouth open. Was this really happening right now? All the pieces began clicking into place. My heart thundered with the combination of everything that had already happened today and everything this amazing man was offering me with his words.

"Say something," Jack said in a whisper. "Please."

I walked toward him feeling lighter and freer than I had been at 10,000 feet.

His eyes were pleading with me as I got closer. By the time I stood in front of him, he'd stood back up and held his hands open by his sides. He looked so handsome in his pilot's uniform even if the short-sleeved button-down was a bit rumpled from the long flight. The four gold stripes on his epaulets glinted in the bright summer sun. I hadn't expected him back until later tonight. I'd planned on surprising him with the news about my skydive after I was safely on the ground. Now

I felt like I was still free-falling, only this time it was a thousand percent better.

"I love you too." The words came out of me in a rush—had been waiting, in fact, for longer than I realized. As soon as the words came out, I felt tears fill my eyes. Stupid fucking emotions. "I'm not sorry for jumping, but I'm sorry I worried you."

Jack yanked me into his arms and bear-hugged me until I could barely breathe. "I love you so much," he said again and again, tucking his face into my neck.

"I missed you," I admitted softly. "I know traveling is part of your job, but I'm still allowed to miss you when you're gone, right?"

"Only if I'm allowed to miss you just as much."

Jack pulled back and met my eyes before leaning in to kiss me. He cupped my face with both hands and poured all of his feelings out in that kiss until I was dizzy.

"Mpfh. Pretty sure the cameras are more in love with the two of you than me."

I turned to see Ryan Fae standing behind me with his hands on his hips and a smirk on his face. Sure enough, all of the cameras were pointed at Jack and me.

Heat flooded my face as I turned back to bury it in Jack's shirtfront.

I heard Millie's unique combination of happy squeal and clapping before noticing the rumble of Jack's laughter through his chest.

He leaned down to press a kiss against my cheek. "I'm sorry for freaking out. Did you, ah, have fun?"

I glared up at him and then turned to make sure the cameras weren't focused on us anymore. I'd heard Ryan trying to corral them back on him now that our drama was over. "No, dammit. I did not," I hissed. "I'm never doing it again, and also fuck you very much if you even think I'm getting in an airplane again for any reason because I am not. Ever."

Jack's laugh was big and boisterous. The stress from earlier was finally gone, and my heart had settled back to a steadier beat.

Jack's eyes twinkled at me. "You're in love with a pilot and you refuse to board an airplane."

I ran a finger along the edge of his jaw and down his throat before grasping his necktie and pulling him in until we were nose to nose.

"I guess you'll just have to find other ways to make me fly."

EPILOGUE
JACK - ONE YEAR LATER

"This is stupid," I muttered. "He's going to hate it."

I looked out across the dark water of Lake Michigan sparkling in the summer sun. It was an absolute perfect day to spend at the park with our closest friends. Millie had offered to bring a picnic lunch for everyone, but Rourke had insisted on having lunch catered instead. Bossy rich bastard.

Rourke bumped me with his chair. "Cut the crap. He's going to love it. He gets off on cheesy shit like this."

I looked down at him. "You didn't curse like this before you started dating Ty. Which is weird because he doesn't curse a lot. Yet somehow he still manages to be a bad influence on you."

Predictably, Rourke's face softened when I mentioned his boyfriend's name. "Tyler Nosen is everything that is good and beautiful in this world."

I made a gagging sound. "And you're calling me cheesy. Right."

"We're back," Ty said in an overly loud voice to make sure I heard them coming. His eyes were wide with a *What can you do?* expression. Teo jogged next to him to try and keep up with Ty's longer stride.

I blew out a sigh of relief. For a minute, I thought he was going to miss the damned thing entirely.

"Sorry about the detour," Tee said, reaching for my hand. "I shouldn't have had the second iced coffee."

I leaned in and kissed him on the lips, trying to hide my nerves. "Will you walk with me closer to the shore?"

"Of course." He let me lead him away from the blankets and camp chairs we'd set up on the grass. "You never told me how the blackjack went. All you did was ask if you could take cash out of the checking account for gambling, but then I never heard if you won or lost. You got in so late last night, I forgot to ask."

I'd flown some women to Vegas for a bachelorette trip for the third time already this summer. One more trip like that and I was going to take Rourke up on his offer to be his exclusive pilot once and for all.

"I didn't end up going. I just had my usual tikka masala and called it a night. I would have called, but that was the night you had the compliance auditors there during your shift."

"Yeah, it was fine. Passed with flying colors. Trinity gave me an extra day off next week to make up for it."

I kept my eyes peeled to the south after I felt the buzz of my phone in my pocket. Sure enough, there he was.

"Hey," I said, pointing. "What's that?"

Teo squinted where I was pointing and then looked at me like I was an idiot. "It's a plane, Einstein." He leaned down to pick something up from the ground. I needed his eyes up, not on a fucking special-shaped rock.

"Yeah, but... it looks like one of Kirk's planes."

He stood back up and squinted again as the colorful plane drew closer. "If one of his guys is screwing around while Kirk is out of town, he's going to kick their ass."

Once the plane was easily visible, the banner behind it became clearer.

"What the..." Tee stepped closer to the shore. The plane buzzed by, low enough to show off its cargo.

Teodor Parisi will you marry me?

I watched his jaw drop as he processed the banner's message. My sister's muffled laughter came up behind us along with the gasps and shouts from our friends who were gathered together for the outing. When he finally turned to look at me, I was on one knee with the ring box flipped open.

I spoke softly enough that only he could hear me. I knew Chelsea was somewhere nearby, recording it all on her phone, but this part was just for the two of us.

"Wanted: one lifetime of lovemaking with plenty of talking. I promise to hold you and love on you with plenty of chitchat and loads of expectations. I prefer to switch things up in the bedroom and would desperately like to take care of you and treat you like you're the most important thing in my world—because you are—at least for the next fifty plus years. Please let me stay forever and hold you; I promise not to be gone in the morning. Willing to exchange last name only."

As I recited the heavily edited want ad, Teo's eyes filled and overflowed. His hands were clapped over his mouth, and the tears made his striking eyes even brighter. He was breathtaking, as usual.

He dropped to his knees and threw his arms around my neck. "Of course I'll marry you, you idiot. I love you."

I wrapped my arms around his back and stood, picking him up until he wrapped his legs around my waist.

"I love you so much, Tee," I whispered against the side of his face. "You make me ridiculously happy."

I glanced up at movement out of the corner of my eye. Chris had arrived fashionably late with his latest temporary girlfriend on his arm. Typical. At least he hadn't let Teo down. As much as I thought Chris was a selfish asshole, he was still one of Teo's good friends. Both of us had talked at length about how we felt sorry for him and wondered if he'd ever stop dicking around and settle down with someone. I thought probably not. The guy seemed to appreciate his playboy lifestyle, and that was fine.

I, on the other hand, appreciated having a home and a partner to return to after every trip. Teo had decorated our new house with color and comfort. I loved it so much. Every time I walked home from the station and entered our little yard, I grinned like a fool. Tee had overflowing pots of flowers on the front porch now that it was summer, and there were tomato and herb plants almost covering our entire, albeit tiny, back deck. Most of the deck had been overtaken by the "cat palace" I'd built to give Waffles and Socrates some "outside time." Who said I didn't have a love language?

Apparently my love language was acts of stupid service. But every time Tee crooned over the cats being able to spend time outside, I was grateful for every splinter the damned thing had given me.

Inside the little house were funky rugs on the hardwoods and framed photos on the walls. I'd made him move his skydiving photo out of the bedroom since it gave me nightmares, but he'd replaced it with an adorable shot of our nephew, Wyatt, who Teo insisted on calling Jet to tease my sister for one of her cornier ideas during the last stages of her pregnancy.

Wyatt was currently being bounced on our niece Bella's slender hip. The fat baby was almost bigger than the skinny ten-year-old could handle, but she adored him. Whenever both sides of the family were together, Bella took charge of Wyatt and my sister went searching for the nearest glass of wine.

Teo began to wiggle in my embrace. "Was it my imagination, or was there a ring?"

I leaned in and kissed the hell out of him first.

As I slid the sugary peach ring over his finger, he squawked. "That's cheating!"

I laughed and brought the real ring out of my pocket. "I thought you might be snacky. It's been thirty minutes since your last piece of candy."

My parents approached with their congratulations. After hugs and cheers all around, my dad began with the trivia. "Did you know that in Ancient Greece, men proposed to women by throwing apples at them?"

Teo's face lit up. "Yes! Oh my god, I thought I was the only person who knew this. It's because Eris, the goddess of chaos, was a total jealous bitch. Excuse my language, Lori."

That was the moment Teo officially became a Snyder.

And trivia night was never the same.

"You need a hobby," I said into his ear. "Besides learning obscure facts."

Tee leaned in to whisper back. "I also know some things about another Ancient Greek named Aristophanes, who came up with 106 ways of describing male genitalia."

Oh.

"So if you want me to share some of those with you... *later*... you might want to appreciate me as the well-rounded erudite pantomath that I am."

"You hooked one of them smart ones," Ty stage-whispered. "Wanna swap?"

Rourke smacked him in the stomach and began muttering even more obscure Greek facts that absolutely zero people around us wanted to hear. Well, except my dad and my soon-to-be husband.

"I don't know what any of that means," I said, pulling Teo closer and moving my hands down to cup his perky ass. "But I do appreciate how well-rounded you are. And I'll be happy to show you how much a little later."

The sound of his laugh was all I ever wanted to hear, and it rang across the waterfront park on and off for the rest of the afternoon as we spent time with friends and family enjoying our lives together.

Want to see how Rourke and Ty got together? Sign up for Lucy's newsletter for a fun bonus short!

If you like enemies-to-lovers and revenge, click here for a steamy full-length standalone. For a limited time only, pre-order Hostile Takeover *for only $2.99!*

LETTER FROM LUCY

Dear Reader,

Thank you so much for reading *Virgin Flyer*! This is my first full-length standalone novel, and I loved delving into Teo and Jack's world.

If this is your first Lucy Lennox book, please check out *Borrowing Blue* which is my most popular title and the story of two men as sweet as Teo and Jack.

If you want to read the bonus short featuring Rourke and Ty, don't forget to sign up for my newsletter here:

readerlinks.com/l/1444214

Be sure to follow me on your favorite retailer to be notified of new releases, and look for me on Facebook for sneak peeks of upcoming stories.

Feel free to stop by www.LucyLennox.com or visit me on social media to stay in touch. We have a super fun reader group on Facebook that can be found here:

readerlinks.com/l/1437680

To see fun inspiration photos for all of my stories, including *Virgin Flyer*, visit my Pinterest boards.

Happy reading!
Lucy

ABOUT LUCY LENNOX

Lucy Lennox is the creator of the bestselling Made Marian series, the Forever Wilde series, and co-creator of the Twist of Fate Series with Sloane Kennedy and the After Oscar series with Molly Maddox. Born and raised in the southeast, she is finally putting good use to that English Lit degree.

Lucy enjoys naps, pizza, and procrastinating. She is married to someone who is better at math than romance but who makes her laugh every single day and is the best dancer in the history of ever.

She stays up way too late each night reading M/M romance because that stuff is impossible to put down.

For more information and to stay updated about future releases, please sign up for Lucy's author newsletter on her website.

~

Connect with Lucy on social media:
www.LucyLennox.com
Lucy@LucyLennox.com

WANT MORE?

Join Lucy's Lair
Get Lucy's New Release Alerts
Like Lucy on Facebook
Follow Lucy on BookBub
Follow Lucy on Amazon
Follow Lucy on Instagram
Follow Lucy on Pinterest

Other books by Lucy:
Made Marian Series
Forever Wilde Series
Aster Valley Series
Twist of Fate Series with Sloane Kennedy
After Oscar Series with Molly Maddox
Licking Thicket Series with May Archer
Virgin Flyer
Say You'll Be Nine
Hostile Takeover

Visit Lucy's website at www.LucyLennox.com for a comprehensive list of titles, audio samples, freebies, suggested reading order, and more!

www.ingramcontent.com/pod-product-compliance
Lightning Source LLC
Chambersburg PA
CBHW060924190726
48286CB00002B/631